FEAR THE PAST

DARK YORKSHIRE - BOOK 5

J M DALGLIESH

EXCLUSIVE OFFER

Look out for the link at the end of this book or visit my website at **www.jmdalgliesh.com** to sign up to my no-spam VIP Club and receive a FREE Hidden Norfolk novella plus news and previews of forthcoming works.

Never miss a new release.

———————

No spam, ever, guaranteed. You can unsubscribe at any time.

CHAPTER ONE

THE OTHERS LOOKED like they were settling in for the night so he stood, turned and lifted his coat from the back of the chair. He slipped his right arm into the sleeve amid howls of protest and laughter accompanying the anecdote being loudly recounted. He shook his head.

"It's getting late and you guys aren't going anywhere."

"It's not late," came the joint response from several around the table.

"I'm driving and I've had too much already," he countered.

"Aww… Jody, just get a cab. The evening's only just getting started."

"I've got a lot on tomorrow."

"That's the joy of being the boss. You get to make your own hours."

"And I still need to pay the bills," Jody replied, shaking his head and zipping up his jacket. Glancing through the window to the car park beyond, he tried to assess whether or not the rain had stopped. The darkness enveloped almost everything in view and what little he could see was masked by the condensation on the panes. "I'll see you guys in the morning," he said, heading off. Glancing back at the small group revelling in their impromptu gathering, he blew out his cheeks and muttered under his breath, "Those of you who make it in any way."

THE PUB WAS POPULAR, even midweek, and he had to pick his way through the bar avoiding elbows, chairs and stools as he went before reaching the side door leading to the car park. The toilets were adjacent to the exit and he hesitated. Did he need to go? No. He'd be home in less than ten minutes and he could wait. The sooner he was out of here the better. Pushing open the door, it swung away from him. The wooden door had seen better days. A length of gaffer tape secured a large crack in the pane alongside chipped paint and multiple dents and scrapes – most likely down to the enthusiasm of the patrons coming and going over the years. The nights here were often rowdy. He had to admit to being involved upon occasion.

Stepping outside the stark contrast to the interior struck him and he shuddered against the cold. Descending the steps to the car park on unsteady feet, he walked towards where he'd parked the car. Calling a cab to get home would be sensible but he dismissed the thought. It wasn't far. Light rain was falling and he looked up at the nearby streetlight to better judge the intensity. It was much the same as when he'd arrived two hours earlier. Had he known the plan, if indeed it was the plan to have a session at the pub, he would've declined the offer. However, it was sold to him as a catch up meeting. To be fair that wasn't unusual and often took place in a pub. More often than not it was also this establishment. It had been a while since he had been into the office and his absence was leading to friction, he could feel it even if nothing was being said. He couldn't afford to allow that to continue and feared it was already too late but, in any event, he'd made the effort.

Jody looked back over his shoulder towards the pub as he approached his car. He could make out the team – his business partner along with their small entourage of administrators – still inside, their movements showing the party was in full swing. Turning back, he eyed his BMW and crossed towards it, fishing out the fob. He smiled to himself but it was tinged with elements of relief and regret. The relief came from the knowledge he'd managed the evening without having to be too vocal. Expecting a grilling for not pulling his weight in recent weeks, he found the absence of business talk refreshing. The regret was born out of keeping secrets. Necessary secrets. After all, that was the nature of the beast but somehow, on this occasion at least, it felt disloyal. *Who was he to talk about loyalty?* Loyalty, a virtue which was by all accounts diminishing in importance within the circle he moved in. Once it had been one of the primary requirements but apparently not anymore. The sense someone had his back was a distant memory and paranoia was now, his closest friend.

Perhaps it had always been this way and what he hankered for was a vision of a nostalgic past that never truly existed. His father always told him people lived in the memories of days gone by and, as a result, missed what was unfolding before their very eyes. Having never understood what that statement meant, it was easy to dismiss but now, many years too late, his father's words made perfect sense to him.

Shrugging off the melancholy that threatened to take root, he opened the door. Not wishing to get rainwater running onto the driver's seat, he took off his coat and threw it into the rear. A sound nearby made him look in the direction he thought it came from. There were two recycling points at the edge of the pub's boundary, large metal deposit bins for clothes by the look of them. Taking two steps forward, he waited for his eyes to adjust to the surroundings. Illuminated only by the streetlights, the surrounding trees and bushes were shrouded in darkness and their gentle sway in the breeze was barely visible. Jody stood still, the hairs on his neck raised as he stared into the gloom. What had he heard? The rain was forgotten and he ignored the fact his hair was now soaked through. Water ran down his face and yet still, he peered into the shadows.

"Is anyone there?" he called, narrowing his gaze. No reply. A car passed by on the road, the familiar sound of displaced water breaking his train of thought. Realising he had been holding his breath, Jody retreated towards the car. Noting the rain driving in through the open door and onto the leather interior, he cursed himself. Irritated at allowing his imagination to run riot, he reached the car and took hold of the frame of the door. With one last look back towards the trees he shook his head, smiling and feeling foolish. "Get a grip, man," he said, under his breath.

Jody didn't hear the movement behind him nor did he see the reflection of the amber streetlights glinting off the hammer head as it came down on the back of his skull. He fell, unconscious before striking the ground. Several more blows followed with the only accompaniment being the sound of his assailant's exertions whilst wielding the weapon. There was no resistance.

Soon, all that could be heard was the sound of the intensifying rain coming down in sheets and striking the tarmac all around him.

CHAPTER TWO

THE LOCALS WERE GATHERING. The persistent rainfall that carried throughout the night was easing and the curiosity along the length of the police cordon was clear despite the hour. DI Caslin sipped at his coffee. It was still hot and he needed it. The sounds of normality came on the wind from the adjoining streets as the residents of York awoke and set about their day with the school run and daily commutes going on as normal. By now this street would usually be bustling with like-minded people heading out to work or arriving to open their businesses for the day but, for now at least, the immediate scene was more reminiscent of an apocalyptic war film than central York. A figure appeared and Caslin recognised the brigade's station officer stepping out from the building, roughly sixty yards away and looking in his direction. He beckoned them forward with a wave of the hand. The structural surveyor had given the all-clear and the investigation could begin.

"That's us, sir," DS Hunter said. Caslin nodded, putting his coffee cup down onto the bonnet of the car alongside Hunter's and they set off. The building was a charred wreck, a ruin set in the middle of a terrace of shop fronts. The adjacent properties were undamaged by the ravages of the fire but unsure of their structural integrity, Caslin and his team were held back until the scene was assessed and deemed safe for them to enter.

"Let forensics know they have access, would you?" Caslin said. Hunter bobbed her head in acknowledgement.

"Any statement, Inspector?" someone called from a distance. Caslin looked over his shoulder and beyond the cordon, spying an approaching journalist. The cameraman walking alongside her was desperately trying to get the footage up and running, giving away her profession. Caslin wasn't surprised. In the current age such events were massive news with the media anticipating headline grabbing acts of terrorism until proven otherwise.

"I'm sure there will be something issued later on this morning but we have nothing to add from the earlier release," Caslin said, continuing his walk towards the building.

Approaching the entrance, the scale of the devastation became clearer. At least it used to be the entrance but now the entire frontage was blown out with rubble, timber and glass strewn across the road. The windows of the surrounding properties in every direction were smashed, their residents evacuated to a safe area at a local community hall. The local supermarket had initially been set up as a makeshift triage centre. The staff working the night shift stepped up to assist the emergency services until the required resources could be marshalled. Caslin eyed the scene, grateful the explosion happened when it did and not during the forthcoming rush hour when a far higher number of people would have been present or passing by. The carnage would have been significantly magnified had the explosion occurred even a short time later.

"DI Caslin?" a voice came to him from inside the building, drawing his attention. From within the blackened interior, Caslin saw the approaching figure of the brigade's fire investigator.

"This is Mark Francis. He's our senior investigator on the scene," Station Officer Wardell said, introducing them.

"Good morning," Francis said, offering his hand to Caslin. "Pleased to meet you."

"DI Caslin and DS Hunter. Is it okay for us to explore?" Caslin asked, taking the offered hand.

"Of course. Just watch your footing, would you? There's a lot of water and the building is precarious in places."

Caslin turned his collar up and indicated for Hunter to join him. The volume of water put down by the three appliances in dealing with the flames, stopping the spread of fire to the adjoining buildings, was such that it now ran from the interior walls and what was left of the ceilings. Many upper floor joists survived the initial force of the explosion only to collapse subsequently due to the intensity of the fire along with the water used to douse it.

"What are we looking at?" Caslin asked. The investigator glanced about them.

"The explosion centred just behind me," he said, gesturing towards the rear of the room they were standing in, roughly at the centre of the building. "Which rules out a gas leak."

"You're certain?" Hunter asked, taking notes.

"Absolutely. The supply comes into the building at the rear due to the proximity of the gas main running along the street parallel to this one. This row of buildings is somewhat unusual in that respect. The seat of the fire is such that I'm quite happy to rule out a gas leak as the source."

"In that case, do you have any idea as to what was the source?" Hunter asked.

"Well, this is only an initial assessment but I'm happy to give you a rundown of where the evidence is taking me."

"Please do," Caslin said, looking the immediate area up and down. He considered it a miracle that anyone survived the blast let alone the accompanying fire.

"Basic fire science indicates there has to be fuel, oxygen and an ignition source to spark the fire that led to the explosion," Francis explained. "Ruling out the most common, that being the gas supply, I'm looking for electrical faults either in the building's wiring or appliances. The seat of the fire, here behind me, doesn't appear to be caused by any dodgy cabling. If anything, I'd say the place was rewired fairly recently. Within the last decade based on the condition of the consumer unit and the installation sticker. It is housed in the kitchen to the rear so was shielded from the blast by an interior load-bearing wall."

"Appliances?" Hunter asked.

"None present in the vicinity of the fire," Francis replied, with a brief shake of the head.

"That pushes us towards arson?" Caslin suggested.

"We still have a lot of work to do but that'll be my working hypothesis, yes," Francis concurred. "Two casualties were found over there," he said, pointing to the edge of the room they were currently standing in. "I believe they were pronounced dead at the scene," he said, looking to Wardell for confirmation.

"Yes, they were pulled from the building by the first responders and pronounced once clear."

"They were in the same room as the explosion?" Caslin asked. The station officer nodded.

"And the other victims?" Hunter asked, looking around.

"I believe they were in the outer reception, closest to the street," Wardell confirmed.

"And they'd be separated from the other two by what...?" Hunter asked, trying to visualise the interior before the force of the blast had ripped it apart.

"A false wall, basic timber studwork faced with plasterboard," Francis said. "Pretty common in a minicab booking office such as this, I'd imagine."

Caslin pictured the building as it had once been. An outer reception or waiting area for customers and drivers to hang around in with a hatch to the interior where the booking clerk would sit, taking calls and dispatching the cars.

"Any sign of an accelerant?" Caslin asked.

"Not that we can see. We will often find a concentration of flame in an area where petrol has been poured, such as when your average pyro empties a can of petrol through a letter box."

"Or when someone is trying to conceal the evidence of a crime by burning the building down," Caslin said, looking around.

"That's right. Those are the two main reasons leading to arson on this scale. We have none of the corresponding evidence here," Francis explained. "Your explosion is what set light to the building."

"What are we looking at?" Caslin asked, sensing this wasn't the result of a tragic accident as he had secretly hoped it would be. This was far more sinister.

"I don't think we're looking at anything particularly sophisticated," Francis stated. "It's an improvised device, fairly small, judging from the lack of structural damage but certainly packing enough of a punch to knock out the frontage as well as all the glass in the general vicinity and set the building ablaze."

"Are you confident this must have been placed here?" Hunter queried. Francis looked at her.

"Rather than anything in situ that may have gone off accidentally?"

Hunter nodded, "Exactly."

Francis thought on it for a moment, "I can't see any scenario where this could be accidental. Unless they wanted to place a firebomb somewhere else and it went off here by mistake. I'm afraid you will have to wait for a more detailed conclusion but I'll liaise with your forensics team once they get on site."

"Let's keep this to ourselves for the time being, if you don't mind?" Caslin said. "I don't want to create a panic. Otherwise people will jump to conclusions and assume it's an act of terrorism and we can do without unjustified reprisals." They all agreed. The initial statement offered to the press implied that a gas leak may have led to the explosion and Caslin saw no reason to change that yet. "Thanks, Mark. May we go further?" he asked.

"Certainly. But don't head upstairs. The floors above aren't likely to come down but they're far from safe to walk on. The cellar is intact and the fire spread upwards so the ground floor and basement are structurally sound although the cellar is flooded for obvious reasons."

Caslin thanked him and left him to get on with the remainder of the inspection. Turning to Hunter, he indicated they should look around. They both took out torches and progressed into the building proper, picking their way through the debris. The going was slow as they were careful not to contaminate any potential forensic evidence.

"Made a hell of a mess," Hunter said, sidestepping a pool of water and shielding her head from the water trickling down from above.

"What did he say the casualty count was?"

"Two dead and three injured. Two of the latter are critical requiring emergency surgery and the other is stable but unconscious. Add that to the residents evacuated during the night and the numbers increase."

"Injuries?"

"A few cuts from flying glass. Shock and a reaction to the cold mainly. The fear of a secondary explosion or building collapse meant they were unceremoniously dragged out, many in their bedclothes and a number of them are elderly."

"Staff or clients inside the cab office?" Caslin asked.

Hunter shook her head. "No IDs yet. Terry Holt is at the hospital trying to get the names and we're working on the assumption that at least two were manning the office and the remainder could be a mix of customers and drivers. There was one car immediately parked outside and that is registered to the business but we don't know who was driving it last night."

"Could have been much worse," Caslin said quietly, angling

the beam of his torch towards the floors above. "And this is definitely one of Fuller's, yes?"

Hunter nodded, "I double checked."

Caslin took in a sharp breath, "Pete's going to be pissed off."

"Who would be stupid enough?" Hunter countered. Caslin inclined his head. She had a point. Pete Fuller was a name to be fearful of, not only in York but across all four counties making up the Greater Yorkshire area.

"He's been gone some time though."

"Who's running the organisation now? Is it still the boys?" Hunter queried.

"Last I heard. Ashton was taking the lead with Carl backing him up and running the muscle."

"Looks like he doesn't have the iron grip that his father did."

"I'm not aware of anyone chancing their arm but maybe someone's taken a view that now's the time," Caslin floated the theory. He hoped that wasn't the case. The three largest crime syndicates operating in the city stuck to their own patches. There was the occasional skirmish as the lower levels tried to make names for themselves at the expense of their rivals but, on the whole, they kept their distance. That approach was good for business and all of them were very much focussed on money above all else.

"Or the Fuller boys are spreading their wings," Hunter added.

"Stepping out from Pete's shadow?" Caslin said.

"And someone wants to put them back in their box."

"We need to speak to them and gauge what their response will be. Nip it in the bud before things get out of hand. Also get onto the National Crime Agency and see if there is any intelligence we're unaware of regarding Fuller and his crew. It wouldn't be the first time they'd neglected to keep us in the loop."

Further conversation was interrupted by the ringing of

Caslin's mobile. Glancing at the screen, he saw it was DC Terry Holt.

"Terry?"

"Sir, I'm at the hospital," Holt began, his tone conveyed he wouldn't be delivering good news. "Another one has died in theatre. Her injuries were too severe."

"That's three. What of the others?" Caslin asked.

"One stable but is currently in a medically-induced coma and the other is still in surgery. I've nothing further on the latter."

"Any idea who they were?"

"I've identified one, a Matt Jarvis. Looks like he was trying to get a cab home."

"If he was in the front office, he'd have been furthest from the explosion so that'd make sense," Caslin explained.

"Got off lightly... so to speak," Holt said before correcting himself.

"I know what you mean. Keep me posted," Caslin said before hanging up. He looked to Hunter, "We had better go and see Ashton."

"I doubt we'll get a warm welcome."

Caslin smiled, "Ashton is level headed... at least, as level headed as you can get when you're a narcissistic sociopath."

"And he's widely considered to be the sensible one," Hunter added with a wry grin.

They stepped out of the building. Looking back, Caslin scanned the mix of damp, charred timber and brickwork still smouldering in the early morning light. The thought came to him that if they didn't solve this case quickly, they might see an escalation in similar acts being committed. The death toll would only increase and the chances of more innocents being caught in the crossfire amplified.

Heading in the direction of the cordon, in place at both ends of the street, Caslin noted their approach was being watched by the journalist who had spoken with him earlier. With a flick of his head, he ensured Hunter had registered her presence to ensure she also remained tight-lipped. Caslin was adamant they needed to keep a lid on this situation for as long as possible. They were prepared for the questions this time and Caslin took a deep breath as they reached her location. A uniformed constable, there to maintain the barrier between the public and crime scene, lifted the tape allowing them to pass under.

"Inspector, any news on the number of casualties?" she said as soon as he was beyond the safety of the cordon.

"A statement will be released later. I'm afraid I have no news for you," he said politely but firmly, leaving no doubt as to his desire to not enter into conversation.

"Any word from Peter Fuller?" the journalist asked. Caslin stopped. This wasn't the office junior sent out to cover a story in the early hours. She clearly knew the lay of the land and had done some homework. He very much wished he hadn't. Stopping, he indicated for Hunter to get the car and turned towards the journalist. The camera was filming across her shoulder and directly at him, including the backdrop of the destroyed building. Caslin shuffled sideways knowing the dramatic scene would now be out of shot.

"We are yet to speak with the owners of the premises in question," he began. "Our thoughts are very much with the injured as well as those who have been temporarily evacuated from their homes and businesses."

"And the cause of the explosion, has it been determined?" she asked, cutting over his last words. Her candour struck Caslin. Many times, in previous situations, he'd have been able to keep talking without really saying anything of real note – the interviewer being happy to get anything out of him. This felt different. "Why are Major Crimes investigating a gas leak?"

"A statement will be forthcoming. Please excuse me," he said and strode away as fast as he could without appearing to be fleeing. Hunter brought the car alongside and he clambered in as more persistent questioning came in his direction. He ignored it, closing the door and Hunter accelerated away. Caslin let out a sigh of relief. He was never one who sought the limelight; always preferring to defer press conferences to those who either revelled in them or were more suited to the experience.

Lowering the visor, he used the vanity mirror to observe the duo watching them drive away. He was impressed. This journalist knew her background. He very much wished she hadn't and figured it would be best to steer a path well clear of her in the future.

CHAPTER THREE

HUNTER EYED a break in the traffic and took the turn into the yard. Three men of Asian appearance were busy rubbing down a Mercedes that positively shone even on a grey morning such as this. One of them glanced over at the new arrivals and indicated for them to drive forward into the bay. Hunter shook her head and instead, reversed the car into an old parking space delineated by fading white paint put down long ago. Shrugging, the man returned his focus to helping his colleagues finish off the car they were working on. On such a wet morning, the men operating the hand car wash would be unlikely to do a roaring trade but that mattered little in the vast scheme of things.

They were parked on an old petrol station forecourt. No longer used, all that remained to indicate the nature of the previous business was the overhead canopy. The attendant's office as well as the pumps themselves were long gone. These little enterprises were popping up all over the city, all over the country. Cheap to operate and occupying sites considered unfit for any other practical purpose, they were cash-based businesses that in themselves were becoming rarer with the advancement of the digital age. Beyond the forecourt to the rear scaffolding rose four stories and no doubt would end up even higher once the building work neared completion. A developer's sign advertised that the properties, luxury apartments close to the city centre, were available for purchase off plan.

"They are branching out, aren't they?" Hunter said, inclining her head towards the building work. Caslin pursed his lips before answering.

"Whilst not missing out on the opportunity to keep their core trade ticking over," he replied, staring at the three men as they waved off a grateful owner, leaving the forecourt in his gleaming vehicle.

Abandoned petrol stations couldn't be developed for many years due to the underground storage tanks potentially contaminating the site and the subsequent risk of explosion. Many of these sites lay to waste as speculative purchasers waited until such time as they were able to exploit the real estate. This was one such a place. The Fullers had several of these car washing facilities scattered around, wedded to other parts of their organisation consisting of fast-food outlets, minicab firms, low-end used car dealerships and dry cleaners. All businesses that handled a high turnover of cash thus making it easy to launder the wealth generated through their drug dealing, protection rackets and other illegal enterprises. Evidently, they were now channelling their funds through legitimate construction projects such as the apartment block currently springing from the wasteland of rotting premises. Built with the proceeds of crime, these apartments would undoubtedly enable them to launder even more money by way of inflated construction costs that were only ever payable on a spreadsheet.

They got out of the car. The wash attendants paid them little attention. Two were now seating themselves on camping chairs and nursing cups of coffee to warm their sodden hands in the absence of a waiting client. A third retreated into a small portacabin, reappearing moments later with a steaming mug in one hand and a mobile phone in the other. He talked into the latter, his eyes never leaving the two newcomers as they crossed the compound in search of the site office in the construction zone.

The area was cordoned off with Herras fencing and they walked along the boundary until they reached the gate. It was open, work on the site being well underway and they passed through. None of the workmen acknowledged their presence amid the sounds of a banksman directing a lorry load of supplies across the site and shouts from a foreman above to his team of bricklayers. They skirted the activity keeping to the sides and picking their way across the churned earth beneath their feet. The recent rainfall, cold weather and the heavy plant combined to turn the site into a quagmire. Scaffold boards were laid in places to make traversing the site by foot easier but even so, the going was tricky.

Noting several temporary buildings, they ended up asking where they could find the office and were directed to one on the eastern edge of the site. By the time they'd located the building word had spread of their arrival. Standing outside but leaning against the door jamb, on a ramp leading up to the door, was a young man in his thirties. He was tall, sporting close-cropped dark hair and warily watched them approach with an impassive expression.

"Good morning, Carl."

"Mr Caslin," Carl Fuller replied. "What brings you here?"

"Your brother around, is he? The two of you are never far apart." Carl indicated inside with a brief flick of the head.

"DS Hunter," Hunter introduced herself, holding up her warrant card before Carl.

"Whatever," he said, locking eyes with her and ignoring the identification. He didn't seem inclined to break his gaze so Hunter did so, following Caslin inside.

The interior was much like any other construction site office. Wipe boards were hanging on the wall with progress charts laid out in schedules of red, blue and a black marker. Plans were laid out on one desk with a line of filing cabinets adjacent as well as opposite. Three men stood huddled around another desk at the far end, deep in discussion, with papers strewn out before them. One, in the middle with his back to them, Caslin recognised as Ashton Fuller. His giant waves of blonde hair, in stark contrast to his brother, saw him stand out without the need to see his face. Of the other two, one was heavy set and much older. Judging by his attire, Caslin figured him to be a contractor whilst the other was far younger and taking a back seat in the discussion.

Caslin cleared his throat and Ashton glanced up in their direction, unsurprised by their presence. Returning to his conversation, he looked between the two men to either side of him seeking their agreement.

"I'll take care of it," the larger man said.

"Good," Ashton confirmed. "Come back to me later, yeah?" The man nodded and turned to leave, paying the new arrivals no attention whatsoever. The younger man also left. He flicked his eyes towards Caslin as he passed in what Caslin figured was a nervous action. He seemed familiar but Caslin couldn't place him. Being a part of the Fuller's crew would mean they'd probably crossed paths at some point over the years. "Detective Inspector Caslin," Ashton said warmly in a welcoming tone. "What brings you here?"

"One of your businesses going up in flames," Caslin said flatly. He noted Carl entering behind them. Glancing back over his shoulder, he saw Carl lean against the wall, folding his arms across his chest in front of him. "What can you tell me about it?"

Ashton momentarily followed Caslin's glance towards his brother before addressing the question. "It is unfortunate."

"Particularly for your employees who were inside," Hunter added.

"Very," Ashton said, expressionless.

"Can you tell us who was present?" Caslin asked.

Ashton nodded. Crossing the office, he retrieved a scrap of paper. Returning, he handed it to Caslin who eyed the list of names. There were four, one woman and three men.

"Sally was working the comms last night. Tom was with her and the other two were drivers," Ashton said. "Any word on how they are?"

"I thought you might be at the hospital," Caslin said. He was being disingenuous and he knew it.

"I have a business to run. Besides, I figured someone like you would be dropping by this morning," Ashton stated, pushing aside the plans atop the nearest desk and perching himself on the edge.

"Sally is dead," Caslin said. "As are two of the others but one is in surgery. They are hopeful."

"Good to know," Carl said from behind him.

"A member of the public is also in a serious but stable condition," Caslin added.

"I'm sorry to hear that," Ashton said. Caslin didn't believe him.

"You haven't asked about the cause," Caslin said, moving further into the office and turning so both brothers were in his sightline. Ashton shrugged.

"Enlighten me," he said, folding his arms.

"Gas leak," Caslin said, watching closely for a reaction. The thought occurred, Ashton must be one hell of a card player because he was unreadable.

"Should be illegal," Carl said, sniffing loudly. "Poor workmanship."

"True," Caslin said, flicking his eyes towards Carl and back to his elder brother. "How's business?"

Ashton smiled, "Booming, Mr Caslin. We're on the up."

"Any of your competition making inroads?" Hunter asked.

"What's that supposed to mean?" Carl asked. Hunter turned to him.

"In a world of finite resources when you want to grow, it always comes at the expense of another, doesn't it?" she asked. "Basic market economics."

"You're a lot smarter than you look," Carl sneered. He was

about to respond further but Ashton shot him a dark look ensuring he kept quiet.

"We are competitive," Ashton answered.

"How about Clinton Dade?" Caslin asked, referencing the Fullers' historical adversary. Carl scoffed, unable to contain his reaction.

"That old mincer!" he said before Ashton could speak. "He wouldn't dare."

"Dare to do what?" Caslin asked. Carl looked to his brother who, for the first time, appeared to drop the mask he so carefully maintained.

"Nothing," Carl muttered, turning his attention to the floor. Ashton took a deep breath and looked at Caslin.

"We've not come across Clinton in quite some time. There's no issue between us," Ashton argued. "Besides, I have a lot of time for the elderly. You have to look out for people, don't you?"

Caslin let the silence hang for a few moments as he assessed the brothers. They also appeared comfortable enough to allow it to continue. Caslin's gaze fell on the eldest who returned it. After a few seconds, Ashton raised his eyebrows initiating a questioning look. Caslin rolled his tongue against his cheek in the inside of his mouth. Reaching into his pocket, he withdrew one of his contact cards.

"If anything comes to you that you think I should know, do give me a call," he said, stepping forward and offering the card. Ashton glanced at it but he didn't make a move to accept it. Caslin reached past and placed it onto the desk alongside him, bringing him into close proximity with the younger man. Before stepping back, Caslin held his position and leaned in close enough that only the two of them could hear his words. "Don't do anything hasty, Ashton. And see to it no one else does either, for all our sakes," he almost whispered, casting a lingering look towards Carl who stared at him with a face like thunder. Stepping away, he added in a voice for all to hear, "We'll be in touch."

"Thanks for stopping by," Ashton replied, unmoved and glancing at his brother. Carl didn't speak as both detectives made to leave the office. They reached the door and Ashton called after them, "Feel free to have your car washed before you go. It's on me." Caslin glanced back at him but didn't respond.

Walking down the ramp, the roar of heavy machinery and their accompanying warning alarms came to ear as the two of them set off across the site in the direction of their car. Hunter looked back to see Carl at the doorway, hands thrust into pockets and watching their departure.

"They're not giving much away," she said, raising her voice to ensure she was heard above the noise.

"You didn't expect them to, did you?" Caslin said. Hunter agreed. "I had hoped appealing to Ashton's common sense would give us time to get it sorted."

"Do you think we managed it?"

Caslin shook his head, "To be honest, I don't know. He was expecting us and I'll bet he's already formulating a response. I know he gives over the impression of composure but he can be almost as impulsive as his little brother, albeit he's marginally more calculating."

"You think he knows where this has come from?"

"He suspects," Caslin thought aloud, "and I reckon he has in mind what they plan to do about it."

"Your instinct is Dade, right?" Hunter asked.

Caslin nodded, "Stands to reason. Despite what he says, there's no love lost between the two families and they don't go too long without stepping on each other's toes."

"Bombing one of their businesses is an escalation. A bit more than *stepping on their toes*," Hunter argued as they reached the car. She unlocked it and they got in. Caslin shut his door, instantly diminishing the ambient noise around them. He looked back towards the building site.

"They have a lot to lose if they're going to get involved in a turf war," he said.

"As would Dade," Hunter countered. "Is there anyone else? Danika Durakovic perhaps?"

"No, I don't see what she would have to gain. There isn't a great deal of overlap. The Fullers think they're big time. The family reputation is fearsome but let's be honest, the crew aren't what they once were. They haven't managed to eclipse their old man. Far from it."

"Not yet, no," Hunter stated. "But what about the possibility you floated earlier? That maybe the brothers are the aggressors here and the bombing *is* the retaliation."

"If that's the case, we had better figure it out before someone ups the ante. Otherwise this is going to get messy very quickly."

Hunter turned the key in the ignition firing the engine into life. Moving off, they negotiated the small queue waiting their turn to be valeted. Circumventing the cars, Hunter drove around the rear of the old petrol station and came to the main road. The skies were brightening as the clouds cleared bringing forth the promise of a better day ahead. Caslin's phone rang and he took it out, noting the call was from Terry Holt.

"What is it, Terry?"

"He didn't survive theatre, sir. That's four out of the five who didn't make it."

"Okay," Caslin said, deflated. Glancing at Hunter he offered a brief shake of the head. She knew what that meant. "Head back to Fulford Road and we'll see you there. When you get back, I want..." his phone beeped to indicate there was another call incoming. Caslin checked the screen, it was Kyle Broadfoot, Assistant Chief Constable and his boss. He figured he had best take the call. "I'll get back to you, Terry," he said, hanging up and switching to the other line.

"Nathaniel," Broadfoot said by way of greeting.

"Sir," Caslin replied. "We're on our way back to Fulford Road."

"Good, you're already out in the field. I need you to swing by somewhere and meet me," Broadfoot said. "I've got something for you to cast your eye over."

"Sir?" Caslin failed to hide his irritation. "The explosion earlier today looks very much like a targeted campaign against Pete Fuller's group."

"And you will be able to fill me in when you get here, Nathaniel."

"Where exactly are you, sir?" Caslin asked, caught off guard. For Broadfoot to be present at a crime scene so close to home before Caslin was even aware of its existence was surprising to say the least.

"East of York. Head towards Pocklington, via Kexby and you won't be able to miss us," Broadfoot said. "I'll expect you along directly." He hung up before Caslin had a chance to reply. Touching the handset to his lips, he was momentarily lost in thought before he caught sight of Hunter in the corner of his eye repeatedly glancing across at him, itching to know what was said.

"Change of plan," Caslin said, looking over towards her. "Head for Kexby."

"Why?" Hunter asked.

"Damned if I know," Caslin replied. "But ours is not to reason why…"

CHAPTER FOUR

THE ROUTE to Kexby was a much-travelled road cutting through farmland and linking various small communities between York and Market Weighton. Aside from the sparsely populated villages there was very little reason to be in the area unless working the land or attached to the small industrial estates peppering the otherwise rural landscape. Passing one such a place, Caslin eyed the liveried police car coming up on their right-hand side. Slowing down, they approached a turning into a gated area used by agricultural machinery to access the fields. Pulling up, they came to a stop alongside the police car. Looking past it, barely a stone's throw away, they could see it was one of three not including the CSI van parked nearby.

A uniformed constable stepped forward and checked their identification before allowing them access. Clearing the highway, Hunter parked beside what she recognised as Kyle Broadfoot's chauffeur-driven car. Caslin got out and looked around. Nestled into the Vale of York, the landscape was flat with trees lining the boundaries shielding the immediate area from passing traffic on the road. The access track ran off in a straight line from the road whereas adjacent to it was a patch of flooded marshland. Reeds grew in abundance nearby and beyond those he could see open water, perhaps stretching for a hundred yards. From the look of its configuration, he figured this was a man-made basin created to drain the fields of excess water.

A group were gathered near to the water's edge and Caslin could make out the lanky figure of his superior amongst the collection of high-vis jackets and white-clad forensic technicians. Both Caslin and Hunter approached as Assistant Chief Constable Kyle Broadfoot spotted their arrival, acknowledging them with a wave and beckoning them over.

"Nathaniel. Sarah. Pleased you could join us," he said, his words accompanied by a cloud of vapour. Despite the presence of the sunshine, the clearing skies belied the freezing temperature hovering barely above zero. Exposed as they were out here in the countryside, the wind chill made it feel several degrees below.

"Good morning, sir," they said in unison. He bid them to accompany him to the water's edge. The forensic team stepped aside to give them space. What they saw was no longer shocking to either of the newcomers. A body lay half into the water, much of the upper torso was submerged. It was clearly a male. Caslin figured him to be in his early thirties. However, the angle in which the body lay, face down in the water, it wasn't particularly easy to judge. There was a significant amount of damage to the rear of the skull with the hair thickly matted with blood. Caslin figured pathology wouldn't need to work too hard to determine the cause of death. The water here didn't flow and therefore it was reasonable to presume the body lay in more or less the same position in which it had entered the water.

Caslin knelt in order to get a better view. The man was dressed in jeans and a checked shirt. It was a casual shirt not an all-weather outdoor item and offered scant protection against the recent weather. Coupled with the jeans and the leather town-shoes they could rule out the man being a hiker or rambler. Looking around this seemed an odd place for a man dressed in this way to be.

"Any ID?" he asked. Broadfoot politely snapped his fingers indicating for something to be passed to him. An evidence bag was swiftly handed over and Broadfoot gave it to Caslin. Standing up, Caslin donned a pair of latex gloves and opened the bag. Withdrawing a wallet from inside, he noted it was wet, presumably having been retrieved from one of the victim's pockets. Flicking through the contents, he came across the driving licence. Even with the face being half under water, Caslin could see it was the same man. "Jody Wyer," he said aloud for Hunter's benefit as much for his own. Continuing to inspect the contents, he noted there was at least fifty pounds present, credit cards and a number of business cards. Caslin teased one out. It was damp and therefore delicate so he took great care not to damage it. The card had the business name, *Blue Line Investigations.* A registered office address in central York, along with both a land line and mobile phone number. He passed the card to Hunter. She scanned it.

"What do they investigate, does it say?" she asked.

"A private investigation agency," Broadfoot confirmed. Caslin flicked his eyes in his superior's direction and then across at Hunter.

"Any sign of the mobile?" Caslin asked. Broadfoot shook his head. "How about a car? Do we know how he got here?" he asked, looking around. Iain Robertson appeared, clad in his white suit. Caslin hadn't realised the head of forensic investigators was present when he arrived. He was caught off guard figuring Robertson would be on his way to the scene of the bombing to liaise with Mark Francis, the Fire Brigade's lead investigator.

"We have fresh tracks set down overnight just over there," Robertson indicated to where members of his team were setting up. "My guess it's an SUV of some type judging by the width of tread and the wheel base. The drop in temperature has set them quite nicely for me."

"I think we can rule out robbery as a motive based on what

they left us," Caslin argued. No one disagreed. "How long would you say he's been in the water?"

Robertson looked at the body, screwing his nose up in concentration. "Bearing in mind the recent weather, I'd suggest a couple of days. No more than that," he said, rocking his head side to side as he offered his thoughts. "Once we get him out of the water, I'll take his temperature and then I'll be able to narrow that down a little for you. Are you happy for us to proceed?" he asked, looking to Broadfoot who nodded.

Robertson called over his technicians and the others stood aside, retreating up the shallow incline to allow them to get on with their work.

"I know you have your hands full with this bombing in the city centre, Nathaniel," Broadfoot said. "But I would like you to focus with an equal measure on this case. I've cleared it with DCI Matheson that we take the reins on the inquiry. Such is the way of things at Fulford Road at the moment I think she was only too happy for us to take it off her hands."

Caslin noted Broadfoot was staring back towards the forensics team as they retrieved the body from the water with an expression on his face that Caslin found unreadable. Usually, he found Kyle Broadfoot to be very matter-of-fact, displaying an innate pragmatism that saw his stewardship of the North Yorkshire Crime Directorate run very smoothly as well as successfully.

"Can I ask what our interest is in this case, sir?" Caslin asked. After all, as homicides went this was a fairly straightforward investigation. "I mean, why should it interest Major Crimes?"

Broadfoot took a deep breath, his gaze passing over DS Hunter and falling onto Caslin.

"Jody Wyer was known to us," he said flatly.

"In what capacity?" Caslin asked, sensing reticence.

"On occasion, he would offer up information if it were mutually beneficial."

"He was an informant?"

"Not officially, no."

"I've never come across him," Caslin said, glancing towards Hunter who indicated the same with an almost imperceptible dip at the corners of her mouth that was missed by Broadfoot, as intended.

"Before your time here, Nathaniel."

Caslin raised his eyebrows and nodded, "Any idea what he was investigating?"

"No, I'm afraid not," Broadfoot stated. "Although, the last communication we had with him he implied he was working on something pretty big."

"When was this?" Hunter asked.

"Last month."

"Did he offer up any more detail than that?" Caslin asked. Broadfoot shook his head. Wyer's body had been photographed and was now being placed into a body bag in preparation for transportation to the morgue where an autopsy would take place. At this point, Broadfoot finally tore his gaze away from the scene.

"No, I'm afraid he didn't," he said, turning and indicating to his driver that he was ready to leave. The officer strode towards the car.

"Was he reported missing?"

"Not that I'm aware, no."

"Who found the body?" Caslin asked.

"A dog walker. That's him over there," Broadfoot said. Caslin turned to see a man talking to another officer a little way off. A Springer Spaniel sat at his feet as he offered his statement.

"Who do we contact as next-of-kin, sir?" Hunter asked. Broadfoot looked at her. "We'll need an official identification."

"That won't be necessary in this case, Detective," Broadfoot said, turning to Caslin. "Keep me posted, would you?"

"I will, sir," Caslin said.

Broadfoot smiled weakly, acknowledging Hunter and set off. His hands were thrust into the pockets of his overcoat and his head bowed as he picked his way across the mud in the direction of his car. The engine was already running and his driver opened the rear door for him, swiftly closing it once Broadfoot was inside. Caslin watched the car leave, the uniformed constable opening the gate to allow them to pass.

"What do you make of that?" Hunter asked. "I've never seen him so pained."

Caslin shrugged, "Me neither. It makes it even more intriguing to find out what Mr Wyer was getting stuck into."

"You think it will be related to his work?" Hunter asked.

"Let's not rule anything in or out," Caslin said. "Maybe he criticised his better half's choice of outfit and we'll have it closed off by dinner time." Hunter laughed. It was a bitter sound.

"I guess there's a first time for everything," she said. "How do you want to play it?"

"We'll not get anything from the bomb site until later today at the earliest. Let's drop in on Wyer's office and see if we can gauge their reaction to all of this."

Caslin felt his phone vibrating in his pocket. Inclining his head in the direction of the car, Hunter nodded and set off. Taking out the phone, Caslin saw it was Karen, his ex-wife.

"Karen," he said, turning back towards Robertson and the CSI team carrying out their inspection of the deceased.

"Hi, Nate," she said, coming across far more upbeat than usual. "I wanted to speak with you about the weekend."

"The weekend?" he asked, immediately concerned there was something he'd forgotten about.

"Yes. You remember, we're away in Copenhagen and we talked about you having the kids?" she said. Caslin's heart sank. He had forgotten about his ex-wife and her fiancé going away for a long weekend. Seeing two crime scene officers hoist the black body bag onto a gurney and wheel it away, struggling in their efforts to negotiate the terrain, towards the waiting transport van, he considered his position.

"Yeah, about that…"

"Nate," Karen said, her tone shifting slightly. "Don't you dare cancel on me. We've had this planned for months."

"I know. You heard about that explosion in the city this morning?"

"No, I haven't seen the news," she said. "Why? What's going on?"

"I can't say but... it's a difficult time—"

"Nathaniel, I am going away on Friday night and you need to be with your children."

"Perhaps Sean could—"

"No, Sean is not taking responsibility for his sister! He can barely look after himself. You know that. I know your job is important to you."

"It's not that it's important to me," Caslin argued. "I can't just drop everything."

"I'm not asking you to drop everything. These are your children, Nathaniel."

"I'm well aware—"

"You're having the children this weekend," Karen said, talking over him. She was emphatic.

"I... I'm sorry. I can't," Caslin replied. The line went dead. He exhaled heavily, casting his eyes skyward. The last thing he wanted to do was let his family down. In the past few months he was pleased with the progress they had made. Lizzie was developing further into the confident little girl he'd always imagined she would be and Sean was on the right track. Granted, it was a tougher climb from the darkness of his world twelve months previously, but things were looking positive. It nagged at him that Karen was still so quick to judge him as being willing to shirk his responsibilities.

Realising there was little he could do, he pushed the negativity aside. There would be a solution and he had a couple of days to think of one. If not... well, he would cross that bridge when he reached it. Turning, he covered the short distance between himself and the car. Hunter already had the engine started. Getting in, he was grateful the heaters were on.

"Everything okay?" Hunter said, clearly reading his expression.

"Nothing a spare me wouldn't cure," he replied. She looked at him quizzically. "So that I could be in two places at once," he explained.

"I could use one of those as well," she agreed. "Do we ever get the balance right?"

Caslin's face split a wry grin as he shook his head slightly, "Tipping the scales the opposite way every now and again would make a nice change though, wouldn't it?"

"Life could be worse," she said softly, watching Jody Wyer being loaded into the unmarked mortuary van. "Shall we go?" He nodded and Hunter pulled away. The constable manning the gate opened it and Caslin acknowledged his efforts with a brief flick of the hand as they passed through.

CHAPTER FIVE

IT WAS mid-morning by the time they arrived at Blue Line's offices. Located on the upper two floors of an imposing old Victorian terraced house, previously residential but now converted for commercial use. The ground floor was assigned to a small architect's firm and the access to the private detective's office was by way of a metal fire escape running up the side of the building. Parking was limited to the width of the building's frontage. Caslin noted the plaque on the wall, sited in the only empty bay denoting where Jody Wyer's car would be parked.

A Jaguar was in the adjacent bay, less than two years old and was designated as belonging to another employee of the company, a T. Mason. Caslin thought the name sounded familiar to him but he couldn't place it. They made their way up the stairs, their feet clattering on the metal beneath them as they went. The recent rain followed by the subsequent drop in temperature made the route up precarious as the water had frozen, but they reached the top without event. Caslin opened the outer door and ushered Hunter into the lobby. The interior had a makeshift appearance to it. The walls were painted white. The carpets were a block-blue colour and thin but hard wearing. Everything around them was functional but could have been any bland office offering any service. Nothing denoted they were in premises specialising in private investigations.

A woman appeared from a small room holding a steaming cup of tea before her and was so startled by their presence she almost jumped at the sight of them. Caslin smiled.

"I'm sorry," he said, glancing back towards the entrance and indicating it with his hand. "The door was open."

She gathered herself swiftly, also apologising. "No, please, it's not a problem. I just didn't hear the door. It was probably the kettle," she said. "How can I help?"

Caslin assessed her. She was in her late twenties, attired in business dress and fastidiously-applied make up and hair. There didn't appear to be a reception of any kind, so Caslin was unsure of whether he was speaking to an employee or an investigator. He took out his warrant card and stepped forward enabling her to see it.

"I'm Detective Inspector Caslin. This is DS Hunter," he said. "And you are?"

"Donna Lafferty," she replied. "I'm Mr Wyer's personal assistant."

"Can I ask when you last saw Mr Wyer?"

"A couple of days ago," Donna said. "He's not been in much this past week or so."

"Is that unusual?" Hunter asked.

"Not really. He's been very busy recently. He's often out of the office for days on end."

"And what about speaking to him... when was that?" Caslin asked.

"The last time?" she clarified. Caslin nodded. "The same time. Two nights ago. Why? What's going on?" She said the last with a tinge of anxiety creeping into her tone as the realisation dawned on her they were there on a business call. "What's he gotten himself into now?"

"Can you tell us what Mr Wyer was working on?" Caslin

asked, but Donna's reply was interrupted by the arrival of another.

"I thought I heard voices," a barrel-chested man said, stepping out from a room at the end of the narrow corridor into the interior. Caslin took his measure, late-fifties, overweight with dark brown hair swept up in a quiff that was almost certainly coloured from an over-the-counter bottle. He approached with an affable manner, a booming voice that echoed in the confined space. "How can we help?" he said, grinning. His face had reddish tones to his cheeks and he was already breathing heavily as he offered Caslin his hand in greeting.

"They're from the police, Mr Mason," Donna said.

"Detectives Hunter and Caslin," Caslin said, taking the offered hand.

"Pleasure," he replied, shaking Caslin's hand warmly. "Tony Mason. What can we do for you?"

"I'm afraid we have some bad news for you regarding Mr Wyer," Caslin said. "We haven't confirmed it officially but a member of the public found Mr Wyer early this morning."

"*Found him?*" Mason replied, a look of surprise crossing his face.

"I'm afraid, we believe Mr Wyer is dead," Caslin stated. Donna emitted an audible gasp whereas Mason appeared similarly shocked.

"I... I... don't understand... He's dead? How?"

"That's yet to be determined," Hunter offered. "Is there somewhere that we can talk? We need to gather a bit of background to help us figure this out."

"Yes... yes, of course," Mason said. "I know how it works. Please, come with me to my office."

Mason placed a reassuring hand onto Donna's shoulder before turning and leading them back along the corridor to the room he'd originally appeared from. Caslin followed with Hunter a step behind. As they made their way, the floorboards creaked and groaned under their weight and the corridor itself felt like it slanted at an angle towards the rear of the building. A sign of the building's age. As they walked, Caslin remembered why he recognised Mason's name. He was a former CID officer based out of Acomb Road Station covering the west of York. Caslin was reasonably confident Mason left the force prior to his arrival at Fulford Road, but he was certain it was him.

They entered the office and were met by another woman seated at one of the two desks present. She was older than Donna, perhaps in her fifties, and a similar age to Mason.

"This is Beth, my P.A.," Mason said, the joviality in his tone no longer evident. Beth rose from her desk and greeted them with an awkward smile glancing across at her boss, aware of how his mood had changed. They introduced themselves to her. "It's Jody," Mason explained, looking to her and offering them both a seat. "He's dead."

"My god," she exclaimed, open-mouthed. "How?"

"We're working on that," Caslin said, noting Donna entering behind them. Her eyes were brimming with tears and Beth quickly crossed over and placed a supportive arm around her shoulder, offering her a tissue. "Can you tell us about Jody's caseload?"

Mason shrugged, "Nothing out of the ordinary."

"What sort of work do you take on?" Hunter asked.

"Run-of-the-mill stuff really," Mason explained. "We do insurance fraud, personal injury claims... Oh, and the usual marital affairs and such like. The former two are a bit of a money-spinner and the latter is... well... commonplace."

"What was Jody currently working on?" Caslin asked. Mason looked to Donna.

"He had three or four cases on the go," she said, her voice cracking.

"Were any of those cases threatening in nature?" Hunter asked. "Anyone taking offence at his attention?"

"Are you saying Jody's been murdered?" Mason cut in.

"What makes you ask?" Caslin said.

"The questions you're asking. I've been there. I know the drill. You said he was found dead. You said nothing about anything suspicious."

"Can you think of any reason someone would wish him to come to any harm?" Caslin asked.

Mason sank back in his chair, shaking his head. "No. None at all. Jody is… was… one of the good guys."

Caslin looked to the other two who both shook their heads. "Was he married?"

"Divorced. A long time ago," Mason stated. "His ex remarried and lives in New Zealand now."

"Any kids?"

Mason shook his head, "No. He never seemed too bothered about relationships either."

"How so?"

"He spent a lot of time on his own. His parents are both dead and he was an only child. All adds up to being a bit of a loner."

"What about his cases?" Caslin asked.

"We don't share caseloads," Mason explained. "We operate under the same umbrella but not in tandem, if you know what I mean?"

Caslin nodded, "How long have you known each other?"

"All his life," Mason explained. "I worked with his father in the job. We were good friends. When I was approaching my thirty, Jody suggested I join him in setting up this business. He was working as an investigator for an insurance company and there was plenty of work to go around. We set up on our own. Our combined experience gave us a decent amount of credibility in the industry, so it was a no-brainer."

"And how is business?" Hunter asked, involuntarily casting an eye around the bare office, devoid of character. Mason noticed.

"Don't let the décor fool you, Miss," he said, narrowing his eyes. "We just don't waste money on stylish furnishings. There's no point. We hardly get clients come through the door as most of our business is corporate related. Much of our time is spent out in the field. Business is punchy right now. We have three teams of investigators plus ourselves and cover a radius of one hundred miles from this very chair. You'll see from my jag parked outside that business has never been better."

"No offence intended," Hunter said.

"None taken," Mason countered. Caslin rolled his tongue along the inside of his lower lip. Hunter was irritated by Mason's belittling reference to her but only he could see it.

"What of Jody's cases?" Caslin asked. "Which was his most pressing?"

"He had a pretty big divorce case that was coming before a court in a couple of weeks," Donna offered, regaining some measure of composure. "And he took on an embezzlement case last month. Other than that, he was working two suspected insurance scams involving personal injury claims. They were both involved in the same accident but Jody figured they were set-ups."

"Can you elaborate?" Caslin asked. Donna looked to Mason who nodded.

"The divorce case is a straightforward investigation to assist a spouse improve the marital settlement from her estranged husband. He was quite abusive and played away so she is highly motivated."

"The abuse. Was it violent?" Hunter asked, making notes.

Donna nodded furiously. "Yes, absolutely. Systematic over the course of a decade. We collected medical records as well as proof of infidelity."

"Proof? In the form of what?"

"Video surveillance in the main," Donna stated.

"Was the husband aware of Mr Wyer's interest?" Donna shook her head. "And the others?"

"A firm in Leeds asked us to look into some accounting discrepancies within one of their client's accounts. They think one of their staff has been syphoning off funds."

"How much?" Caslin asked.

"We had only just begun but already we've noted twenty thousand is missing and it looks like it will rise far higher the further we go back."

"And the insurance scam?" Hunter asked, looking up from her pocket book.

"Two high value cars colliding with each other," Donna explained. Caslin figured he knew where this one was heading. It was a popular scam. "One was a Mercedes, the other a BMW and both were written off. The total value of the car owner's claims, including personal injury, were well over a hundred thousand pounds. Plus, there are subsidiary claims from passengers totalling over five figures per claimant."

"I'll bet the accident happened on an empty street in the middle of the night?"

Donna nodded. "Don't they always?"

"And where were you with those cases?"

"Jody figured both sets of people knew each other, so he was building a case trying to link them."

"In what form?" Hunter asked. Both Donna and Beth looked towards Mason once more. He remained stoic, unflinching. "Donna?" Hunter pressed.

"He didn't say," she replied, looking to the floor.

"We'll need names, contacts… regarding everything Jody was working on," Caslin said to Mason, figuring nothing would come out of the office without his say-so. "I can obtain a warrant if you prefer?"

"That won't be necessary, Inspector," Mason said. "You'll have our full cooperation in this matter."

"Thank you," Caslin said.

"When was the last time you saw Jody?" Caslin asked Mason.

"Two nights ago. We had a bit of a knees-up in the pub under the guise of a team meeting," Mason explained. "It was a cracking night."

"And how was he? Did he seem out of sorts, distracted perhaps?"

Mason thought about it, glancing at his colleagues and frowned, "Come to think of it, he wasn't his usual self. Don't get me wrong, I couldn't put my finger on why but he wasn't really up for a night out."

"True. He left early before it all got going," Beth confirmed.

"Did he say anything that might indicate why he wasn't participating?" Hunter asked.

"He was driving and so only had a couple of drinks," Donna said. "But no, other than that, he was quite normal as far as I could tell. A bit quiet maybe but no one likes being the sober one at the party, do they?"

"I guess not. Did Jody leave his computer here by any chance?" Caslin asked.

"No. He uses a laptop and always takes it home with him," Donna confirmed.

"We'll take a look at his home address then," Caslin said, taking out two of his contact cards and giving one to both Donna and Beth. "Well, if you think of anything I might like to know, I'd appreciate it if you would give me a call."

"Be assured we will," Mason said, sitting forward. "Tell me, which CID do you operate out of?"

"We're based at Fulford Road," Caslin replied, meeting Mason's eye and ignoring Hunter's glance.

"Nice station," Mason stated.

"Yes, it is," Caslin said, stepping forward. Mason rose as Caslin offered his hand. "If we need a positive identification to take place, would you be willing?"

"Of course, yes," Mason confirmed.

"Right you are. We'll be in touch."

DESCENDING the stairs to the outside, Caslin felt eyes on their back as they reached the street. Glancing over his shoulder, he caught a glimpse of Donna and the larger-than-life figure of Tony Mason watching them from above. Looking back, he met Hunter's eye as they crossed the road in between oncoming traffic to where the car was parked.

"A penny for them?" she said.

"What's that?"

"I know that face," Hunter explained. "What is it about them that has got you thinking?"

Caslin shook his head, smiling, "You started out over at Acomb Road. What do you know about Tony Mason?"

"He left before I went into CID," Hunter stated. "But I remember him as a well-liked DI. A little too old-school perhaps for the modern era."

"Meaning?"

"Well, he'd bend the rules if he thought it would get a result. That sort of thing."

"I see," Caslin said, reaching the car and heading around to the passenger side. Hunter unlocked it and they both got in.

"Not unlike someone sitting not too far away from me now," Hunter said with a wry smile. Caslin laughed. "Tell me, why didn't you say where we worked?"

Caslin looked at her with a questioning glance. "I don't know what you mean."

Hunter turned the key and started the engine. "Yes, you do. You told him we were based at Fulford Road."

Caslin stared ahead, assessing the traffic despite the fact he wasn't driving. "That's my problem, Sarah. You see, we are based at Fulford."

Hunter smiled, "You implied we were Fulford Road CID and didn't mention we were Major Crimes…"

"Who work out of Fulford Road," Caslin countered, grinning. "He didn't ask. I just didn't correct his assumption."

"You don't trust him."

Caslin inclined his head, "Did you notice how they both looked to him for their lead."

"Beth and Donna?"

"Yeah. Every time they were asked a question, they ran it past him first."

"He is their boss," Hunter stated in mitigation.

"Yes, he is," Caslin said, returning his focus to the traffic levels before adding, almost as an afterthought, "and no... as things go, the people I have a hard time trusting, apart from ex-cons... are ex-coppers. I don't trust him. Not one little bit."

CHAPTER SIX

THE SOUND of trains clattering through the nearby station in central York carried to them, metal upon metal shrieking as the carriages came to a halt. A muffled public address system announced forthcoming arrivals and platform updates.

"Looks like nobody's home," Hunter said, peering at the darkened interior through the shuttered blinds of the bay window. They were standing outside an unassuming brick terrace. Part of a row of twenty houses separated from the road by a knee-high dwarf wall. The street was narrow and lined on the opposing side by similar properties. Parked cars were interspersed with large gaps that would be filled once residents returned from work later in the evening. The buildings traditionally housed railway workers well before the advent of the motoring age. Even with minimal outside space, on-street parking and the accompanying noise of the city, they were still in a desirable location being so close to the city centre and its transport links.

"He lived alone," Caslin stated, stepping back from the front door and glancing towards the upper windows, his continued knocking remained unanswered. Two properties along, he noted a passageway to the rear of the terrace. Such was the nature of the construction rights of way were granted to the rear of neighbouring houses, allowing access to your own gardens via their boundaries. "Let's take a look around the back."

They made their way along and cut through the passage, barely a shoulder's width of space to the interior. Emerging from the darkness into a courtyard they were overlooked from the rear of the houses in the next street along. Almost all the properties had extended their living space to the rear as well as into the attic space, maximising their footprints. There would be little privacy to be had. Almost every window they looked at was shrouded in net or drawn curtains, despite it being the middle of the day, to ensure prying eyes were kept out. Gardens were fenced off or built up with imposing brick boundaries, each with a gate to allow access for your neighbours to pass through. Turning to their left, Caslin blindly reached up and over, unlocking the bolt at the top of the gate. Presumably, if you didn't know it was there, you might think the garden more secure than it actually was. Caslin doubted it would deter even the most incompetent of burglars.

Passing through the first garden they saw no one. Entering into the next, they startled a young woman standing at the window of her kitchen running herself a glass of water before the sink. She didn't recognise them and the look on her face was more one of surprise than suspicion. After all, they weren't dressed as you would expect a burglar to be. Hunter brandished her warrant card at the window, encouraging the occupant to come to the rear door for a word. She did so willingly. They exchanged names as well as greetings.

"Mrs Dempster," Hunter began.

"Natalie, please."

"Natalie. We're looking at your next-door neighbour's house," Hunter explained, leaving out the fact they had found his body. "Have you seen anyone there recently?"

"Jody?" she asked. Hunter nodded. "No, I've not seen him for a while. To be honest, he's hardly ever home. Keeps all kind of strange hours and so do I, so I often don't see or hear him for days on end."

"What is it you do?" Hunter asked, making conversation.

"I'm a nurse at the hospital," she replied. As if working out why they might be there for the very first time, she asked, "Is Jody all right?"

"No, I'm afraid Mr Wyer was found dead this morning," Hunter replied.

"Oh my god," Natalie said, glancing away and leaving her mouth wide open. "Poor Jody."

"Has there been anything unusual that you have noticed in the last few days or weeks?" Caslin asked. "It may have seemed innocuous at the time but now… perhaps not?"

Natalie shook her head, "No. Nothing out of the ordinary."

"Did you know Mr Wyer well?"

"Quite well, yes. We would share an evening every now and again," she explained. "We're not best friends or anything but I like him. Plus, he gets on with my partner which always helps."

"What kind of neighbour was he?" Hunter asked. "Did he socialise much? Have wild parties, guests at all hours, that type of thing?"

Natalie shook her head, "No, nothing like that. He was a quiet guy. Seemed to keep himself to himself, you know? Shame really."

"How so?" Caslin asked, interested.

"Well… I get the impression he was a little brow beaten. He was that sort of guy."

"Brow beaten? By whom?"

"It's just my impression but some people just aren't good at socialising, are they?"

"Did he have any friends? Regular visitors?" Caslin asked.

"You know what, if you'd asked me that any time in the last two years, I'd have said no but there has been a woman coming by recently. I mean, he never had a girlfriend as far as I knew and I did wonder whether he was more inclined the other way, if you know what I mean?"

Caslin nodded. "So, this was a girlfriend? Did you ever meet her?"

Natalie shook her head, "No, I only caught the odd glimpse of her coming or going. She might not have been a girlfriend. She might have been another type of lady friend, who knows?"

Caslin considered what she was implying, "A regular visitor... friend with benefits, perhaps?"

Natalie shrugged, "Maybe. He didn't strike me as particularly successful with women nor did he seem too bothered about that fact."

"What do you put it down to?"

"Certainly not a lack of character. He was a great guy to be around but I'd say he was carrying a lot of baggage. He always seemed weighed down by life."

"Right," Caslin said, nodding. "Did you get a name for this woman?"

"No, can't say I ever did. I'd know her if I saw her again though. She stands out. A redhead – flame red. Natural as well, not from a bottle. Believe me, you'd know her if you saw her."

"A bit of a knockout?" Hunter asked.

Natalie agreed. "That's why I'd be surprised if they were a couple. I mean, Jody's a lovely guy and really successful with his business and everything but... well, he's not a looker."

"You mentioned Jody was weighed down. Can you elaborate on that? Did he ever say anything about it?"

"As I say, it's just my impression. I remember he found it tough when his dad was ill. You know, the getting to and from the hospital, arranging care and stuff? He did a lot for his old dad."

"They were close?"

Natalie frowned, "I'm not sure about that. I mean, he didn't speak highly of the man. I think it was more of an ingrained sense of duty that he carried... or had drummed into him."

"His father was overbearing?" Hunter clarified.

"I'd say so, yes. Not that Jody ever mentioned it directly but... you pick up on things, don't you?"

"Okay, thanks," Caslin said, glancing to Hunter before looking at Wyer's house next door. "Mr Wyer lived alone?"

"Yes, he did. Do you need to get in? I have a key."

CASLIN UNLOCKED the back door giving access to the kitchen. Stepping inside, he flicked the nearest switch bathing them in a flickering fluorescent light that eventually settled. Entering an empty property for the first time always felt a little eerie. Storm clouds were gathering and in such a built-up area very little daylight permeated the interior. Like the others in the row, Wyer's property was extended at the rear leaving the middle section of the house to cope with even less natural light. They listened for a moment but quickly decided they were indeed alone. Even so, they had to check.

Leaving Hunter to explore the ground floor, Caslin made his way upstairs. The treads creaked and groaned under his weight as he climbed them. There were two bedrooms off the landing as well as a family bathroom to the first floor with a narrow staircase curving up towards the converted attic. Casually inspecting both rooms, Caslin noted they were in a decent state of dress. The larger of the two was furnished with a king size bed and lined with contemporary wardrobes. Flicking through them, he found suits and clothing, all neatly pressed and on hangers. Jody Wyer was fastidiously neat with his attire.

Heading into the second bedroom, located to the rear, he found a spare bed that didn't appear to be in use at present. There was no sheet or bed covering. Even the associated duvet was curled up and lay at the foot of the bed. One wardrobe filled a corner to the right of the chimney breast and upon closer inspection only housed spare bedding and empty coat hangers.

Clicking the double doors shut, Caslin turned and headed back onto the landing and into the bathroom. In contrast to the master bedroom this area needed a thorough clean. Scale was building up on the mixer taps and around the base of the shower mildew was leading to mould along the length of the sealant. *Nobody's perfect,* Caslin thought as he opened a mirrored cabinet set above the sink.

Careful not to disturb anything, he eyed the contents. Alongside the over-the-counter medicines commonly found in family bathrooms, Caslin spied a bottle labelled *Paroxetine*. From personal experience, he knew that to be a medication prescribed for treatment of depression. Using the end of a pen, Caslin manoeuvred the bottle so as he could fully read the label confirming that it was indeed Wyer's and also making a mental note of the dated label. They were recent. The neighbour was correct, Jody Wyer was indeed weighed down by something. Returning his attention to the surroundings, Caslin found his attention piqued by something else. Leaning into the shower cubicle he scanned the toiletries present in the rack. There was an assortment of bottles, shampoo, conditioners, organic facial-scrubs and the like. Hearing footsteps on the stairs he called out so Hunter knew where he was.

She entered the bathroom. Even with two adults present the room was still a good size. Originally, they'd have been standing in a third bedroom with the only bathroom facilities being the pre-war outside toilet.

"What do you make of that?" Caslin said, indicating the toiletries. Hunter looked in and immediately clocked what he was referring to.

"Since when do you guys care about colouring conditioner?" she asked, smiling.

"Particularly to bring out your natural red..."

"Wyer has dark hair, doesn't he?" Hunter clarified, thinking back to the body being pulled from the water.

"Second toothbrush as well," Caslin stated, pointing at the cup sitting beside the basin. Hunter looked over, curious.

"What about clothing?" she asked.

Caslin shook his head, "No. All the cupboards and drawers are full of Wyer's... unless she has a masculine style."

"That's not the impression Natalie gave us."

"No. It certainly isn't," Caslin agreed. "Did you find a mobile or laptop downstairs?"

Hunter shook her head, "No. You?"

"Still one more floor to go," Caslin said, gesturing towards the upper staircase.

They made their way up together. The attic was set out as a home office with a desk at the far end, butting up against the chimney stack. Several filing cabinets lined the adjacent wall and a large cork board was attached to the wall opposite. Hunter inclined her head to say she would check out the desk while Caslin inspected the notes pinned to the board. There were several sticky notes with single words or times scrawled upon them. They made little sense without context. What drew Caslin's eye was a map, unfolded and pinned up. This was an ordnance survey map. The area covered began just south of Middlesbrough and stretched down the east Yorkshire coast ending just past Scarborough. Inland, the map went as far west as Pickering.

Many weekends of Caslin's youth were spent walking the moorland and coastal paths of that region and therefore he also knew this wasn't a map picked up off the shelf of any tourist information office. This was a custom order, one purchased directly from the national mapping agency of Great Britain. On it, Wyer had placed pins in certain areas whereas other points were circled in red pen. The significance of these locations was unclear but Caslin found himself curious. Initially, he wondered whether this was related to the divorce case Wyer was working. Could they be locations of trysts between illicit lovers? That theory was quickly disregarded unless the couple had a fetish for old quarries, cliff-top paths or abandoned lime kilns. The random nature of the locations only served to intrigue him further.

"Any sign of his tech?" Caslin asked over his shoulder not taking his eyes from the map.

"No. I have a charger, hard wiring for access to his hub but no computer. I can't find a note pad, diary, mobile, or anything that tells us what his plans were. If I had to say, I reckon his office has been swept clean."

"They didn't clear all of this," Caslin said softly. Hunter came to join him just as he took out his mobile phone. Stepping back, Caslin ensured he got the board in focus and took a few shots with the camera.

"What is it?" Hunter asked, inspecting the board.

"No idea. But I'll wager this is what he's been spending time on."

"What did Donna say he was working? Divorce case, embezzlement and car insurance scams, wasn't it?" Hunter asked.

"That's what she said," Caslin agreed.

"I don't see how those cases fit in on this map, do you?"

Caslin shook his head, "No. I wonder if Wyer was doing something off the books."

"That'd make sense. Broadfoot said he was working something big. That doesn't sound like a divorce case or an insurance scam."

"And they had only recently taken on the embezzlement case and Broadfoot said he'd been working on something for a while."

"Whatever it was, it could have been what got him killed. Do you think this redhead might have something to do with it?"

"We're going to have to track her down and ask," Caslin replied. "Even for a quiet guy, you'd think he would have mentioned her to someone."

"Mind you, do you think his colleagues know he was offering information to Kyle Broadfoot?"

Caslin raised an eyebrow, "Perhaps he's very good at keeping secrets."

Further conversation was halted by Caslin's ringing mobile. Taking it out of his pocket, he glanced at the screen and saw it was DC Terry Holt back at Fulford Road.

"Sir, uniform have located Jody Wyer's car."

"Good. What state is it in?"

"I'll text you the address."

"Any joy from the networks regarding his mobile phone?"

"I'm still waiting, sir."

"In the meantime, can you dig out as much as you can regarding Tony Mason? He's a former DI at Acomb Road as well as Jody Wyer's business partner."

"Will do, sir. What is it I'm looking for?"

"Anything and everything, Terry. Thanks. I'll catch—"

"Sir? Some of the guys back here are asking why we took over the Wyer case?"

"Which people?"

"Oh... you know, people, people."

"When I know, you'll know, Terry," Caslin said, hanging up. Hunter looked at him with a quizzical expression. "Tongues are wagging about our interest here."

"I must admit, I'm curious too," she replied. Caslin smiled just as his phone beeped. It was a text from Holt.

"Come on. Let's take a look at Wyer's car."

CHAPTER SEVEN

JODY WYER'S Seven-Series BMW cut a solitary figure in the car park of the pub. Perhaps it was the police presence combined with the onset of rain that kept the footfall low. Only a handful of punters were propping up the bar as Caslin looked out of the window, seeing the liveried police car maintaining the integrity of the crime scene.

"How long has it been there?" he asked the landlord, a round-faced twenty-something dressed in a black T-shirt and jeans.

"It was here two nights ago when we locked up and hasn't moved since."

"Do you know the owner? Was he a regular?" Caslin asked, glancing around the interior. It was clean, tidy and distinctly lacking in character. This was a chain pub resulting in a décor that was bland and inoffensive whilst trying to tip its hat to a bygone age. In his opinion they'd failed miserably.

"Yeah, I've seen him in here," the landlord stated, acknowledging a customer who was waving an empty pint glass in his direction. "Can I get you a drink?"

Caslin declined, "Was he here the other night, when you first noticed the car?"

"Aye, yes he was."

"What time did he leave?"

"I don't know exactly but it was early. Well before closing."

"Did he leave with anyone?"

"No idea, sorry," he replied with a shrug. "Any idea how long until I get my car park back?"

"No idea," Caslin replied with a shrug. "Sorry."

The landlord frowned and turned away and crossed to the opposing counter to serve the waiting patron.

"He was helpful," Hunter said. "Shall we take a look?" Caslin nodded and the two of them left the bar and walked out into the car park. The rain was steadily falling. Not persistent enough to drench you but hard enough to become very quickly irritating. Caslin turned his collar up and thrust his hands into his pockets as they crossed the saturated tarmac, rainwater pooling on the patchwork, uneven surface. Approaching the black car, they both donned latex gloves. Caslin eyed the interior. There was a jacket lying haphazardly across the back seat as if it were casually thrown there. Apart from that, there was nothing in view. The car was as neatly presented as Wyer's house. Caslin lifted the handle on the driver's door and found it unlocked. Casting a glance across the roof of the vehicle towards Hunter, he opened it.

Dropping to his haunches, he inspected the interior of the cabin. The side pocket of the door was empty without even a discarded fuel receipt or crisp packet. Hunter opened the opposing door and examined her side. Checking the lining of the upholstery, Caslin looked for any telltale indications of a struggle – blood stains, a scuff to the edge or a tear in the stitching – but there were none. Meeting Caslin's eye following her initial inspection, Hunter shook her head.

"Not a lot here is there?"

"He keeps things clean, doesn't he?" Caslin replied. "Glove box?" Hunter opened it, rifling through the contents. She pulled out the owner's wallet containing the service record and maintenance manual. Putting that aside, she took out an in-car charging kit for a mobile phone and what Caslin assumed was the locking wheel nut.

Shrugging, Hunter blew out her cheeks. "That's it," she said, disappointed. Caslin popped the manual boot release and they both walked to the rear of the car. Lifting the lid, they found what they were expecting – a clean, carpeted lining with nothing present that didn't belong. Closing it again, Caslin turned and looked around them, surveying the scene.

"We'll have to confirm that this was where the office outing took place," Hunter said, thinking aloud. "But it stands to reason. He either met someone here in the car park and left with them or he decided to walk from here."

"Didn't take his coat though," Caslin said.

"Let's gather as much of the CCTV as we can from the surrounding area. We might catch a break."

"Good idea," Caslin said, pursing his lips.

"What are you thinking?"

"Just that…" he left the thought unfinished, turning his head and scanning the tree line behind them. He cast his eyes up and took in the streetlights as well as the pub's minimal exterior illumination. "Not a bad place to jump someone," Caslin said, turning to Hunter and then scanning the floor nearby. She considered the theory. Caslin stepped away from the car and dropped to his haunches, reaching out but not touching the floor. He looked to the heavens and then back at the ground.

"What is it?" Hunter asked, coming alongside.

"The tarmac is wet, so it could be a trick of the light but I think this is blood," he said, moving his hand in a circular motion indicating a patch of the car park that appeared a darker shade than that surrounding it. "It stands to reason Wyer would have taken his coat off when he reached the car and was about to get in. That's why it's unlocked with the coat on the back seat. Do you have your torch?"

"Yes," she replied, reaching into her coat pocket.

"Can you put some light on this?" he asked. Hunter set the beam to where Caslin pointed. The damp patch shone with a tinge of red. Caslin looked past the car and into the trees beyond. "There's a great place to keep an eye on things," he said, looking from there back towards the pub. "You've got a decent sightline to the exit door from the pub into the car park. Likewise, anyone entering by car. There's nothing behind the trees there to note your presence, only the gable wall of those buildings. You're totally concealed."

"You think he was ambushed?" Hunter asked.

"If it was an opportunistic robbery why didn't they take his wallet? And why didn't they just leave him where he fell?" Caslin pointed to the ground at their feet.

"They went to a lot of trouble to get rid of the body but he was always likely to be found," Hunter said. "Maybe it was a robbery that got out of hand and when they realised he'd died, they panicked. Perhaps they got rid of the body because it would tie them to this area."

Caslin had to admit her logic was credible but not flawless. "The car ties it to the area though and they didn't move that. We'd better put a call in to forensics and let Iain Robertson know he has another crime scene."

"He'll be happy," Hunter said, smiling.

"Ahh… he loves being miserable," Caslin countered. "It gives him something to complain about."

"TERRY, talk to me about Tony Mason," Caslin said, momentarily distracted by his mobile ringing. Picking it up off the desk, he registered the caller before quickly dismissing it and sending the call to voicemail. Putting down the handset, he turned back to DC Holt and indicated for him to continue.

"Anthony Mason, resident here in York and a former detective inspector with North Yorkshire Police. Previously a DS with Greater Manchester," Holt stated, walking over to the information board and pointing to Mason's photograph, sited alongside one of Jody Wyer. "Companies House has him registered as a director of *Blue Line Investigations*, a limited company formed five years ago as a joint enterprise between the two of them."

"What do we know about the company?" Hunter asked.

"All required filings with HMRC have been carried out on schedule. Their position is solvent with a healthy cash position," Holt said. Hunter made a note. "I checked out their website. The services they offer are much as you described: corporate investigations, insurance fraud, marital disputes."

"And Mason himself?" Caslin asked.

"The performance reviews in his personnel file were variable."

"How so?"

"He earned glowing reports throughout his early career as he climbed the ranks until hitting a downward trend in the latter years of his service. I'd interpret that as a result of a change in commanding officer alongside a shift in how we were managed."

"Is that your polite way of saying he was proper old-school in his approach to policing?"

Holt nodded enthusiastically. "He received several complaints regarding his conduct in the last three years up until he hit his thirty and retired," Holt said, referring to his notes. "One of those complaints came from a fellow officer."

"Wow," Caslin said, glancing towards Hunter. "He was probably keen to get out of the door."

"Those aren't the greatest highlights on file for him though," Holt said. "He was the subject of an investigation by Complaints nearly a decade ago."

"What was their interest?" Caslin asked, finding his curiosity piqued. The Complaints Division were responsible for investigating serving police officers, covering everything from conduct to corruption.

"His financial affairs," Holt said. "He was the victim of two counts of common assault. One in 2006 and another, more recently, in 2011. The latter saw him hospitalised for over a week."

"How does that tie in with Complaints?" Hunter asked.

"There was the suggestion that this resulted from debts he had run up."

"Who with?"

Holt shook his head. "The investigations didn't go anywhere. Complaints ended theirs with a reprimand placed on his file relating to his gambling habits, recommending an ongoing process of monitoring. The thinking was that he'd left himself open to manipulation with his debts which, as you both know, is a big no-no."

"What about the assaults?"

"In 2006, the case remained unsolved. Mason claimed he had no knowledge of his assailants and there were no witnesses. In the second case, the charges were dropped when Mason himself refused to press charges. I think that was the final nail in his career. Shortly after, he was shifted across to Acomb Road to see out his thirty."

"Any suggestion as to who he owed money to?" Caslin asked. "Are we looking at loan sharks or backstreet bookies?"

Holt shrugged, "Sorry, sir. I don't have that information. I'm going to go through the archive and gather the related names and I'll run them through the database for prior convictions and known associates. I might get a steer from that. I had a thought though. If he hit the financial buffers perhaps there was a pattern in his personal life that coincided with it?"

"Go on," Caslin encouraged him.

"He moved house on several occasions in the last ten years and not only at times matching a redeployment. Now, bear in mind it's only a cursory examination but each time he was downsizing and moving to a less desirable area."

"Cashing in to fund his lifestyle?"

"Or to stem his losses," Holt countered.

"Great work, Terry." Caslin smiled, turning to Hunter. "I reckon we should pop back and have a word with Mr Mason. I think he is holding back on us a little."

"Agreed," Hunter said and they both stood up.

"Let me know what you find in the archives," Caslin said. There was a knock on the frame of the door to their office. Simon, the civilian clerk from the station's front office ducked his head around the door.

"I'm sorry to interrupt, Inspector Caslin," he said tentatively. For a man who was notoriously unaware of how mundane people generally found his presence to be, he was however, acutely aware of how Caslin felt towards him – largely disinterested.

"What can we do for you, Simon?"

"I've taken three calls for you, Mr Caslin," he said. "They are all from your father. He is trying to get you on your mobile but is not having much luck. Is there a problem with your phone?"

"No. Not at all," Caslin replied. Hunter looked away and Terry Holt turned his back stifling a grin, both well aware Caslin was being short and yet equally aware Simon wouldn't notice.

"Oh… right. Well, he's asked that you return his call when you are free."

"Thank you," Caslin said.

"He has called three times," Simon said, watching Caslin pick up his mobile and put it in his pocket.

"Thank you," Caslin repeated.

"If he calls again, what should I say?"

"Use your imagination," Caslin said, pulling on his coat and signalling for Hunter to join him. They both walked out, Hunter smiling at the bemused clerk who was trying to make sense of the exchange.

"That was mean," Hunter said playfully as they made their way along the corridor.

"I don't know what you're talking about," Caslin said with a wry grin. "Heads up," he added under his breath as DCI Matheson rounded the corner in front of them. She indicated for them to stop as they approached.

"Nathaniel," she said, also acknowledging Hunter with an expression serving to advise her that her presence was not required.

"I'll meet you downstairs," Hunter said to Caslin who nodded. Matheson waited until the detective sergeant was out of earshot before she spoke.

"As much as I appreciate your Major Crimes Unit picking up some of CID's caseload, I was wondering what your interest in the Wyer case is?" Caslin smiled. That was a popular question at present.

"Interest is ongoing, Ma'am," he replied. Caslin was confident her words of appreciation were genuine since his own recruitment to Kyle Broadfoot's crime bureau had left Fulford Road's resident investigation team shorthanded. Particularly with Caslin's insistence on taking both Terry Holt and Sarah Hunter along with him, a decision that decimated the operational effectiveness of Fulford Road's CID. Replacements were either in place on a secondment basis or in the process of being reassigned. Nonetheless, the upheaval was significant. "Besides, we have an ongoing commitment to support you until such time as Fulford Road is back to the appropriate headcount." Matheson smiled but Caslin saw past it.

"Your political nous is improving, I see," she said.

"Thank you, Ma'am."

"In the meantime, can you offer me any reassurance that this bombing will not be repeated any time soon?"

"I wasn't aware that'd been confirmed," Caslin said. Matheson frowned, her patience tested. Caslin had to concede some ground, "Early days. We don't have a motive yet but the ownership of the business is more likely to be part of the inspiration than a random act of terror. That's my instinct talking, just to be clear."

Matheson accepted the statement with good grace, "Thank you, Nathaniel. If you need my help, just let me know."

"I will, Ma'am," Caslin said. "Thank you."

The DCI moved off and Caslin increased his pace, eager to hook up with Hunter and head over to see Tony Mason. Previously, he hadn't known what to expect but having met the man, Caslin didn't like him. He knew the type, bold, brash and a devil to unpick. Mason would only offer the information he knew Caslin could easily find out in other ways. Wyer wasn't talking to those around him regarding what he was working on or if he was, they weren't willing to reveal it. Either way, Caslin knew there was more information to be had and he intended to find out what that was.

CHAPTER EIGHT

APPROACHING MASON'S OFFICE, they spied his white Jaguar pulling out into traffic and set off in the opposite direction.

"What do you want to do, call in at the office or…"

"Follow him," Caslin said. "We're already heading that way. Outside of the office he may just drop his guard and you never know, maybe he'll give us more."

Hunter kept pace with Mason's car maintaining a comfortable distance with several vehicles in between them. They passed out of the city centre heading north towards the outskirts of York before cutting east. The residential area of Rawcliffe was to their right, bordering Clifton which was the direction they were travelling. Hunter saw Mason's indicator flicker on as he took a turn onto the Clifton Moor industrial estate, the last vestige of development before they reached the countryside. The traffic was lighter here and she eased off allowing him to put a little distance between them to remain unnoticed before she also took the turn.

Mason pulled his Jaguar into a scrap metal yard, easily identifiable by the towering stacks of wrecked cars visible above the perimeter fence. Hunter pulled up a few hundred yards away. To get any closer risked their presence being revealed as the nearby businesses were set back from the highway by some distance leaving too much open ground in which to try and conceal themselves.

"Leave the car here and let's see if we can get a little closer," Caslin said, getting out of the car. Hunter did likewise having reached over and grabbed her camera from the glove box. Falling into step alongside him, she hooked her arm through his to simulate being a couple. Together, they made their way along the path on the opposite side of the road from the scrap yard, casting casual glances in that direction as they passed the entrance. Emblazoned with a bold, blue and white sign signifying *MacEwan's Metals*, Mason's car was parked before the site office but no one else was visible. They kept moving so as not to draw attention to themselves but Caslin looked to their right and the building on the opposite side of the road. It was a two-storey distribution warehouse of some kind belonging to a large logistics firm. "This way," he said to Hunter, guiding her in the direction of the entrance.

Once inside, Caslin flashed his warrant card and sought access to the upper floor. The site manager was accommodating without prying, happy their presence had nothing to do with him or his team. He showed them into his office which overlooked the frontage giving them an uninterrupted view of the scrapyard. Caslin thanked him and they were left alone. A few minutes passed and they waited. The only movement came from the operation of a large crane, bending and scooping up a mixture of tangled metal and dropping it into a hopper to await the crusher. They didn't have to wait too long before figures emerged from within the office.

Mason appeared first. Even from this distance his pink cheeks looked far flusher than they had previously. His expression was fixed and he didn't look happy. Another man followed closely behind. He was older. Caslin figured he was in his late sixties with swept back hair that appeared almost white in contrast to his tanned skin, judged most likely to be natural rather than fake. He was gesturing as he talked and it looked very much as if Mason was the target of his ire. The latter turned and replied in kind raising his arm and pointing a finger in an accusatory gesture. Seconds later another came from within the office. Clearly, this man was the calming influence who sought to reconcile the other two.

"Recognise any of these guys?" Caslin asked.

"The peacemaker is David MacEwan," Hunter said. "He's been around a bit but I don't know the other one."

"I thought I knew him," Caslin said quietly. "I didn't realise he was back from Spain though."

"Nor did I," Hunter said.

"What about the guy with the white hair?"

"No idea."

"Get some pictures, would you?"

Hunter took out her camera, zoomed in on the trio and snapped away. The heat of the conversation subsided and they continued to talk but it was clear they hadn't reached a resolution. Mason clambered back into his Jaguar, slamming the door shut and rapidly firing the engine into life. The wheels spun in the gravel as he turned the car around and drove out of the yard, accelerating away at speed once the car reached the tarmac of the highway.

The remaining men continued their conversation and they were joined by another, a younger man who approached from the left and was previously shielded from view by the perimeter fence. Hunter ensured she had him in the frame as well. Moments later, he disappeared again before reappearing minutes later at the wheel of a red Mercedes. He got out leaving the engine running. They watched as MacEwan shook hands with the white-haired man and they shared a joke about something. The latter got into the car and the driver shut the door for him.

"Make sure you get that index," Caslin said, taking out his phone and putting a call into the control room.

"I've got it," Hunter confirmed as the vehicle left the yard taking a right and heading out of the industrial estate. Returning her focus to MacEwan she snapped the final picture of him and his associate as they dropped out of sight, back into the office.

"Right, thanks," Caslin said, hanging up on his call. "The Police National Computer check on that Mercedes has it registered to a hire car company based at Manchester Airport. We're going to have to get onto them directly to find out who's driving it."

"He certainly didn't get that tan in Yorkshire. Not at this time of the year," Hunter said dryly. "Should we go and have that chat with Mason now?"

Caslin shook his head, looking at his watch, "No. Let's find out a bit more about the new figures before we do. Mason looked pretty pissed off with whatever the conclusion of that discussion was. Related to Wyer, do you think?"

Hunter thought on it. "MacEwan's a career criminal. We've had him a couple of times over the years but he's always managed to slip through the net when those around him end up doing serious time. It's a strange acquaintance for an ex-copper to be associating with."

"We need to know who the unidentified man is and see where he fits in," Caslin said.

"MacEwan's been sunning himself for the past few years," Hunter said. "Maybe that's one of his business partners from over there."

"Perhaps," Caslin said. "Whatever's going on, Mason is rattled."

"WE'RE NOT LOOKING at anything particularly complicated here," Iain Robertson said, addressing the group. Kyle Broadfoot was in attendance at the briefing of the initial forensic analysis of the bombing. Caslin perched on the edge of a table to the left and Terry Holt was seated with Hunter. Robertson turned and pointed to a sketch of the minicab offices owned by the Fullers. On it, Robertson had placed pins labelled with the names of the victims to denote where he believed they were standing at the moment of the device's detonation. "I think the explosion originated here," he said, indicating the back office, located in the middle of the building behind a stud wall separating the waiting area from the front lobby. "Two of the victims were present in the room, judging from the severity of their injuries."

"What was the nature of those?" Broadfoot asked.

"Massive trauma. First-degree burns and lacerations. Both of them lost limbs as a direct result of the blast," Robertson explained. "The other employees were standing in the lobby."

"We believe they were drivers," Holt added.

"One of them was most likely about to take the fare of the waiting customer," Robertson said. "The former two were standing as the blast occurred and were struck by glass from the dispatcher's sliding screen. It shattered, sending shards of razor-sharp glass directly at them. The customer was either seated or lying down on the bench and I think this was the stroke of fortune that saved his life. Although caught in the blast, being in the corner saw the shock wave strike him but most of the debris flew above and past him. Bearing in mind he was half-cut from a night out, I wouldn't be surprised if he'd fallen asleep while he waited."

"You said the device wasn't complicated?" Caslin asked.

"That's right. We're talking about an improvised explosive. No doubt, homemade but no less deadly. I'm not expecting to find a complex chemical structure to this."

"And do we have any idea yet as to how it made its way into the building?"

"We recovered the hard drive related to the internal CCTV from the rubble. It was stored upstairs and so was protected from the worst of the blast. That's the good news."

"What's the bad news?" Caslin asked.

"The cameras were switched off thirty minutes before the

bomb went off," Robertson confirmed. An air of deflation swept throughout the room.

"Can we find out from the footage who was present in the building at that time?"

Robertson nodded, "I gave it to your man, there."

Holt stood up and crossed to his desk. Bringing his computer out of hibernation, he transferred the pictures to a projector before heading over and drawing the screen down so the others could see. Starting the footage rolling, Holt drew their attention to the time stamp in the bottom right-hand corner. It was forty minutes prior to the detonation. The images were split screen with nine camera angles displayed at the same time, a mixture of the interior and exterior of the building.

"We've identified five of the people we can see here and the sixth is a member of the public," Holt said, pointing them out. The customer was sitting with his feet up in the waiting area. One of the staff members, presumably a driver, came out and the two of them left the waiting area to go outside. "These four remaining are the victims along with another customer who appears in the waiting room in about eight minutes," Holt said, "whereas, this guy here," he indicated a figure approaching the rear of the building through the yard, "we are yet to identify."

They all strained to make out the details of the man's face. There was precious little light in the immediate vicinity. The figure wore a hooded jumper, pulled up over his head, and he didn't look in the direction of the cameras even once.

"He's been here before," Caslin said, watching him punch in an access code and unlock the door to the rear and pass straight through. Stepping into the dimly lit hallway behind the office and adjacent to the staff kitchen, they got their first proper view of him. Camera angles could be deceptive but he appeared to be a clean-shaven, white male, roughly six feet in height and carrying a small backpack. The image was low quality monotone and anything more discernible about his appearance was not forthcoming. "Can you clean that up at all, Terry?"

"No, sir. Not easily at any rate but I'll give it a go."

They watched as he entered the back office to be greeted by the four occupants but again, he didn't make eye contact with the camera. The staff present appeared to pay him little attention and continued their conversation. The hooded man crossed the room and made a show of retrieving something from the corner of the room but the action was predominantly out of shot.

"Definitely familiar," Hunter observed. Moments later, he returned to the door and stepped out back into the hall. Two of the occupants glanced in his direction as he left but it was unclear if communication followed or not. The figure reappeared on the hallway camera walking back out the way he had come in only this time he moved at pace. "No backpack," Hunter said. Holt sped up the film by a factor of three. The staff went about their business with nothing of note taking place until the footage ceased.

"At least we have our bomber," Broadfoot stated.

"Although, it's going to be highly unlikely we can identify him from that. The only witnesses who could identify him would be those present and they're all dead," Hunter said.

"No. He was well known to all of them. That's one of the Fullers' own right there," Caslin stated. "It was an inside job. He's a member of their organisation. No one batted an eyelid as he walked in and out."

"Do you think the Fullers know?" Broadfoot asked.

Caslin shook his head, "I didn't get that impression when we met with them." He looked to Hunter who shook her head to signify she agreed. "We could ask Ashton or Carl but they'd never let on. We'd just find another dead body in a couple of days."

"Or not," Hunter said. Caslin agreed. "It's a bit odd the footage going off when it did. Presumably, you reckon it was set to switch off?"

"Aye," Robertson confirmed. "Someone intentionally went into the system the day before and set it to shut the cameras off."

"You'd think that was to hide the bomber coming in but they got their times wrong."

"That's it," Robertson said. "Take another look at the time stamp. The clock was wrong on the system. They programmed it right but didn't factor in the timing was out."

"The big question for me is who put him up to it?" Caslin continued.

"Could be an internal power play," Holt suggested. "Between the Fullers themselves."

"Who stands to benefit most from the Fullers taking a hit like this?" Caslin asked.

"Clinton Dade is the obvious answer," Hunter replied. "But why now? Everything has been pretty cool between those two. It's not like the old days when Pete was knocking about."

"Gangs used to fight it out after the pubs closed back then," Caslin said. "Business has moved on. Everyone's a bit more professional these days. Or at least that's what we've gotten used to."

"Go and pay Dade a visit, would you?" Broadfoot said to Caslin, leaning forward and resting his elbows on the table in front of him and cupping his hands beneath his chin. "Suss him out and see if he orchestrated this. If their respective organisations are reheating the old antagonisms, I want us to get ahead of the curve rather than where we are right now."

"Will do, sir," Caslin said.

The meeting was adjourned and they split up to go about their tasks. Caslin called Hunter and Holt over to him.

"Terry, can you dig around MacEwan and see what he's up to at the moment but do it quietly. If he's friendly with one local ex-copper, like Mason, then he may be friendly with more. In the meantime, Hunter and I will call in on Clinton Dade and see what he makes of all of this. Chase up the hire car company regarding the Mercedes as well, would you?"

CHAPTER NINE

THE HEAD WAS THROWN BACK with an accompanying laugh, genuine and booming, projecting across the room. He was a slightly built man, tall and rangy, and one apparently able to skip the onset of middle-age spread. The diamond studs adorning his earlobes matched the chain around his neck visible beneath the collar of a neatly pressed, pink and white striped shirt. The depth of his voice surprised Caslin based solely on his outward appearance. However, he wasn't surprised by the reaction to their visit. His eyes flicked towards Hunter who was unimpressed. The two men standing either side of Clinton Dade remained impassive, not sharing the humour.

"You find the deaths of four people amusing?" Caslin asked.

"I think your attempt to bring it to my door is," Dade countered, the smile fading. Caslin met his eye. There was a gleam of confidence carried within the gaze. If Dade was even slightly thrown by the police presence in his office, then he hid it well. He was a shrewd operator having walked the path of criminality for several decades without falling foul of the law. A handful of convictions during his rise through the criminal ranks was all that put a blot on his copybook but they were distant memories. "I should be offended by your visit," he said, tilting his head to the side and casting an eye to one of his associates who stepped forward.

"I am," the younger man said, fixing Caslin with a stare and failing to hide his animosity towards them. He was tall, powerfully built and wore his hair short, bleached a ridiculous blonde colour setting it in stark contrast to his dark eyes and skin tone.

"And you are?" Hunter asked, drawing the gaze onto her.

"Minding my own business," he replied. Dade raised a hand and placed it gently on his associate's forearm. Caslin saw it as a commanding but affectionate movement.

"Don't worry about Alli," Dade said. "He doesn't care for the attentions of the police."

"If that's the case, perhaps he should make better choices regarding the company he keeps," Caslin said.

"Perhaps," Dade agreed, a half-smile creeping across his face. "So, one of the Fullers' establishments goes up in flames and you look to me? I should expect it to be fair."

"Wouldn't be the first time you and Pete came to blows and dragged the rest of us into it," Caslin said.

"Ancient history. Besides, Pete and I haven't had cause to cross each other's paths in years."

"Largely because he's been inside for decades," Hunter argued.

"Has it been that long?" Dade said, relaxing into his chair and dropping his shoulders ever-so-slightly. "Time certainly flies. What brings you to me?"

"He was sentenced to a minimum of twenty-seven years," Caslin said, stepping forward and placing his hands on the edge of Dade's desk in a very deliberate attempt to undermine his authority by invading his personal space and signifying there was no barrier before him.

"So?"

"So, he's in the home stretch," Caslin stated. "Knowing the type of man he is, I'll bet he has plans for when he gets out. I wouldn't be surprised if you factor in some of them." Dade grinned but on this occasion the humour appeared contrived.

"And what? You think I'm getting in first?" he said. "What possible motivation would I have?"

"Destabilising Pete Fuller's power base before he can get out would be advantageous to you," Caslin said inclining his head thoughtfully. "Particularly bearing in mind the feelings he holds towards you."

"You seriously think I'll be top of his list after two decades behind bars? I wouldn't be surprised if he fancies leaving it all to the boys and putting his feet up somewhere. Maybe he'll head to Cromer. Besides, two more years is a long time in the nick. Anything can happen to an old man."

"You're the same age, aren't you? School friends, if I recall correctly?" Caslin said. Dade nodded slowly.

"A different life."

"What actually happened between the two of you, anyway? It was well before my time but I'm still curious," Caslin asked.

Dade took a deep breath. "It was all a long time ago."

"You tread on his toes? Steal one of his girlfriends?"

"Now, that would have been even further back," Dade said with a grin.

"And yet probably still relevant."

Dade sat forward bringing him ever closer to Caslin who remained leaning forward. The two were so close, Caslin could smell the other's breath.

"Bombing a rival's business is just not my style," Dade explained. "Far too volatile in nature. It would open up the prospect of similar events befalling my own. That wouldn't make a lot of sense."

"Where the two of you come into it sense goes out of the window," Caslin countered.

"Now you listen to me, Mr Caslin," Dade said pointedly, lowering his tone to one of controlled aggression. Now they were seeing a representation of Dade's formidable reputation.

"Whatever befalls Pete Fuller, as well as his boys, has nothing to do with me. I'm a businessman. That is all. The past is where it is… where it belongs… and I have no intention of revisiting it."

"If not you, then who?" Caslin asked, holding the gaze for a moment longer before stepping back. Dade also relaxed if only a little.

"You should be looking closer to home," he suggested.

"The Fullers?"

"Exactly," Dade said. "You imagine this is all a result of some long-term power struggle between me and Pete? Your assertion is flawed from the outset."

"How so?"

"Pete still runs his enterprise from his cell make no mistake about that."

"Through his sons, yes," Caslin stated. "So, what's your point?"

"Maybe you're looking at the wrong struggle," Dade said softly. "By your logic, I'm not the only one to have something to lose when the big man gets out."

The door to the office opened behind them and both Caslin and Hunter turned. The arrival stopped abruptly upon catching sight of them.

"I'm sorry, Boss," he said. "I didn't realise you had company." Caslin took in his measure. He was in his early thirties and struck Caslin as familiar but he couldn't place him.

"I know you, don't I?" he asked the newcomer who appeared slightly perplexed. Sensing they were there in an official capacity, his eyes narrowed as he responded.

"I don't think we've met," he said.

"DI Caslin."

The young man shook his head and moved past him, "No. Never met."

"You must forgive Mark, Mr Caslin," Dade said, by way of an apology.

"The young men you surround yourself with are ill-mannered, Clinton," Caslin said, following Mark's passage with his eyes still trying to place him in some context within his memory. The comment made Alli bristle once more.

"I'll be sure to have a word," Dade replied. "Now, if you'll excuse me. We have a business to run."

"If I find out you have anything to do with this, Clinton. There will be no way of stopping me. If you bring a war to the streets of my city, I will tear you down one piece at a time," Caslin said in an icy tone, leaving no one present unclear on the depth of his motivation.

"Any problems with Pete Fuller are all of his own making" Dade said, matching the tone, "and they have nothing... *nothing* to do with me."

Caslin exhaled, flicking a glance to the associates now lining up behind their boss. All of them displayed hostile expressions. He cracked a smile.

"We'll be seeing you, Clinton."

REACHING THE CAR, Caslin waited for Hunter to unlock it and glanced back towards Clinton Dade's nightclub. The purple and blue colouring adorning the building looked strange in the gloom of the afternoon. Once night fell and the neon lit up, the place would be jumping. One of York's most popular clubs it was the jewel of Dade's organisation and where he could be found most of the time. Having been in and around the criminal fraternity for all of his adult life, it was the illegal rave scene of the early 1990s that saw him make his step up in the food chain. As legislation caught up, he was able to transfer the skills as well as the contacts he'd accumulated and adapt to a rigid presence in the club scene. Now with a string of clubs stretching across the Greater Yorkshire area providing an air of legitimacy to his business affairs, Clinton Dade was a major player. One of the key distributors of illegal drugs across the city, he used those revenues to fuel the rest of his business empire.

"Do you think he's on the level?" Hunter asked.

Caslin admitted he wasn't sure. "It's a tough call. You could make a case for his being behind it but at the same time…"

"His reasoning is just as plausible," Hunter finished for him. Caslin nodded his agreement. "Is Fuller likely to get out soon?"

Caslin shrugged. "Parole boards are unpredictable. I wouldn't like to second guess them. If it were up to me, he'd never see the light of day."

"And what Dade said about the Fullers?"

"Keep it in mind," Caslin suggested. "We'll have to pay Pete a visit."

Hunter started the car and pulled out from the side road turning left in the direction of Fulford. Caslin's phone rang: Terry Holt.

"Sir," he began, "I've got a response on the red Mercedes. The hire car. It was leased to a man by the name of Brian Jack three days ago."

"Arriving at Manchester Airport?"

"Yes. I've been onto the border force and he flew in on the 9:15 flight from Almeria."

"Spain," Caslin reiterated for Hunter's benefit glancing over to her. She smiled. "What do we know about him, Terry?"

"Nothing, sir. Brian Jack doesn't appear on any of our records. No priors, no convictions, arrests – the man is a ghost."

"Can you search through the database and see if he's a known associate of anyone we know?"

"Done it, sir. Like I said, he's a ghost. I have no record of him at all anywhere in the UK… ever."

"Is he a foreign national?"

"Arrived on a British passport, sir."

"How can that be?" Caslin said, thinking aloud. "He exists. We were looking at him earlier."

"I'm going to check it out, see if I can find when the passport was issued and to which address and so on. Maybe it will become clearer."

"Good. Pass the car's index around and have everyone keep an eye out for it," Caslin said. "I don't want him pulled over. Run it through the number plate recognition database and see if we can see where he's been. We need to know who this guy is and finding out where he's spending his time might help."

"I've got an idea on that, sir. I'm going to try and get into the car's telematics."

"Tele… what?" Caslin asked.

"Telematics, sir," Holt explained. "Modern cars are pretty much run by computers now and top end marques are selling assistance packages as part of the deal."

"Breakdown cover and so on?"

"More than that even. They can track you pretty much like we can an aeroplane. The car's internal computer sends out a ping, similar to a plane's transponder, and that gets relayed through cell towers to the manufacturer. That way, they know where you are when you need their assistance."

"Are you telling me you'll know where he is?"

"And where he's been," Holt added. "Before you get your hopes up though, let me flesh it out first."

"In case it doesn't work, Terry?" he asked playfully.

"That's about it, yes, sir."

Caslin hung up, "The world is moving forward at pace, Sarah."

"Sir?" she asked, confused.

He shook his head indicating for her not to worry about it. Turning his eye to the passing landscape, he mulled over the details of what he learned from the conversation with Dade. The CCTV from inside the minicab office was indicative of an inside job. It must have been a member of Fuller's crew who placed the bomb. No one else would have found the office so accessible. The hacking of the security system would have been possible via an external source but the suspected bomber was clearly known to the occupants. At the very least they were acquaintances and possibly even friends. Dade implied the Fullers had their own internal tug-of-war going on but for that to escalate into bombing one of their own establishments was bordering on lunacy.

"That guy, the one who came in right before we left," Caslin said. "Where do I know him from?"

"I know," Hunter agreed. "I had the same feeling but I can't place him. What was his name... Mark, was it?"

"Yes, that was it," Caslin said. "It'll come to me."

CHAPTER TEN

THERE WERE no skid marks visible on the road. The volume of rainfall overnight left a visible sheen on the surface. Caslin looked back up the road, analysing the curve of the bend as well as the adverse camber. An open stretch of highway such as this would undoubtedly see traffic moving at speed over and above the set limit for the road. They were surrounded on both sides by farmland, flat and fertile, running alongside the River Ouse. The highway was raised above the level of the land to keep the road open should the flood plain ever be required. Looking in the direction of travel, Caslin followed the route of the car. The four trenches gouged into the grass verge denoted where the vehicle left the road, doing so at a sideways angle with the driver having lost control in what must have been a four-wheel drift.

Grateful for the road closure, a police cordon was currently in effect a half-mile to the east and west, Caslin began the short walk back to the impact site. Several officers were walking the length of the road one hundred feet in each direction to try and spot any debris that may indicate the occurrence of a collision leading to the accident. Caslin reached the verge and circumvented the forensics officers, measuring and documenting where the car had left the road. Stepping up on to the bank, he looked down on the activity beneath him. Hunter saw him and offered a wave beckoning him down by way of a short path to his left. He acknowledged her but remained where he was for another moment, surveying the crash site.

The car left the road at a significant speed striking the verge at an angle with enough momentum to lift the car up and over, flipping it into the air before coming to rest on its roof at the foot of the embankment. Pieces of metal, plastic and broken glass were strewn all around them due to the car's collision with a copse of trees on its way through before coming to rest. The mangled wreckage was such that Caslin knew no one would have stepped from it alive. Checking his footing, he descended the bank to be met by Hunter as he found stable ground.

"Just the one occupant in the vehicle, sir," she said.

"Brian Jack?"

"Yes, sir," Hunter confirmed, glancing back at what used to be a prestigious make of car but was now good for nothing apart from scrap. "Early assessment suggests he would have died upon impact. We think he clipped several trees before coming to a stop where you see it now."

"Any witnesses to the car leaving the road?"

"No, sir," Hunter confirmed, looking at her notes. "Nor is there anything to indicate what caused him to lose control."

"Was he on the phone?"

"The car's bluetooth wasn't in sync with a mobile phone."

"Hire car… he might not have bothered. Have we found a handset?"

"No, not yet but we haven't finished the search. Judging by how fast we think the car was travelling, the area to cover is going to be pretty large."

"What about the victim?"

Hunter produced an evidence bag and Caslin could see a wallet within it. She passed him a set of latex gloves and he put them on while she opened the bag and removed the contents. Passing it over to him, Caslin inspected them. There were several credit cards, none of which were registered to UK banks. They appeared to be Spanish. There were business cards for a swimming pool cleaning company along with a property maintenance firm. All of them carried the name of Brian Jack.

"Pool cleaning must be quite lucrative," Caslin said, casting an eye over at the smashed Mercedes.

"We're in the wrong business, sir," Hunter said.

"Tell myself that every day," Caslin smiled. He returned the cards to the folds of the wallet and checked the remaining pockets. Apart from approximately two-hundred pounds in cash there was nothing of interest. Passing the wallet back to Hunter, she resealed the evidence bag. Caslin walked over to inspect the car itself.

Coming to the driver's side, he found the door open. The angle, along with the severe warping of the shape, indicated a forceful impact. Iain Robertson, clad in his forensic coveralls, was knelt by the door analysing the interior. The body of Brian Jack was visible beyond him, suspended upside down and still sitting in the driver's seat. As he approached, Caslin could see the deceased man was held in position by more than merely the seatbelt. Coming to stand behind Robertson, Caslin knelt and looked up. The branch of the tree had been torn from the trunk by the force of the collision but not before punching through the windscreen and piercing the body of the driver. The branch now protruded through the body and also the rear of the seat. Easily measuring four inches in thickness, it had punctured Jack's right-hand side, travelling in a diagonal direction upwards and exiting the body just below the left shoulder blade. The windscreen itself had shattered but the glass was held in place, sprayed with blood spatter, as was the roof of the cabin.

"That had to hurt," he said aloud, drawing Robertson's attention.

"How much he would have known about it is another matter entirely," Robertson replied, greeting Caslin.

"Let's hope so," Caslin said with a frown. "It certainly made a mess of him."

"Yes, it did," Robertson sighed. "His right hand has been partially severed at the wrist. Cause of death will probably be penetrating force trauma but I'll leave that to Alison to confirm."

"Any idea how long it will take you to free him up?" Caslin asked, considering when the body could be shipped to pathology for Dr Taylor to begin her examination.

"You got somewhere you need to be?"

Caslin laughed, "Any early thoughts?"

"A few," Robertson said, standing up. "I think the car was travelling in excess of seventy miles per hour when it left the road. Judging from the impact on the verge, I'd suggest before he lost control he was going even faster. The speed would have declined as the car lost grip and the driver lost control but there was no way he would have made the bend in the road, not at that speed. I'll put a proper calculation together later."

"Have you got a cause?"

"I can rule things out rather than in at this point," Robertson explained. "Once we can get what's left of the car back to the workshop, we'll strip it down and analyse the mechanicals. It's virtually brand new though, barely ten thousand miles on the clock if I had to guess. I haven't been able to reinitialise the digital dash but the index has it as registered this year. Tyre treads show minimal wear and a cursory inspection of the brake disks hasn't thrown up anything to make me think they are faulty. I'll caveat that by saying you'll have to wait before I will go definitive on that."

"Could we be looking at something non-mechanical?"

Robertson eyed him warily, "You're expecting foul play?"

"Wouldn't rule it out," Caslin said, scanning the length of the car.

"I'll check out the obvious, brake lines, fuel lines and so on. Likewise, once I'm able to download the files from the engine management system, I'll run the diagnostics. There's always the possibility of a power-steering failure. Should that happen at high speed or any speed above forty, for that matter, keeping the car on the road could become problematic. There is also this," Robertson said, pointing to the rear and indicating for Caslin to join him.

They walked to the back and then around to the nearside of the car. The ground was wet and slippery and both men took care with their footing. Caslin took in the damage to the bodywork, it was substantial. Robertson pointed out a specific section of the rear-quarter panel, just behind the wheel. The body of the car was scuffed from the edge of the arch back to and including the moulded bumper. Caslin questioned the finding with a flick of his eyes. Robertson produced a powerful Maglite and aimed the beam on the paintwork. Caslin looked closer.

"What am I looking at?" he asked.

"Red paint," Robertson said.

"The car is red, Iain."

"Look closer," Robertson pointed out, inclining his head to where he was focussing the beam. "It's a different shade of red." Caslin moved closer and at first, he couldn't make it out but as his eyes adjusted, he saw the scrape. Roughly half an inch wide with a couple of smaller scuffs running above the largest, the paint here appeared to be of a darker shade. "More of a burgundy, I would suggest."

"Agreed," Caslin said. "A collision with another vehicle?"

Robertson shrugged, "I wouldn't jump to a conclusion. You'll need to contact the hire company. There's every possibility it's historic and unrelated to the accident. This could easily be the result of poor driving in a car park somewhere."

"It could also be a PIT manoeuvre?" Caslin suggested, referring to the pursuit intervention technique where a fleeing vehicle is tagged at that specific point of the bodywork, causing the car to shift abruptly sideways and out of control. To carry out such an action at speeds in excess of seventy miles per hour on this type of road would lead to a catastrophic outcome. Casting an eye across the scene, Caslin figured that this description was certainly apt.

"The thought had occurred," Robertson said. "Have you identified any reason why he would be a target?"

"Not yet but there's quite a lot of movement around this guy and I'm yet to figure it out."

"WHAT DO we have on Brian Jack?"

"Not a lot, sir," Hunter said. "I've checked with both Europol and Interpol and he isn't on either of their radars."

"I've also made some discreet inquiries about his business interests in southern Spain, sir," Holt said. "He has a number of low-key contracts with the ex-pat communities located in and around the city of Alicante and further along the coast as far as Torrevieja."

"What kind of contracts?" Caslin said, staring at their information board and almost willing a connection to reveal itself.

"Principally in property management and maintenance," Holt confirmed. "Smaller apartment complexes rather than your large hotel chains."

"No issues with the local police?"

"None reported, sir." Holt tossed his pen onto the file before him. "His businesses started up from scratch three years ago. I spoke with a very helpful lady who is chair of a group representing the interests of UK citizens abroad."

"Sounds political," Caslin said, frowning.

"You would think, wouldn't you?" Holt said with a grin. "They are more of a social club from what I can gather. Organising the lawn bowls competition and barbecues."

"And she knew him?"

"Well enough. She said he was popular and had rapidly established a presence over there."

"And business was good?"

"She thought so. Although, she did voice her bewilderment at why a man of his age was so driven to launch a business at his time of life. I got the impression most of them were keen to focus on leisure time more than anything else."

"He was a bit of a workaholic?"

"That's not how I took it, sir. She raised his health as being a particular issue."

"What about it?"

Holt shook his head, "Didn't give me the specifics. I don't think she knew. Could have been gossip."

"Have any links to MacEwan surfaced or other known contacts?" Caslin said, looking to Hunter. She shook her head. "Nothing."

"Keep digging. Brian Jack came back to the UK for a reason and we need to know what it was. The last time we saw him he was looking decidedly unhappy. Why?"

"We'll keep at it, sir," Hunter stated. Caslin stood up and reached for his coat.

"Alison Taylor has the pathology report on Jody Wyer's death ready for us and I'll see if I can draw the preliminaries out of her regarding Jack's demise while I'm there."

Caslin stepped out of the office and almost bumped into Kyle Broadfoot who was coming the other way. He stopped him in his tracks glancing over his shoulder in such a way that led Caslin to assume he didn't wish to be overheard.

"Sir," Caslin said.

"Where are we with the Wyer case?" he asked. Caslin was momentarily thrown. The more pressing case was surely the bombing in central York.

"Progressing, sir," Caslin said. "But at this stage we are still short of any motive although we have several lines of inquiry to follow up on. I'm just heading over to pathology to discuss the manner of his death with Alison."

"I'll walk with you, if you don't mind?" Broadfoot said,

gesturing with an open hand for Caslin to come alongside. The two men set off and Caslin felt a little awkward. His superior was taking such an interest in this particular case that he sensed there was more going on than he knew. He chose to test the waters.

"What can you tell me about Jody Wyer, sir?" Caslin asked as they walked.

"A fine young man."

"You knew him well?"

"Well enough, yes."

"In what capacity?" Caslin asked. Broadfoot stopped, turning to face him. "Sir," Caslin added as an afterthought.

"Why do I get the sense that you are investigating me, Nathaniel?" Caslin raised his eyebrows and exhaled heavily. "Probably because I am, sir," he said, seeing little sense in dressing it up. "Figuratively speaking. I wouldn't say you're not being straight with me but let's be clear, you're not telling me everything that you know."

Broadfoot drew breath, glancing along the corridor as a uniformed officer came into view before passing through a doorway and disappearing once again. "I knew Jody," he said under his breath. "I have a relationship with him beyond his use to Major Crimes."

"I see," Caslin said. That wasn't the response he'd anticipated. "What's the nature of it?"

"Personal," Broadfoot explained. "I knew Jody's father, Keith, quite well. He was my mentor when I came through the ranks."

"I didn't realise you came through the ranks, sir?" Caslin said honestly. He'd always figured Broadfoot to be what the rank and file referred to as a 'plastic' – a policeman recruited from university and advanced up the chain as swiftly as possible having never actually seen any front-line action. If Broadfoot was offended, he didn't show it.

"It was a short-lived period," he explained, "but one that shaped my views of the service. Keith Wyer was a top detective and when he asked me to be Godfather to his son, I wouldn't have dreamed of saying no." Caslin did some mental arithmetic.

"I understand that he lost his father relatively recently."

"That's right."

"Bearing in mind Jody's age…"

"I know where you're going, Nathaniel. He was a surprise to both his parents. A welcome one, I assure you. I think Keith and Sandra found it difficult… having a child so late in life. Sandra passed away some years ago. She never even got to see him graduate from school."

"Is that why you want us on this case, sir?" Caslin asked. "I'd understand. I mean… I don't need to tell you it's probably not something you should be involved in… but I understand."

Broadfoot shook his head, "I'm not using your resource to settle a personal outrage, Nathaniel. Jody contacted me a few weeks ago and said he'd come across something he thought I should know."

"And that was?"

"Genuinely, I don't know," Broadfoot said, lowering his voice. "But he wouldn't have come to me without being sure I would be interested. That's not his way."

"He must have said something."

"Only that he was gathering information and once he had it straight in his own head, he would bring it to me. I asked if I could help but he declined."

"How did he sound?"

"Looking back, I would say stressed. Agitated," Broadfoot said. "He has always been quite an anxious chap. Therefore, his mannerisms often reflected that. I didn't think too much of it at the time but now…"

Caslin glanced about them. They were very much alone in the corridor. "I'll get to the bottom of it, sir."

"Thank you, Nathaniel," Broadfoot said with gratitude before his expression clouded over in a show of apprehension. "And I know I've no right to ask this of you but—"

"It will remain between us, sir," Caslin said, understanding the fear. "Tell me, did Jody ever mention a new girlfriend to you? Perhaps, someone he may have met recently."

Broadfoot thought hard on it before shaking his head. "No. I'm sorry. He didn't mention anyone. Was he seeing somebody?"

"It would appear so, yes," Caslin replied. "I'll get on then, sir."

"By all means," Broadfoot said, giving him his blessing to leave. "Oh… and, Nathaniel?" Caslin stopped, looking back over his shoulder. "Thank you."

"Don't mention it, sir," Caslin said, acknowledging the sentiment.

CHAPTER ELEVEN

THE HINGE on the refrigerator door creaked as it opened, the handle snapping shut once released. The sounds echoed throughout Dr Taylor's pathology laboratory. Caslin shuddered, feeling the cold.

"How do you spend all day in this?" he asked, referencing the artificial light and the somewhat sterile surroundings they were standing in. Alison Taylor laughed.

"Some people surround themselves with the living," she explained, "while others, prefer the peace and quiet."

"You don't have children, do you?" Caslin asked playfully. She returned his smile.

"It's not only children that people like me choose to avoid. Some of the adults are more than irritating," she said, inclining her head in his direction.

"That's cold," he countered.

"A lot like your friend here," she said, pulling out the rack upon which Jody Wyer lay. Reaching over, she grasped the fastener and unzipped the bag drawing it down to just below his chest. Leaving Caslin to take his first look at the deceased since he was pulled from the water, she crossed to her desk and returned with her notes in hand.

"How did he die?" Caslin asked, as she ordered her paperwork.

"He suffered a low velocity impact to the back of his skull. A depressed fracture formed at the impact point leading to a severe contusion as the bone fragments ruptured the subcutaneous blood vessels. On the periphery, I found further fractures radiating out from the impact point," she explained, producing x-rays from her file. "You'll see here," she passed him one of them. "The radiating fractures stop when they meet the sutures."

"You said it was low velocity?"

"Yes. Human bone is relatively elastic in form, you'll probably be surprised to know. The response of the bone to the strain, or load if you will, depends on the velocity and magnitude of the force. A slow load would lead to injuries consistent with a car accident, for example, falls from height or an assault. Whereas a rapid load, or higher velocity, is attributed to ballistic injuries, discharge of firearms, munitions or explosives and so on."

"Any chance of his death resulting from a fall?"

"No, I don't believe so," Dr Taylor explained. "In general, specific types of load will produce characteristic fracture patterns. Low speed injuries involving a wide area typically produce linear fractures. When the force is applied over a wide surface such as with a fall from height it allows the kinetic energy to be absorbed and thus results in smaller injuries. Whereas a localised application of force is far more destructive. The shape and size of the object used to apply the load is highly associated with the resulting fracture pattern."

"So, he was definitely struck with an implement," Caslin said, nodding gravely.

"Without doubt. When the head is struck with or strikes an object with a broad flat surface area, the skull at the point of impact flattens out to conform to the shape of the surface against which it impacts."

"That elasticity you mentioned?" Caslin asked, she nodded. "How quickly did he die?"

"I would have thought you're looking at minutes rather than hours."

"We are working on the theory that he was assaulted in a car park in the town and then the body was later dumped in the water," Caslin explained.

"Yes, Iain Robertson was good enough to pass on his initial thoughts," Dr Taylor said. "I think you are correct."

"Any suggestion of the type of weapon used?"

"A hammer is my best guess. The effusion of blood into the surrounding tissue is such that the weapon was rounded and evidently packing a hefty weight. Blows from a stick, bat or some kind of rod will often leave parallel linear haemorrhages. These injuries are rounded and even though the end of a stick *could* also result in a similar pattern due to the length of those types of weapon, the edges would likely be irregular and the lengths greater as they come in contact with the skin."

"A hammer," Caslin repeated almost to himself.

"There are two reasons why I think he died shortly after the attack."

"Go on," Caslin said.

"Firstly, the extent of the bruising. Usually these injuries see a blue colouring appear within the first few hours and, as I'm sure you know, these colours change as the tissue reacts to the spread of the blood giving rise to some magnificent colouration."

"It has been known on occasion," Caslin said with a wry smile.

"You'll see swelling, damage to the epithelium, extravasations and coagulation... to name but a few."

"I'll take your word for it, Alison."

"These occur within hours of the injury providing it happens ante-mortem and that's why I can be confident he died almost immediately."

"There wasn't much of that?"

"Totally absent in this case," she confirmed. "Secondly, if the victim had been alive when he was placed in the water, he would have ingested a significant level of sediment in doing so as he sought to breathe. Whether he was conscious or not is largely irrelevant. I would not necessarily expect to find indications of that in his stomach but certainly there would be large deposits within his lungs and there is no sign at all."

"He was dead when he went into the water," Caslin stated.

"Absolutely," Dr Taylor nodded. "His lungs were clear of water, so he didn't drown. Prior to death, he exhibited no signs of poor health. I would say he was above average in his general levels of diet and fitness. Toxicology reports came back as clear of any illicit substances."

"What about prescription drugs?" Caslin asked. "I came across a bottle of anti-depressants with his name on at his house."

"Yes, I picked up on that but they were low-level doses indicative of a mild approach to his treatment."

"Rather than?"

"In all likelihood, a condition that was either being managed at an early stage or one not considered to be too debilitating, rather than one needing a sterner intervention," Dr Taylor concluded. "However, his GP will be better placed to confirm his treatment."

"Great," Caslin said, looking past Alison towards her autopsy area as if he was searching for something.

"If you're wondering how I'm getting on with the RTA victim, I haven't started the procedure as yet," she said, raising her eyebrows.

"I *was* thinking about getting your initial thoughts," Caslin said doing his best to mask his impatience. Dr Taylor's face split a broad smile.

"Well, it's a good job I know you as well as I do then," she said, zipping up Jody Wyer's body bag. Caslin stepped back to allow her room to slide the tray back into the refrigerator. He closed the door ensuring the latch locked into place. "This way," she said to him as he passed back the copies of the x-rays he was still holding.

Leading him through to her office, she put Wyer's file down and picked up another, handing it to Caslin. He opened the manila folder and perused the contents.

"What am I looking at?" he asked.

"He was in a bit of a state once they managed to get him out of the wreck," she said. "As I say, I've not begun the autopsy yet but when I assessed him upon arrival, I noted several surgical procedures had taken place. Nothing that looked particularly fresh but even so, clearly planned surgical procedures."

"For what?"

"You'll have to wait for confirmation of that, I'm afraid. However, I do have a working theory," she said. "Now, due to the delay in cutting him out of the vehicle, I set to work on some of the blood samples Iain's team were able to provide. He sensed you were keen to get a move on with this one, so we thought we'd get ahead."

"And?"

"Toxicological reports indicated a blood-alcohol level that proved definitively he hadn't been drinking. Nor was he under the influence of any substance as far as I can tell. However, the tox screen did come back with some interesting results."

"Interesting how?"

"There are significant levels of a drug called *Pembrolizumab* in his system," she said, pointing to a chart that Caslin had before him. "This is a relatively recent addition to the arsenal used to treat cancer, one of eleven new drugs approved by the European Medicines Agency last year. It is the first cancer immunotherapy drug that has shown, in some cases, a greater efficiency than chemotherapy in first-line treatment of non-small lung cancer."

"Lung cancer?"

"But that's not all. Although considered a clinical

breakthrough and widely available it is not one that we use in a large capacity here in the UK. So, that got me thinking."

"Where does he undergo his treatment?"

"Exactly," she explained. "I ran a check in our database and found no hits under his name in the UK. Your understanding is that he is resident in Spain, is that correct?"

"It is."

"Stands to reason. Spain is one of the medical tourism hotspots when it comes to cancer treatments," she said. "Their clinics have excellent ties with research institutes and their pricing structure and success rates often makes them an excellent choice in comparison to travelling to the US or Israel, for example."

"I'll bear it in mind," Caslin said. "This is all very fascinating but how does this move us along?"

"I was surprised that a UK citizen with such a condition has no medical history whatsoever in their home nation. I would have expected to be able to locate some medical history of some description."

"Good point. We only have him appearing on the Spanish radar a few years ago. He must have lived somewhere and it doesn't appear to be here."

"I suppose he could have been living previously almost anywhere," Dr Taylor continued. "On a hunch, I explored the idea further by looking for some of the telltale signs that give away where medical treatment takes place."

"What type of signs?"

"Dental work is one of the most common. The amalgam fillings we use are of a different composition to that used on the continent for example."

"I would never have known," Caslin said. "Any luck?"

"Yes. His teeth showed many signs of decay and I can spot our fillings quite easily. Some of the work was done many years ago, so he was certainly treated in the UK. I took his prints and ran them through the system."

"We've already done that," Caslin said. "We didn't get a hit."

"Not through a PNC check, no, but you didn't run it through the Ministry of Defence files, did you?"

"No, we didn't," Caslin said. "Did you find a match?"

Alison Taylor nodded, "Yes. Royal Navy. He served twelve years."

"Go on," Caslin said, captivated. He knew her well enough to know when she was holding back.

"His real name is Philip Bradley. He was a Lieutenant but that's not all."

"Well?" Caslin asked, fostering his impatience.

"He was recorded as having died two years ago," she said, reaching across and leafing through a couple of pages in the file Caslin was holding and only stopping when she reached a copy of the official death certificate. Caslin scanned the document. A brief inspection revealed the dates corresponded more or less with Brian Jack's appearance in southern Spain.

"Well, I'll be damned," Caslin mumbled.

"PHILIP BRADLEY," Hunter said, approaching the noticeboard and attaching his MoD photograph next to a shot of David MacEwan, taken the day before when they observed the meeting at the scrap yard. "He served in the Royal Navy on a succession of deployments. He was present on HMS Invincible when she was sent to the Falklands."

"Any issues with his record?" Caslin asked.

Hunter shook her head. "No, his record was clean. I have his performance reviews here and he is described as both competent and diligent. However, his final appraisal back in 1983 stated he wasn't considered as having the *necessary potential for further advancement*. He left the navy eighteen months later."

"He wasn't going anywhere," Caslin said. "Where did he go next?"

"You'll not believe it, sir," Hunter said. "He came to us."

"The police?"

Hunter nodded, "Yes. He was originally from Leeds, growing up in Chapel Allerton in the north-east of the city. He joined North Yorkshire Constabulary straight from his time with the navy and remained there until he transferred over to Greater Manchester in the late 1980s. He served with them reaching the level of Detective Chief Inspector until his registered time of death two years ago."

"Well, yesterday he was looking good for a guy who's been dead for two years," Caslin said, staring intently at the photograph on the board. "How was his demise reported at the time?"

"He was apparently killed aboard a yacht in an accident sailing in the North Sea," Hunter read out from her notes.

"What type of accident?" Caslin asked.

"The boat caught fire. There was an explosion," Hunter said. "The crew managed to issue a mayday call and the coastguard dispatched a helicopter along with a crew from the nearest RNLI station. When they located the ship, it was burnt out with the survivors having decamped into a lifeboat."

"And Bradley?"

"Killed in the initial explosion," Hunter said.

"At least, that's what was recorded," Caslin stated the obvious. "Witnesses?"

"Yes, sir. There were three others crewing the ship including the captain and owner of the vessel."

"If Bradley was declared dead, they must have recovered his body," Caslin said. Hunter nodded.

"Yes, the RNLI attempted to recover the vessel but it sank as they towed it back to port. What they thought was Bradley's body was fished out of the water and later identified as his."

"Well, we know that wasn't the case," Caslin said. "Who identified the body?"

Hunter returned to her notes, "Scott Tarbet. The boat's captain. He was Bradley's cousin and so was taken at his word.

The other two witnesses confirmed seeing the boat go up in the explosion with Bradley aboard."

"And they were?"

"Greg Tower and Toby Ford," Hunter said.

"What do we know about them?"

"Greg Tower is deceased. Died in a car crash last year," Hunter confirmed.

"Are we sure of that?" Caslin asked with no intended sarcasm.

"I'll look into it, sir."

"And the other... what was it... Ford?"

"Toby Ford, sir," Hunter said, hesitantly. Caslin picked up on it as did Holt, lifting his head from the notes he was making. "Chief Superintendent Toby Ford is still serving with Greater Manchester Police, sir."

"Now that does make things interesting, doesn't it?" Caslin said with a smile. The other two failed to see anything amusing about it. "Terry, I want you to go through Bradley's time with GMP. See what his career highlights were. By all means take a look at his time with us as well but Manchester is more likely to be relevant. It's interesting that our friend Tony Mason also served with the same constabulary. I wonder if you'll find an overlap between the two. Did they work together or have any affiliations with each other? It's a bit of a coincidence for them to be moving in this circle without having some sort of shared past. Let's see how far it goes back but be discreet, Sarah," he said, turning to Hunter, "any idea of where the captain of the boat is now?"

Hunter returned to her notes, "Tarbet is registered at an address in Whitby."

"Good," Caslin said. "I love a trip to the coast."

CHAPTER TWELVE

PASSING out through the last remaining suburb of the north-eastern edge of Whitby, Caslin looked over his right shoulder as the water came into view. He could see the ruined remains of Whitby Abbey standing proudly on the point overlooking the town commanding as much attention now as it would have done over the previous centuries. As the coastal road descended closer to sea level, the white caps of the waves on the North Sea appeared ominous. The car was buffeted by the wind and although the skies were clear of the brooding storm clouds of recent days, there was no guarantee it would remain so.

They were heading to Sandsend, a couple of miles out of Whitby. A small village located along the route of the three-mile beach running all the way to Whitby's harbour. The approach road had a large hotel and golf course to one side with the sand and sea to the other. Along the length of the final mile of the descent were parking facilities, only a car's width but running top to tail down to the village. For most of the year space would be at a premium, however, currently in the off-season and with the weather cutting, many people were driven inland and away from the coast.

Turning his gaze out to sea, Caslin expected to see

windsurfers, kayaks and the like. Today, the sea was empty beyond the cargo ships passing by in their designated lanes, hugging the coast for its safety and security. Hunter pulled off the road near to the base of the hill parking as close as she could get to the village. Caslin could see their destination. Getting out of the car, he drew his coat around him as the sanctuary of the interior was traded for the bitter easterly wind. The red flags were up along the shoreline denoting the water was off limits, deemed far too dangerous, hence the lack of activity. A few dog walkers braved the conditions, enjoying their time when the animals were permitted on the sand.

Caslin stepped over to the fence looking down at the immense concrete construction of the tiered sea wall defending the coastal cliffs from the ravages of nature. He tasted the salt on his lips as he cast an eye along the beach towards Whitby. The view was obscured by what appeared to be fog but Caslin knew better. The wind was whipping up the sand into a mist of sorts, obscuring the town in the distance.

"I bloody love this place," he said under his breath.

"What's that, sir?" Hunter called to him, returning from purchasing their ticket from the parking meter.

"Nothing," he replied, gesturing for them to head along the path. On the opposite side of the road, facing the sea, were a run of Victorian terraced houses along with a smaller group of more recent buildings. They all had signs picketed outside denoting they were for sale. For a brief moment, Caslin wondered what it would be like to live here but quickly dismissed the notion. There was no way he'd be able to afford one of those along the seafront.

At the foot of the hill they found the road narrowing as it turned inland before crossing an inlet by way of a narrow stone bridge. Cars travelling in opposing directions needed to take turns in crossing. On the seafront itself, they walked past a tourist information office, a snack bar and an outfit where you could hire kayaks or surfboards. None of them were doing a roaring trade. Beyond those buildings, they entered an area set aside for the numerous small fishing boats pulled from the water and placed behind the sea wall.

Ahead of them was the lifeboat station, its doors open with both the main boat, rigid-hulled inflatable and all-terrain track vehicle present and ready to be called upon. A few more commercial enterprises completed the run of buildings but they passed these. Calling at Scott Tarbet's address earlier, they were directed here. The neighbours advised them he spent much of his time out on the water and even on days such as this could be found pottering around the sailing club. The sailing club was little more than a shack and a launching station for the locals to set off from or lift their boats from the water.

One man could be seen sitting in the stern of an aging fishing boat. They approached him. He glanced over at them before returning his focus to what he was doing. As they came closer, Caslin could see he was either repairing or inspecting a net.

"Scott Tarbet?" he called up.

"Depends on who's asking," the man replied.

"Detective Inspector Caslin," he said, brandishing his warrant card. The man briefly looked down at them but clearly didn't pay much attention to the identification.

"In that case," he said, putting the mass of blue netting down and standing up. Coming to the port side, he leant on the edge with both hands. "What can I do for you?"

"We wanted to speak to you regarding your cousin, Philip Bradley," Caslin said. "Specifically, about the day he died."

"Why on earth do you want to drag all that up for?" Tarbet protested. "I can't see as there is anything more to say."

"Nice boat," Caslin said, casting a glance over it. Tarbet nodded.

"Yeah," he said, glancing from bow to stern. "It's seen better days but it gets me out on the water."

"A bit of a change to what you used to go out on the water in, isn't it?" Hunter asked, referencing Tarbet's former yacht. The man stared at her. She had touched a nerve, intentionally or otherwise.

"Yes, it is," he replied with no edge to his tone at all. "I'm presuming you know what happened to the last one then?" he said, looking first at Caslin and then to Hunter. They both nodded. "Ah well, it was all a long time ago. We used to love going out on the water, the wife and me. These days... it's just not the same anymore."

"This your boat?" Caslin asked. Tarbet looked at him. Then he looked away.

"Yes, this is my boat," Tarbet asked. "What of it?"

"Your last boat was more of a yacht wasn't it?"

"Things change," Tarbet said, glancing at Caslin.

"No one could blame you for losing your passion for sailing."

"I still have the passion just not the money," Tarbet stated. "My lifelong dream was to have a boat like that. I guess you should be careful what you wish for."

"Did the insurance not cover a replacement?"

"Insurance didn't pay out. The bastards."

"I read in the file that there was some sort of question mark as to how the explosion occurred," said Hunter.

"Then why are you asking?"

"Humour us," Caslin said.

"Question mark, you say? That's a euphemism. Like things weren't shit enough already," Tarbet said, his shoulders dropping as he visually deflated. "As you've most likely read, they felt there was some kind of tampering with the fuel line. I'd wanted that boat all my life and they reckon after eighteen months I would burn it just for the money? Ridiculous. The insurance money wouldn't have been enough to replace the damn boat."

"Did you fight it?" asked Caslin.

"Still am," Tarbet said. "But you didn't come all this way to talk to me about my insurance claims, did you?"

"No, we didn't," Caslin confirmed. "We wanted to ask you when was the last time you saw Philip Bradley?"

Tarbet fixed him with a stare. His expression was mixed, one of anger and mild confusion. He held the eye contact for longer than was comfortable almost as if he was trying to gauge what answer Caslin might really be after. "What?"

"You heard me right," Caslin said. "I want to know when you last saw your cousin."

"Are you taking the piss?"

Caslin shrugged, "No, I'm deadly serious."

"Well, if you are then you'll already know," Tarbet said. "I last saw him two years ago."

"The night he died?"

"Yes," Tarbet said, anger edging into his tone. "Not far from this spot," he continued, looking over his shoulder and out at the North Sea. "And I see him every night in my dreams."

"You identified his body, didn't you?" Hunter asked.

Tarbet turned his gaze on her, "Yes. What of it?"

"So, you would be very surprised to hear that Philip was alive and well until yesterday morning?"

"What?"

"It would appear your cousin Philip has been living in southern Spain for the last couple of years," Caslin said.

"Don't be daft," Tarbet dismissed the notion, his eyes narrowing slightly. "I watched him die out there… on my boat."

"So, he would like us all to believe," Caslin said. Tarbet looked at him trying to take a measure of Caslin's integrity, unsure whether Caslin was on the level.

"Are you serious?"

"We are interested to know who it was you identified as your cousin," Hunter said. "Because somebody was buried but we know for certain it wasn't Philip."

"But… but… it *was Philip*. I'm sure it was," Tarbet stammered.

"Apparently not," Caslin said. "How could you have been mistaken?"

"He was so badly burned," Tarbet said, a confused expression on his face, thinking hard. "But I recognised his wedding ring and the clothes he was wearing matched his. At least, that's what I remember. You must have made some kind of mistake."

"Quite sure we haven't," Caslin said. "What about the other two on the boat with you that night?"

"What about them? They were Phil's mates, not mine."

"Had you not met them before?"

"No, I hadn't. Phil asked me to take them out on the water as a favour. If I'd known how it was going to turn out I would have said no."

"What can you tell us about that night?" Caslin asked.

"We had had a good day. They were a decent enough bunch of guys. I wanted to head back in but they insisted on staying out. They wanted to see the coastline lit up after dark. The weather was good, so I didn't see any harm. Phil wanted to go below and put his feet up. I figured it was a mixture of alcohol and the waves. Some people really struggle once they're out on the water. To this day I still don't know what happened but there was a fire. It quickly took hold."

"The fuel line," Caslin said.

"So they say. I was bringing the sails in so that we could return to the harbour. I always did so under the motor and it was when I initiated the engine that everything went wrong. The controls didn't respond and I went to go below to check what was going on and that's when I saw the flames. I called out to Philip but he didn't answer."

"What happened then?" Hunter asked.

"The others began to panic," Tarbet stated. "I can't blame them. It was dark and we were some way off the coast. The electricity shorted out soon after and we were thrown into complete darkness. I had to rely on battery backups to put in the emergency call. It was an easy decision to make to abandon ship. At least it would have been if Phil had been with us. I had no choice."

"The three of you left together?" Caslin asked.

Tarbet nodded, "We pulled the life raft and got off as quickly as we could. We kept calling for Phil but he never answered and he never came back above deck."

"And you are sure he was still below?"

"I don't see how he could not have been," Tarbet stated. "Then there was the explosion."

"The report we have says the yacht sank as it was being towed back to port. Is that right?"

"That's right. The boat capsized. The explosion must have holed it under the water. The water put the fire out so by the time the lifeboat crew got to us they were able to retrieve Phil's body before the boat sank."

"How was his health in the time before the lead up to his death? I mean, before the accident at sea?"

"How do you mean?"

"Are you aware of any illness that he was suffering from?" Caslin asked. Tarbet thought about it for a moment before shaking his head.

"Fine as far as I know but he probably wouldn't have told me, anyway. We weren't all that close," he said. "Why do you ask?"

"It doesn't matter. I'm just trying to get a picture of the man. Have you any idea why he would fake his death?"

Tarbet shook his head, "No. It's like something out of a film."

"How often did you see each other?" Hunter asked.

"On and off... occasionally, family events and suchlike."

"Are you surprised by any of this?"

"Damn right, I am," Tarbet said with a snort of laughter. "You say he died yesterday? What happened?"

"Car accident."

"What was he doing?"

"That's exactly what we are trying to find out," Caslin said. "You identified him because you were his closest next-of-kin. You mentioned his wedding ring, was he married?"

"Divorced. He had been for a while. Marion went on some around the world trip with her sister. When she got back, she didn't fancy waiting hand and foot on Phil anymore."

"She left him?"

"Quicker than you can book a plane ticket!" Tarbet said, shaking his head. "Don't blame her, really."

"Why not?"

"Phil was a control freak, always had to be the one to make the final call on everything. I'll bet she couldn't breathe."

"You seem remarkably calm about all this," Caslin said.

"What were you expecting? Did you think I would jump up and down... scream or something? Not really my thing. Listen, I've got several years on you, son, done a few more laps of the track if you know what I mean? There's not a lot that will surprise me these days."

"I thought you might be pissed off. If a relative of mine screwed me over, I would be pretty annoyed."

"Well that's where you and me differ, isn't it?"

"I guess it is, yes," Caslin said. "Are you married?"

Tarbet nodded slowly "I was."

"Did she take off with Marion as well?"

"No, she died last year, but thanks for the memory."

Caslin looked away. He was seeking to ruffle the man's feathers but hadn't expected that answer. Now he felt pretty small and justifiably so. Hunter glanced at him. She didn't have to say anything. Her disapproval was evident in her eyes. "I'm sorry, I didn't know."

"How could you?" Tarbet said, his tone icy. "Are we done?"

"Yes, we're done," Caslin said. "For now."

"You need me to identify the body again?" Tarbet asked. Caslin wasn't sure if he was being serious or whether he was deliberately on the wind up.

"No, I think we will manage. Besides, you did such a good job last time. Enjoy the rest of the day, Mr Tarbet," Caslin said, turning and walking away.

"I'm not sure he deserved that," Hunter said, catching up and falling into step alongside him.

"Maybe he did, maybe he didn't," Caslin said. "Think about it. There was a body retrieved from his yacht after the fire. If it wasn't Bradley, then who was it? Somebody died and no one seems too bothered about who that was. Unless you are going to tell me, Bradley sneaked a dead body onboard without anyone knowing then he must be in on it. If not, then I'll feel suitably bad for the next couple of hours. Fair enough?"

"Finding out that his cousin is still alive didn't throw him much, did it?"

Caslin shook his head. He was reluctant to read too much into Tarbet's response. After all, people react to events in different ways, this job taught him that. Although, it was certainly possible that Tarbet was in on this from the start. The question then became: the start of what? Passing the building that housed the lifeboat, Caslin noted a member of staff aboard the rib, set alongside the main boat. Nudging Hunter with his elbow, he indicated for them to step inside. Their arrival was noted as soon as they passed through the double doors.

"Can I help you with something?" the man said, stepping out of the rib and coming to greet them. Caslin held open his wallet and displayed his warrant card.

"Detective Inspector Caslin," he said, introducing himself. The man made a cursory inspection of Caslin's identification before nodding an acceptance of who he was talking to. "Are you a crew member of the lifeboat?"

"For the last fifteen years," the man said, "what can I do for you?"

"Do you remember a yacht catching fire, a couple years ago?" Caslin asked. "Four-man crew. Three were rescued and one was pulled dead from the hull."

"I remember. We get called out a lot but that one was always going to stick in the mind."

"What can you tell us about it?" Hunter asked.

"Not a lot more than you will be able to read in the official reports, I should imagine."

"Nothing stood out as unusual?" Caslin asked.

The man smiled. "That was a weird one, I'll tell you that. It's not unusual for boats to catch fire but rarely do they explode. Not like that anyway."

"The insurance company thought the same," Caslin said. The man bobbed his head. "Unsurprising," he said. "Not a lot of things made sense that night. The explosion was just one of them."

"You've got my attention," Caslin said. "Tell us about it."

"Not much to tell you, not really. Apart from the boat going up in such a manner as I've never seen before, not in thirty years at sea. No, it was more the reaction of the crew that struck me at the time."

"Reaction?" Caslin said.

"If it were me, I would have been shitting myself but they were pretty calm when we plucked them out of the water."

"We were just talking to the skipper," Caslin said. "He described the others as panicking."

"Not when we got there. You would have thought they'd hailed a taxi. It was really weird and I wasn't the only one to think so either."

"Do you know the skipper, Scott Tarbet?" Caslin asked. The man met his eye and glanced away. "I see him around, yes. We're not friends, though. I don't think he has many friends."

"Why not?" Hunter asked.

The man laughed.

"You've met him. He's a hard man to like," he explained. Checking his watch, he raised an eyebrow. "Is there anything else because I really need to be somewhere?"

"Thank you for your time," Caslin said. The man left and

headed into his office, turned off the monitor on his desk and then picked up his coat which was hanging next to the door. Caslin looked at Hunter. "Do you still think I was out of order?"

Hunter shook her head. "What do you want to do now?"

"I think we should talk to the others on the boat that night, don't you?"

"Well, we know Greg Tower is dead and that leaves only one other person on the boat that we can speak to."

"What's up, Sarah?" Caslin asked playfully. "Are you worried Chief Superintendent Ford won't be pleased to see us?" Hunter shook her head. Caslin was right. They needed to speak to Ford but at the same time, the man she was walking with didn't always respect the rank.

CHAPTER THIRTEEN

THE DRIVE from the east coast of Yorkshire across the Pennines to the west of England took just shy of three hours. It was a good job they called ahead. Chief Superintendent Ford agreed to wait for them, albeit under protest. It was well after dark when they reached the station in Manchester. Hunter's satellite navigation system had struggled once inside the city limits, frequently dropping its connection but they managed to make it to their destination all the same. They were escorted up to the chief superintendent's office by a constable from Greater Manchester Police. Knocking on the door a voice from inside bid them to enter. Caslin opened it, allowing Hunter to pass through first.

Hunter was surprised to see Kyle Broadfoot sitting in a chair opposite the chief superintendent. Visually taken aback, Broadfoot smiled at her reaction.

"Pleased you could make it so quickly, sir," Caslin said from behind. Hunter looked over her shoulder at him. "Sorry, Sarah. I forgot to mention I had asked Assistant Chief Constable Broadfoot to join us."

"Detectives Caslin and Hunter," Broadfoot said, introducing them to Toby Ford.

"Caslin?" Ford asked.

"Yes, sir," Caslin said, stepping forward and offering his hand. Ford stood to meet it. "I'm sorry, have we met?" he asked.

Ford shook his head. "I… don't believe so, no. Now that you two are here, perhaps you could tell me what all this is about?" the chief superintendent said, his tone shifting from an unexpected display of familiarity to one of barely masked irritation.

Hunter cast a nervous glance towards Caslin. For his part, Caslin took Ford's attitude in his stride. He was tall and rangy, appearing to have the physique of a cyclist with barely an ounce of fat around his athletic frame.

"I can see you're a busy man, sir," Caslin said, noting Ford checking his watch. "We'll keep this as brief as we possibly can. I'd like to talk to you regarding your association with DCI Philip Bradley." At the mention of the name, Caslin noticed a brief flicker of something cross the chief superintendent's face. Perhaps it was surprise at the mention of a man who had been dead for two years or perhaps it was something else entirely. Either way, Caslin found his curiosity piqued.

"Bradley?" Ford said, sitting down and frowning. "What about him?"

"Specifically, sir, the night he died… for the first time."

"What on earth do you mean, *for the first time?*" Ford asked, looking directly at Kyle Broadfoot. Broadfoot didn't reply but held the gaze for a few moments before raising his eyebrows in a gesture that implied an answer should be forthcoming. "If you're here, then you know what happened to Philip. He's been dead for two years. Now, what's all this about?"

"That's exactly what we're trying to find out, sir," Caslin said. "The issue is, if he died on that boat, just as you, Scott Tarbet and Greg Tower stated, then how come he's lying in my morgue having been killed in a car crash less than two days ago?" Ford's eyes narrowed and his lips parted. "Sir?" Caslin pressed for a response.

"Nonsense," Ford said, dismissing Caslin with evident scorn.

He looked again to Broadfoot, "Sir, surely this is a waste of both our time?"

Broadfoot remained impassive, "You need to listen, Toby, and then you need to provide an answer."

Ford, visibly frustrated at his superior officer's response, returned his attention to Caslin. "Philip Bradley died on that boat. I saw it happen with my own eyes," he said emphatically. "Someone has made a mistake."

"Our pathologist performed a fifteen-point fingerprint check," Caslin said, referencing the thorough examination Dr Taylor carried out. In some jurisdictions a nine-point fingerprint match, where a set of prints have that many similarities, was legally admissible in court. Alison Taylor matched Bradley's to a far greater level of accuracy making it almost a statistical impossibility that the body was anyone else's. "DCI Bradley was alive and well until his car left the road two days ago. Can I ask where you were two nights ago, sir?"

"And what the hell kind of question is that for you to ask me?" Ford said with thinly-veiled aggression.

Hunter bit her bottom lip but Caslin held his ground. "It's a simple enough question, sir, and I would like an answer."

"As would I," Broadfoot said, sitting forward in his seat, breaking Ford's angry stare at Caslin and towards him instead. "If it makes you feel any better, imagine it was your superior asking you the question?" Ford softened in his demeanour. Now, Hunter understood why Caslin requested Broadfoot's presence. "I'll help you. Where were you two nights ago?"

"I... I... was at home," Ford stated flatly. "I resent the need to answer the question, sir. You said Philip was killed in a car accident. Your question implies you suspect foul play?"

"The investigation is ongoing," Caslin said. "Can you think of any reason why he would have faked his own death?"

"None whatsoever."

"And yet, that was his choice," Caslin countered. "He went to great lengths to ensure he was able to vanish. Approaching the end of his service, DCI Bradley was due his retirement, associated commutation from his pension plus the pension itself…"

"And?" Ford asked.

"That's a lot to leave behind," Caslin said. "He never re-entered his previous life as far as we could tell. No access to his bank accounts, credit cards, family members… he dropped out of sight with a snap of the fingers. Why would he do that?"

"I have not got the faintest idea."

"He executed his plan brilliantly. It's almost hard to believe he was able to manage it unassisted."

"If he had assistance, Inspector, it certainly didn't come from me," Ford countered, fixing him with a stare. "I assure you, I am as curious as you are."

"DCI Bradley. Was he a decent officer?" Caslin asked.

"Very," Ford responded immediately without needing time to consider his answer. "A man you could always rely upon."

"He didn't have any financial issues that you are aware of. Challenging relationships… troubling cases or the like?"

"No," Ford stated. "Nothing that I am aware of."

"Forgive me, sir, but this isn't making any sense. A lifetime spent in service to his country. The respect of his colleagues and yet, here we are. These aren't the actions of a man whose character everyone speaks of so highly."

"I can't answer that, Inspector. All I can do is describe the man I knew and I fail to understand why you have brought this to me."

"Your witnessing of his death gave it credibility," Caslin said. "You must know how it looks?"

"Let me be clear, Inspector Caslin… Kyle," he said, turning to Broadfoot. "I have no knowledge of these events. As far as I am aware, Philip Bradley died two years ago in a fire at sea. Now, is there anything else?"

"Not for the moment, sir, no," Caslin said. Ford stood as Kyle Broadfoot did as well. The latter offered his hand to Ford.

"Thank you for your time, Toby," Broadfoot said as they shook.

"I hope I was of some help," Ford replied. "Please do let me know the outcome of all of this."

"Oh, rest assured, sir," Caslin said, "should we need to speak to you further, I'll certainly be back." Ford glanced towards him and the expression of polite familiarity slipped for a moment before being masked by a smile.

"You are welcome, Inspector Caslin. I will be only too pleased to assist you in any way I can," he said, coming from behind his desk and offering his hand to Caslin by way of a farewell. Caslin shook it, locking eyes with the senior officer.

"One more thing," Caslin said, not releasing his grip. "How did you feel that night, out on the boat?"

Ford's smile dropped. "I was terrified, Inspector. By any measurement, the scariest experience of my life."

Caslin nodded, releasing Ford from the handshake. "I can imagine. How close were you to the other officer on the boat that night, Greg Tower?"

"We were friends."

"Close friends?"

"Yes, very. I don't suppose you're going to tell me he's still alive as well, are you?" Ford replied, with a hint of sarcasm.

"I wouldn't rule it out," Caslin countered, assessing Ford's body language. It didn't tell him anything. The man looked stern, focussed. Earlier he appeared off balance, mentally at least, but now, he came across confident and rigid. "Thank you for your time, sir."

They left the office and Hunter dropped back a step as Kyle Broadfoot chose to walk alongside Caslin. The upper floors of the station were nigh on deserted. The majority of the offices were empty with the building's lighting switching to their minimal evening settings, leaving shadows all around them. Conversation could be entered into freely as concerns about being overheard were non-existent.

"You went in pretty hard on Toby," Broadfoot said, glancing over his shoulder to Hunter. She was unsure of whether she should drop back a little further and remove herself from the conversation entirely. Broadfoot didn't give her that impression, so she stayed where she was.

"I know," Caslin said. "It was intentional."

"What do you make of it?" Broadfoot asked.

"The calmest bunch of terrified men I've ever come across," Caslin said, drawing a perplexed expression from his boss.

"Meaning?"

"This is bigger than we think."

"In what way?"

"I need time," Caslin said, "and I can't promise you I won't step on more toes."

Broadfoot stopped, turning to face him. "Whatever it takes," he said directly to him before glancing at Hunter. "Whatever it takes," he repeated. Broadfoot left the two of them in the corridor, striding away.

"He's certainly motivated," Hunter said quietly.

"Personally involved," Caslin added, his gaze drifting past Hunter towards the chief superintendent's office as the door opened. Toby Ford stepped out of the room. Closing the door behind him before he noticed their presence, he met Caslin's eye but only briefly. Locking the door, he returned the keys to his pocket and turned on his heel. He set off, walking in the opposite direction to them briefcase in hand and with his coat across his forearm. "What did you make of him?"

"Defensive," Hunter said. "I think he knows more than he was letting on. You went easy on him… at least, by your usual standard anyway."

"He's not as good an actor as Scott Tarbet. I'll give you that," Caslin said, watching the departing figure make the turn at the end of the corridor and disappear from view. "He was surprised though."

"Surprised that Bradley was alive or that we'd come across him in a car crash?" Hunter asked.

"There's a question," Caslin said. "Instinct tells me he was surprised we ended up in his office."

"Maybe they've been in contact?" Hunter suggested. "Although, we're reaching when all we have is your instinct to go on."

"Philip Bradley picked those specific people to be on board the boat when he checked out," Caslin explained. "We need to know why?"

"He needed his cousin's boat," Hunter said, "and the other two were serving police officers. You could see them as a strange choice or a bold one."

"Their presence gave it an air of credibility," Caslin said, thinking aloud.

"Exactly," Hunter agreed. "And if they were co-conspirators, then their standing would deflect the focus of the investigators away. It's almost as strong as having a judge or a priest on your side in court."

"It didn't deter the claims assessor, though," Caslin countered.

"What would Ford, Tarbet and Tower have to gain from helping him?" Hunter asked. "I mean, they would need to benefit in some way, wouldn't they?"

"I wonder if when we figure out what Bradley had to gain, then that question will be answered."

"Are we any closer to understanding that?"

"No," Caslin said with a shake of the head. "We're still some way off. Bradley saw fit to hide, or the need to run, from something. We should focus on trying to find the link between all of these names. Once we do that, it will start to come together."

"What should we do with Chief Superintendent Ford?"

"I'd love to put some surveillance on him and see what he does next but we don't have the resources... nor the authority,"

Caslin said with regret. "So far, the only links we have are between Bradley, Mason and David MacEwan. Those on the boat are either willing participants or unwitting contributors to a cover story."

"Or both?" Hunter said, Caslin had to concede the point because all they had were theories at present.

"Let's focus on MacEwan and Mason, pull a few threads and see what unravels."

"If Iain Robertson is right, who do you think pushed Bradley's car off the road?"

Caslin shrugged, "Mason's jag is white, isn't it?"

"Yes."

"Let's run a check against everyone we've come across and see if anyone owns a red car. I doubt it will be that simple but you never know."

"You think whatever brought Bradley out of hiding also got him killed?"

"I'll put money on it."

CHAPTER FOURTEEN

"BRADLEY HAS CERTAINLY BEEN CLOCKING up the mileage on that hire car, sir," Holt said as Caslin took off his coat and pulled out a chair. Surprised to find Terry Holt was still hard at it when they eventually returned to Fulford Road, both of them were intrigued to find out what he'd uncovered. "I've downloaded the telematics data from Bradley's car and that has given us reference points for everywhere he's been in the past few days."

"Remind me. What does it tell us?" Hunter asked.

"As long as the engine is running, the system will send out a ping rather like the transponder of an aircraft. This is registered at respective cell towers along the car's route and relayed back to the manufacturer. It's kind of like low-jacking via the GPS network."

"What's he been up to?" Caslin asked, turning his focus to the board as Holt crossed to it. There were a series of coloured pins placed strategically on the map denoting Bradley's movements. A cursory analysis saw he had come to York directly from Manchester upon picking up the car at the airport.

"I've not placed every ping on the map, sir. There really isn't a need but any major route along with a deviation has been catalogued."

"Where did he spend most of his time?" Caslin asked. Holt retrieved his notes and then came back to the board.

"Like I said, he got about a bit. We have him visiting MacEwan's scrapyard on two occasions. One of which was observed by you and the other was the previous night. Now, the information relayed to us will only respect the location of the tower the car's system is communicating with. Therefore, we can't be certain as to who or where he was actually visiting. There is still a degree of supposition going on, on our part. Because you witnessed him there the following day, I'm assuming he went in the day before but equally, he may have been staking the place out from the outside. We have no way of knowing for certain."

"Understood," Caslin said. "Go on."

"Every night, he returned to this location," Holt pointed to a place on the map roughly six miles from the outer limits of the city. "There's a hotel and spa in this area so I figured he was staying there. I called them and was able to confirm he checked in on the day he arrived from Spain under his known alias. He was staying there alone and to their knowledge, he didn't receive any visitors."

"When was the last time he was there at the hotel?"

"His key card was activated on the morning of the day he died, sir. No one apart from the housekeeping staff has entered the room since. I've asked them to keep the room isolated until we can get a chance to go over and check it out."

"Good man," Caslin said. "What are the other highlights of his travels?"

"Mostly, he spent his time in and around York, sir. However, there was one notable deviation that I found very interesting."

"If you're about to tell me he drove up to Whitby, I warn you now, I'll be ecstatic," Caslin said, casting a wry grin in Hunter's direction. She smiled.

"Sorry," Holt dashed his hopes. "Although, he did head to

the coast. He set off east, out of York and took the A64 in the direction of Scarborough."

"Heading for a Victorian coastal seaside resort? Maybe he was missing the lasagne and chips that he gets served up by the ex-pats back in Spain."

"Didn't make it that far, sir," Holt carried on, ignoring Caslin's tangent. "He turned off at Staxton, then continued on before re-joining the coastal road and travelling south."

Caslin thought about the route, attempting to visualise it in his head. He hadn't been that way in years. "Towards Bridlington?"

Holt nodded, "But he took the turn off at Reighton, heading down to Flamborough."

"What was he doing there?" Hunter asked.

"The telematics put him stationary out at Flamborough Head," Holt explained. "The signal was switched off for several hours. I'm presuming he parked up there. It was reactivated when he started the car that evening."

"Could have been meeting someone?" Caslin suggested.

"Could have fancied a walk along the coast and a visit to the lighthouse?" Hunter countered, before adding, "Although, I doubt it."

Caslin laughed, "I don't know. It's a stunning patch of coast. Does he have any connections in the area we are aware of?"

"None that I've come across as yet, no," Holt explained. "It is possible I will the further I go through his old case files but he was in CID for a long time."

"I know, it's a lot of data to sift through," Caslin said, reassuring him. "Has he been anywhere else?"

"He was in and around Selby for an afternoon," Holt said, glancing back at the board.

"Selby?" Caslin repeated.

"What about it, sir?" Hunter asked, perceiving Caslin's far-away look as significant.

"Nothing," Caslin explained, shaking his head. "Just reminds me that I've not called my father back."

"Wasn't that days ago?" Hunter asked, frowning.

Caslin sighed. "Yes. What are you, my ex-wife?" he retorted. She laughed. "What was he doing there?"

"He drove around the outskirts of the town in the morning before backtracking in the afternoon. He stopped around here," Holt indicated a section of the map where he'd drawn a circle to mark the range of the cell tower, "and the car was inactive for a little over two hours before he set off."

"Where did he go then?" Caslin asked.

"Back to his hotel, sir."

"All right. Keep digging. What else have you got for me?"

"I'm ploughing through his case files, sir," Holt said. "I'm looking for a crossover between the names we have but nothing has flashed up in the database as yet. I started with the most recent and I'm heading back through his career. I'm viewing these as the quick wins because pre-late 1980s, the files were not computerised. I've submitted a request for the archives to be released to me. Ours are easy to come by but I'm waiting on those from Greater Manchester."

"Any idea when they'll come over?" Hunter asked.

"Should be tomorrow," Holt confirmed. Caslin looked at his watch. It was late.

"Okay, let's call it a day and start afresh tomorrow," he said. "I'll head over to the hotel and check out his room. You two can go home and get some rest."

"I'll come with you," Hunter said. Caslin didn't object as he stood up, pulling the coat off the back of his chair and putting it on. Holt collapsed his folder before rubbing at his eyes. He'd spent hours trawling through paperwork and was obviously happy for the respite. Caslin silently approved of his attitude. When accepting the offer to head up the unit, Caslin insisted on bringing his own team with him. Hunter's inclusion was a simple decision whereas Terry Holt was a bit of a gamble. That in itself had a certain sense of irony to it, what with Holt's background of borderline gambling addiction. The young detective constable had made a concerted effort to refocus on his career, making the journey from a struggling detective to an efficient and respected member of the team. The opportunity to prove himself was something he'd grasped with both hands.

"I'll close up, sir," Holt said as Caslin and Hunter were ready to leave. They left him to shut the office down and entered the corridor. Fulford Road was deserted, their footfalls echoing on the polished floors.

"Stephen won't mind you working late again?" Caslin asked in passing. Hunter shrugged. "I know you've been pushing yourself recently."

"Don't worry about it," she replied, glancing at him and pursing her lips momentarily. He sensed there was more that she wasn't saying.

"Everything all right?"

"Stephen left last month," Hunter said, her expression remaining impassive. Caslin could have kicked himself. He had no idea.

"I'm sorry I mentioned it," Caslin said.

"It doesn't matter. Don't worry," she replied.

"Are you okay?"

"I will be," she said, looking at him and smiling. She gently elbowed him in the forearm. "Honestly, it's okay. I think it's for the best. We've been hanging on for a while now. Both of us have been kidding ourselves, and each other, that it's going to work."

"How's Stephen?"

"Relieved," she said. "I think he was putting in far more effort than I was towards the end."

"I'm sorry," Caslin said, feeling for her. "Anything I can do?"

"Not talk about it," she suggested, inclining her head.

"Understood," Caslin replied, with a smile.

A QUARTER OF AN HOUR LATER, they pulled into the car park of the Royal Hotel and Spa a few miles outside of the city. The restaurant was open to the public and judging by the number of vehicles present, the establishment was doing a roaring trade. Bradley's choice of a hotel made sense. With a two-hundred room capacity, he would be able to blend into the background rubbing shoulders with guests, diners and spa visitors. For a man not wanting to stand out it was a solid plan. He could come and go without anyone paying him much attention at all.

Caslin had called ahead and upon showing his warrant card at the reception desk was ushered towards the duty manager's office. They were greeted shortly by a young woman, Caslin assumed was in her early twenties. The thought occurred to him about how young management appeared to him these days, wondering whether it was just him getting older or the next generation developing faster.

"Has anyone entered the room since we contacted you earlier today?" he asked her.

"No," she said. "There's been no activity recorded since housekeeping did their rounds this morning."

"Did they report anything unusual after they went in?" Hunter asked.

"Nothing was noted in the file," she said. "The staff are off until the morning but I can ask them if you'd like?"

"Thank you," Caslin replied. "And he checked in under the name of Brian Jack?"

"Yes, he did," she replied, checking her register.

"Can we see the room?" Caslin asked.

The manager led them out of the office and across the lobby to the elevators. Minutes later, they stepped out onto the second floor. Approaching room 243, the manager produced a key card to grant them access. Caslin accepted it from her asking that she waited outside. Entering the card into the slot, the LED changed from red to green and the the latch clicked. Caslin eased the door open. The interior was shrouded in darkness. Stepping forward, he placed the same card into another slot on the wall just beyond the entrance. As soon as he did so, the lights came on.

The room was a familiar layout for a high turnover chain hotel. The bathroom was off the entrance hall to the left. A few metres further they entered the bedroom consisting of a double bed, a small two-seater sofa and a workstation fixed to the wall with a chair underneath. A television was mounted on the wall above the desk. A suitcase lay open beside the bed with the top leaning against the wall. Caslin knelt alongside and inspected the contents indicating for Hunter to look around. The suitcase proved not to be of interest with only a few changes of clothes folded neatly and stacked atop each other. Hunter returned from the bathroom shaking her head in response to his unasked question.

"Nothing in there," she said, crossing the room to the workstation and continuing the search. "Here we go…" she said in a tone that caught Caslin's attention. He had just come across a passport in the exterior pocket of the suitcase. He brought it with him as he crossed to join Hunter, flicking through the pages as he walked. It was in the name of Brian Jack. The photo matched.

"What have you got?" he asked.

"Laptop," she said, glancing at what he held in his hands. "Is that legit?"

"It's genuine," he replied, holding up the passport. "It was issued four years ago, so it's pretty much up to date regarding the components. The anti-counterfeit foils and digital biometrics are present. This means he'd been planning his demise for a minimum of two years prior to the fire onboard the yacht."

"We'll have to get this back to the station," Hunter said, pointing at the computer. "It's locked but… this is interesting," she said, drawing Caslin's attention to a folder that she'd found alongside the laptop. Opening the flap, she withdrew the first sheet and passed it to him. Caslin scanned the document. It was a print out of a spreadsheet. There was a list of countries down the left-hand side of the sheet with the corresponding columns representing months of the year. The spreadsheet was populated with figures represented in sterling, some lodged in red, others in green. The passage of the charted figures went back for the previous twelve months. What the figures related to however, was totally lost on him. "Did you check out the source?" Caslin noted the small print at the head of the page.

"SLG Exchange," Caslin read aloud. "What's that?"

"A trading company," she explained.

"Trading what?"

"Not that kind of trading," Hunter said with a smile. "They facilitate trading on the markets. That looks like one of their market reports. You can pay them and they'll produce these for investors. For a fee, obviously."

"I didn't know you were into commodities?" Caslin asked. Hunter grinned.

"Stephen is a FOREX trader," she said. "Didn't you know?"

Caslin shook his head. "Can't say I remember. What are the figures relating to? Any idea?"

"No, sorry. It doesn't say," she said. "Perhaps his browsing history will tell us." Caslin focussed on the figures seeing them in a different context. They appeared to be documenting the rise and fall of a certain commodity recorded in a dozen countries around the globe. Making a basic assumption that red denoted falls and green, rises, he noted the rough trend saw this commodity's value on the increase in the previous six months.

"On its own it may as well be written in hieroglyphics," Caslin said.

"Then there's this," Hunter said, passing him a copy of an ordnance survey map. Caslin put the copy of the spreadsheet down and took the map. It had been opened and refolded in such a way to leave certain sections of the map facing to the outside. The first location that leapt out at him was Flamborough Head. The area was circled in ink with some handwritten notes alongside but Caslin struggled to make out what they were, such was the writing style that made it almost unreadable.

"Holt said telematics put Bradley out at the Flamborough lighthouse, didn't it?"

"Yes, for several hours."

"Fancy a day out at the coast?" he asked under his breath.

CHAPTER FIFTEEN

THE SURROUNDING landscape was flat with barely a tree in sight as the sea came into view in front of them. The sky was clear and brilliant sunshine forced them to lower their visors as they drove along the appropriately titled *Lighthouse Road*. A line of single-story dwellings lay along the route, all facing out to sea. To the left of them was a golf course hugging the coastline that stretched north towards the Flamborough Cliffs. The village of Flamborough itself lay behind them a short drive inland, safe from the aggression of the sea battering the area.

They passed the original lighthouse, an octagonal structure built from chalk hundreds of years previously. The line of residences retreated inland as the road opened out into the approach to the point. A beacon stood proudly at the side of the entrance to the grounds of the lighthouse, its brazier empty and now only lit for ceremonial purposes at certain times of the year. The approach road narrowed again with open ground to either side of them, less so on their left as the land slipped down towards the water below. The popularity of the site for tourists was reinforced by the first building they came to. It was wide, squat, and two-thirds of it given over to a cafeteria whereas the remainder was occupied by a shop selling souvenirs. The lighthouse was a visitor attraction as were the coastal paths heading north up the Heritage Coast or south-west, back towards the larger population centre of Bridlington.

Caslin passed the café and followed the pitted tarmac road around to the rear and the parking situated closer to the lighthouse itself. This building stood in excess of eighty-five feet towering above the attached ancillary buildings and dominating the landscape. This section of the UK coast proved treacherous for shipping with many wrecks falling foul of the combination of violent North Sea storms and the hidden dangers beneath the surface. Caslin pressed the start/stop button and the engine died. A whirring sound continued for a few seconds as the systems set themselves and then all was quiet. The sound of the bitter north-easterly wind hammering the outside of the car was all he could hear. Hunter looked around. Clearly, she had never been here before. Caslin had, many times.

"What would Bradley be doing all the way out here?" she asked, appearing perplexed. "Not coming for a round of golf?" she half-heartedly suggested. Caslin smiled. There were some hardy souls venturing out on the course, visible to them from the approach road. The sun was shining and that was all the invitation some people needed.

"Let's go for a walk and see if we can get an idea of what he might have been here for," Caslin said, cracking the door open and being hit by a blast of cold air. Getting out of the car, Hunter joined him, wrapping her coat about her and squinting as she faced the sun, sitting low in the sky.

Caslin looked around. The residences stretched behind them in a crescent shape some distance away. There was the possibility Bradley had visited any one of these places but they'd failed to find any associations, loose or otherwise, with the registered occupants. Heading over to the lighthouse, the compound of which was encircled by a five-foot-high boundary wall fashioned from brick, Caslin noted the side road running behind it and down almost to the cliff edge. There were a handful of minor structures present on a prominent outcrop and by the look of the attached antennae, he guessed they were monitoring equipment related to the fog warning system. As for the lighthouse itself, the tower was fully automated, dispensing with the need for a traditional keeper as were almost all of those in the UK network. The wall offered them a little respite from the prevailing wind but that passed as they came around to the northern side.

A path led away from them with a signpost revealing the route of the *Way Marker Trail*. Caslin glanced about them. The business selling souvenirs was closed. A brief inspection of the sign indicated they were operating out of season opening hours. Unsurprising as footfall was light at this time of year. However, the café was open and they passed through a gate to the adjoining garden seating, an assortment of picnic benches, and entered the building. A handful of people were present. A small group of ramblers by the look of them, taking a winter hike along the coast. They approached the counter, Hunter producing a photograph of Philip Bradley. The lady staffing the counter was in her forties with dyed hair that was growing out to reveal grey shoots against the fading blonde.

"Have you seen this man around here recently?" she asked, offering up the picture. The woman looked at it closely, turning the corners of her mouth downwards and shaking her head.

"Not that I recall," she said, eyeing them curiously. "Are you police or something?"

"Yes, we are," Hunter explained with an apologetic smile producing her identification.

"Thought so," she replied. "You all walk funny."

"Is that right?" Hunter said, inclining her head. "Are you sure you haven't seen him? It would have been three days ago."

"Not me. Hang on a second," she said, stepping away and looking back into the kitchen area, standing on tiptoes as she strained to see over the coffee machine. "Geoff!" she called. Moments later a man appeared from the rear. He was short, barrel-chested and balding. He approached them warily giving Caslin the once over as he got closer.

"What is it, Mary?"

"Police," she said to him. He raised his eyebrows in response.

"What can I do for you?" he asked.

"Have you seen this man?" Hunter asked, sliding the photo across the counter towards him. "He would have been here a few days ago." The man eyed the picture but he didn't register a notable response. His gaze lingered enough for Caslin to think it was worth a nudge.

"He would have been driving a red Mercedes," Caslin said.

"Yeah, now you mention it. I think he was here."

"Are you sure?" Hunter pressed.

"He parked in front of the lighthouse, over there," Geoff said, looking out across the tables and chairs and through the large picture window. "That's restricted parking and he didn't have a permit."

"You checked?" Caslin asked.

"No, don't be silly," he explained, "if you work here long enough you get to know the cars and who owns them. It doesn't really matter this time of year but he'd be screwed in the summer. Traffic wardens love coming up here."

"Did you see him with anyone?" Caslin asked.

Geoff shook his head. "No. I mean, he may have been with someone but he was on his own when he came in here."

"Did you speak with him?"

"Only to serve him. He had a coffee and sat down over there," he said, pointing to a table by the window.

"What did he do?" Hunter asked. "Did he speak to anyone?"

"Not that I saw. He just drank his coffee, staring out of the window."

"Then what?"

"Then nothing. He left."

"That's it? You saw him drive off?"

"No. I remember seeing the car was still there when I went out for a smoke but I didn't see him again."

"Any idea where he might have gone?"

"No, sorry. He could have gone for a walk. He was dressed for it," he said. Noting both Caslin and Hunter's interest, he continued, "You know, casuals. Decent all-weather coat. I presumed he was going along the trail. Some people prefer it in the off-season, fewer people to get in their way."

"Thanks for your help," Hunter said and they turned away from the counter. Crossing the café, they went to where the proprietor said Bradley had been seated. Looking out of the window all that was visible was the coastal scenery, the lighthouse and the associated car park. "Meeting someone?"

"Possibly," Caslin said, following her line of sight. "Maybe he was early or arrived to check the area out." Returning to the service counter, he drew both Geoff and Mary's attention. "Do you have any CCTV?"

"No," they replied in unison.

"What about outside, to the car park?"

"No," came the reply, only this time from Geoff alone. "Why would we need it out here? There's nothing worth stealing."

"Fair enough, thanks," Caslin said. Taking out one of his contact cards, he passed it to Mary who accepted it, scanning the details printed on the front. "Just in case anything comes to mind after we've gone," Caslin explained.

"Sure, okay," she said, nodding and then turning and walking over to a cork board mounted on the wall behind the till point. She pinned his card alongside notices put up on behalf of the locals regarding anything from lost cats to cleaning services.

The two of them left the café, Hunter acknowledging the couple's help with a wave as she passed. Stepping out, they were once again buffeted by the wind. They crossed the road to the top of the coastal walking path. Glancing down, Caslin could see the land slipping towards the sea. There were warning signs mounted indicating for people to stick to the marked trail and to follow the detours when they came upon them for their own safety. Noise from behind made them turn as they were approached by the same group of ramblers who were in the café when they arrived. They stepped aside to make room for the walkers who thanked them. Almost as an afterthought, Caslin caught the attention of the second to last member of the group as she came past. She was a lady in her seventies, Caslin guessed.

"Can I ask where you are heading today?"

She stopped, smiling at his interest, "We're heading up to Thornwick Bay past the Flamborough Cliffs. It's stunning on days like this. Well, on any given day to be fair."

"I'll bet," he replied, nodding and smiling warmly. "Tell me, what are the highlights along this route?"

"Many," she said. "The cliffs themselves are well worth a look as are the views on their own but all along this coastline there's so much history. There are the old smuggler's caves and with the frequent land slips the scenery changes every time you walk it. It's tremendously exciting. Are you considering heading along the path?"

"No, not today," Caslin said. "Another time. Enjoy your day." She bid them goodbye and set off to catch up with her friends who were waiting a short way off.

"This is a strange place for a meeting," Hunter said, looking back towards the car park. "I can think of any number of places in and around York that I'd rather head to. Why drive all the way out here?"

Caslin scanned the area, "Neutral ground? I mean, you'd stand out to the locals but that's about all. It's certainly a place that the rest of the world wouldn't pay attention to. There must be a particular reason. Bradley came here for something, must have done."

"What do you want to do?" Hunter asked, glancing at her watch. Caslin screwed his nose up in a mock grimace hearing the sounds of the waves crashing against the rocks as the wind dropped. They'd achieved as much as they were going to.

"We'll head over to Full Sutton."

HMP FULL SUTTON was a Category A prison situated to the north-east of York, near Pocklington, with six hundred male inmates. A purpose-built maximum-security institution, its primary function was to house some of the most difficult, violent and dangerous prisoners currently incarcerated in the UK. Within the walls also stood the Close Supervision Centre, often referred to as the prison within a prison, housing those considered to be the greatest threats to both the public and national security. The approach road left visitors under no illusion as to where they were headed. The small village of Full Sutton was set to their left, average-size family homes, dwarfed by the facility to be found barely a stone's throw away. Signage indicated where they were, directing them towards the administration and visitors' entrance.

Caslin pulled into the car park and located one of many free spaces, bringing the car to a stop. A works compound was off to the prison's right-hand side surrounded by its own security fence and razor wire. The entrance to the prison lay before them, a brick structure protruding out in stark juxtaposition to the imposing walls running the perimeter. The entire compound was illuminated by towering floodlights placed strategically every thirty feet along the perimeter ensuring the open ground around the facility could not be breached unseen.

Approaching the pedestrian entrance, Caslin eyed the security bollards, painted yellow, sited in such a way as to make ram-raiding the administration block an impossibility. Likewise, they passed through the main door with its mechanically-operated security gate that would keep out even the most ambitious of attackers. Official signs were erected leaving entrants to the institution in no doubt as to what their legal requirements were, what would not be tolerated, as well as the consequences of failing to adhere to the visitation rules. All prisons were detached from the trappings of the free society but here, you really were stepping into a world alien to most.

The reception was manned. Family visitations were underway and the lobby was empty. They approached the counter, Caslin noting the glass was easily an inch thick. Feeling the need to lean towards the speaker of the intercom which wasn't necessary, he identified himself by way of his warrant card, as did Hunter. The man behind the screen asked, with a somewhat disembodied voice, for their warrant cards to be deposited within the tray before them so he could inspect them properly. They did so. The sound of sliding metal carried as they closed the lid and the prison officer opened the other side. They waited patiently as he transcribed some details and then conferred with a colleague who glanced in their direction. Their warrant cards were returned to them.

"Please approach the door to your right," the officer advised them, pointing the way. Caslin thanked him. They stepped away and heard a buzzer sound as the lock disengaged. The door came open and an officer appeared from behind it beckoning them to accompany him. Then they headed into the bowels of the prison passing through locked door after locked door. Minutes later, they emerged out into the open and were escorted across a yard towards a square building, two storeys high. Glancing around, the facility was a collection of secure compounds within the inner walls of a greater one. Every building's approach was by way of a tunnel of chain-link fencing and secure access points. The hospital was visible as was what appeared to be a sports hall with an all-weather pitch attached on one side. Again, all were visible through layers of security, perhaps unsurprising seeing as this prison housed mass-murderers, terrorists and those at the top end of the criminal food chain.

Caslin saw a woman appear from inside a building they were passing, a toddler in her arms. Looking past her, he saw what looked like a soft-play area. He was momentarily taken aback. Their escort appeared to notice.

"That's the visitor's centre," he explained. "We have recreational facilities for the children. It makes it less intimidating for them and let's face it, far more appealing for families to spend time together."

"Nice," Caslin said. "Maximum security has come a long way."

"Don't let the image fool you," the officer countered with a dry laugh. "Some of them will still cut your throat as soon as look at you. Your interviewee included," he said the last, with a tilt of the head for emphasis.

"Does he cause you any trouble?" Caslin asked.

The officer shook his head. "Not really. He's an old timer. He understands how these things work."

"How do you mean?" Hunter asked.

"Lags of his generation know the boundaries. There's a mutual understanding between us and them. They know why they're here and it's our job to keep them in. It's not quite respect but that's as close a description as I can think of," he explained. "We all know where we stand."

"And the difference between them and the next generation?" Caslin asked.

"Boundaries. They'll push it to the max and don't mind taking one of us down if it comes to it. The experienced inmates keep a lid on it most of the time but if it does go off, then things go awry very quickly."

"Like a couple of years ago?" Caslin asked, referencing a riot that broke out making national news at the time.

"Just like that," the officer agreed, reaching for his keys as they came to yet another locked door. "Drugs were getting out of hand and we needed to have a crackdown, reassert the authority. You can imagine how popular it was for us to be disrupting their supply of spice?"

"Drugs are your biggest problem?" Hunter asked.

"Generally speaking, yes," the officer stated. "That and keeping the headcases from killing the paedophiles and the ex-military from topping the jihadis… and all of them from trying to give us the odd kicking."

"Sounds like fun," Caslin said with intended sarcasm.

"I'm starting to think I should have tried harder at school," the officer replied, smiling and leading them into the next building.

They found themselves in an inner lobby, standing before a security desk. Here they were reminded of the rules regarding prisoner interaction. Then they were asked to sign another form before being led into an adjoining room. Here they waited. It was only a few minutes before a second door, at the opposite end of the room from where they entered, swung open and a man was led in. Caslin took his measure. They had never met. He was in his late sixties and cut an imposing figure. Once powerful and muscular but now his frame was visibly sagging. Despite that fact, Caslin could tell if it came down to it this man would still be able to hold his own in an altercation with someone half his age. Hawkish in appearance, he carried himself with the confidence that could only be derived from the solid assurance of his position as well as a core self-belief in his own status. He eyed Hunter momentarily before turning his gaze on Caslin. There it remained, his eyes narrowing. Caslin was in no doubt he was conducting much the same assessment of his visitors as they were of him.

"Take a seat, Mr Fuller," Caslin said, polite but firm.

CHAPTER SIXTEEN

PETE FULLER PULLED out a chair and seated himself placing his hands on the table before him, palms down. Rolling his tongue across the inner edge of his bottom lip, he maintained eye contact with Caslin.

"To what do I owe the pleasure, Inspector Caslin?"

"You were expecting me?" Caslin asked. It was as much a statement as it was a question.

"My boys said you would probably be paying me a visit," Fuller stated, leaning back in his chair. Caslin could tell he was standing before a career criminal. Fuller had that look about him. He was not intimidated being interviewed by the law.

"You must be a little disheartened at one of your businesses being attacked in that way?"

"So, it's an attack is it?" Fuller asked in a light-hearted tone. He lifted his hands from the table and crossed his arms in front of his chest inclining his head slightly, holding Caslin's gaze. "The news said it was a gas leak."

"You and I both know that isn't true," Caslin said, stepping across to the table and pulling out a chair of his own. Sitting down, he leaned forward placing his elbows on the table. "I wanted to know what your thoughts were?"

"You're the detective."

"It must be maddening for you," Caslin said. "What with you being who you are."

"How so?"

"A man of your stature being stuck in here as someone attempts to do an end run on you," Caslin said, glancing off to the left at nothing in particular. "I'll bet you're itching to find out who did it? Unless of course, you already know."

"I'm quite sure my boys can handle it," Fuller stated evenly.

"Yes, I've met your boys," Caslin said. "Ashton appears quite level headed. Carl, on the other hand, seems to be wired just like his old man. At least, the old man of his youth."

Fuller smiled at that. "They share my best qualities," he stated.

"Although, on this occasion they may well have gotten in over their heads," Caslin said drumming his fingers on the table and inclining his head. "They've acquitted themselves quite well running your enterprises. The uneasy peace between them and your competitors has been advantageous... for a decade or so, maybe more?"

"And your point is?"

"They've managed to steer clear of any major drama with your adversaries," Caslin said. "But this is different. This is a new phase and I'm not sure they're ready."

"Is that so?" Fuller asked with animosity edging into his tone. "It's a tough business."

"Particularly so where Clinton Dade is concerned," Caslin said narrowing his eyes and watching for a reaction. At the mention of Dade's name, Fuller's eyes widened in the slightest indication that Caslin might be touching a nerve. He noticed. "You and Clinton go back a long way, don't you?"

"We do."

"Is it fair to say you're not exactly on friendly terms?"

"Aye, you could say that," Fuller said raising his left hand

and leaning his face against thumb and forefinger. His index finger stroked his chin as he eyed Caslin expectantly.

"Any idea why Dade would want to start up a little fracas between you? It seems rather odd timing after years of amicable relations."

"Dade is a funny old goat," Fuller said. "It must be all that time he spends with those young boys of his."

"You and he were close once, weren't you?" Hunter said from the other side of the room. Fuller glanced in her direction and smiled.

"A long time ago, lass," Fuller replied.

"What did happen between you two?" Caslin asked.

"A minor disagreement between friends."

"Friends don't go to war with each other over minor disagreements," Caslin said.

"That depends."

"Depends on what?"

"The manner of the disagreement," Fuller said sitting forward in his chair. "As well as the nature of the friendship," he added.

"There's always another way that we could view this," Caslin said. "You must be looking forward to getting out of here. Not necessarily Full Sutton but out of the system completely. How long have you got left to serve… two years, maybe three if you don't have a positive parole board but no more than that?"

"Far less than that."

"In which case, soon you will be moved to a Category C prison to prepare you for returning to society the changed man that I'm sure you are."

"So, what's your point?"

"Maybe this bombing is a response to something you've done. Are you looking to reassert your presence?" Caslin asked locking eyes with the man sitting opposite him. Fuller smiled but it wasn't genuine.

"And you think I'm that stupid?"

"You wouldn't be the first to start acting like he's already out when into the final stretch," Caslin said. "And besides, don't insult my intelligence by making out you have nothing to do with your business interests while you are in here. I'm certainly not that stupid."

"Well, you have to keep your hand in, don't you?"

"We had a chat with Clinton the other day. He was all about the business as well," Caslin said.

"There you go then."

"He thought animosity between you would be bad for both of you. Of course, he's probably drawing on previous experience, isn't he?"

"You keep on pushing that, don't you?" Fuller said fixing Caslin with a stare.

"The word on the street is that the two of you were thick as thieves on your way up. But something happened along the way. Just when the two of you were hitting the big time you had a falling out. Care to comment?" Caslin asked. There was the briefest flicker of a reaction. If they were playing poker Caslin would have known something was up.

"Water under the bridge. I don't think Clinton will be coming for me and as far as I'm concerned..." he drew a deep breath, "the past is the past and that's where it should remain. Is that clear enough for you, Mr Caslin?"

"How's the family?" Caslin asked.

"Well enough."

"Ashton and Carl will be looking forward to your return," Caslin said before sucking air through his teeth, "or maybe not." Fuller raised an eyebrow in a gesture of curiosity at Caslin's intimation but offered no comment. "After all. Despite your obvious influence, they've had their hands on the reins for years. It'll be quite a wrench to step back into your shadow, I'd imagine."

"So, they bomb their own business?" Fuller countered. "No

wonder the crime rates are soaring if your level of ability is the new benchmark."

Caslin was about to respond but was interrupted by his phone ringing. Taking the handset out of his pocket he allowed his gaze to linger on Fuller as he took the call from Terry Holt.

"Sir, I've got an update for you on Bradley's case files."

"Terry, can it wait?" Caslin said barely concealing his irritation at the interruption.

"No, sir," Holt explained. "You are going to want to hear this. Believe me, it's relevant."

"Go on then, make it quick," Caslin said.

"The files from Greater Manchester came over this morning and I'm going through them. The indexing is pretty good I have to say. I was looking for a crossover between Bradley and MacEwan and I found one, albeit it's a little tenuous. Do you remember the Manchester airport securities raid back in the 80s? It was headline news. I don't remember the details because I was just a kid but it rang a bell. Once I looked it up, I remembered hearing about it at the time."

"Was that the raid on the customs clearing house?" Caslin asked. Fuller was still looking at him, an impassive expression on his face.

"Yes, that's the one, sir. An armed gang hit the clearing house in the early hours escaping with an estimated haul of around £22 million worth of cash, gold and gems. As I said that was estimated with the true value never fully being revealed. And don't forget those are the values of the day, it would be a lot more now."

"How much are we talking?"

"Even a conservative estimate would put today's figure at somewhere north of £120 million," Holt stated. "And I'm not sure how much you know about the detail but there was a lot that went unrecovered."

"And how does this tie our boys together?" Caslin asked,

reluctant to reveal names of an ongoing investigation in front of his present company.

"Bradley was a detective chief inspector assigned to the securities raid investigation," Holt said with obvious excitement. "MacEwan was a known associate of Fuller's and was therefore interviewed at the time."

"How was he involved?" Caslin asked.

"Nothing stuck to him, sir. It looks like he was part of the scramble to find someone responsible for such a high-profile crime. MacEwan wasn't interviewed again nor did his name appear anywhere else in the inquiry."

"Do we know who interviewed him?"

"No, sir," Holt explained. "I don't have the transcript, only a reference to the interview with the date it took place. Some of the files haven't materialised from the archive but I'm chasing them up."

"We need to know. If the DCI was in on the interview, it'd be hard to believe they wouldn't recognise each other when they met the other day," Caslin said.

"If not, there is the possibility they didn't know each other. At least, not at the time," Holt said. "But you're going to love the next bit."

"Go on."

"Who do you think we know that is currently doing time for the raid on the customs clearing house?"

"Don't tell me," Caslin said, locking eyes with the man sitting opposite him, "am I sitting in front of him?"

"Only if it's Pete Fuller," Holt said, "and there's one more thing you should be aware of. We knew Jody Wyer's father, Keith, was a serving police officer. What we didn't know was that Bradley was once Keith Wyer's DCI."

"They served together," Caslin repeated.

"At the time of the raid, yes."

Caslin hung up the phone, slowly placing the handset on the table. He looked across his shoulder behind him towards Hunter.

She remained expressionless but he knew she was curious as to what information he had just received, assuming it was significant.

"Now that was very interesting," Caslin said, his lips parting and forming a smile. "You remember Detective Chief Inspector Philip Bradley?"

"Old friends," Fuller replied with a nod of the head.

"Instrumental in your incarceration, I understand?" Caslin said.

"With friends like that who needs enemies, right?"

"He's dead," Caslin said, watching intently for a similar flicker of recognition as Fuller had offered previously. On this occasion the inmate was unreadable with the only reaction being a controlled release of his breath.

"That's a shame. The good often go too early," Fuller said quietly. "My condolences to the family."

"I'm sure they are heartfelt," Caslin said. "And your old friend, David. Heard from him recently?"

"David is a common name, Inspector. I'm afraid you'll have to be more specific than that."

"MacEwan," Caslin said, his gaze narrowing. "Or have you not seen him since you were sent down?"

"Lucky Davie," Fuller said with a smile. "Last I heard, he'd emigrated."

"No, he's very much back in the game," Caslin countered, inspecting his fingernails casually. "I do wonder what he's up to though. Making friends. Influencing others. Quite the character. Nice tan."

"I'm pleased for him," Fuller said but his tone belied some buried resentment. Caslin, however, was unable to interpret how deep those feelings ran. The ice-cool exterior had thawed a little. They were onto something. Caslin could sense it.

THEIR DEPARTURE COINCIDED with the end of visiting times and they found themselves navigating the exit of Full Sutton along with around thirty relatives. Some of those rubbing shoulders with them were downcast, seeing loved ones under such circumstances was emotionally draining. Others, perhaps with more experience, appeared to take it in their stride. A couple even joked with the officer escorting them to the reception. Once clear of the main entrance, Caslin and Hunter picked up the pace to get clear of the pack.

"That puts a different slant on events, doesn't it?" Hunter said once Caslin had filled her in on the details of Holt's phone call. "I wasn't expecting that. Do you think both events are linked? Wyer's murder as well as the bombing?" They reached the car and Caslin leaned on the roof looking across at Hunter and fiddling with the key fob in his hands, mulling over his response.

"Possibly. The characters are interconnected to a point beyond coincidence, so to dismiss the link would be foolish but as for how, I don't know?" he said, pursing his lips. "Are they directly related or is one symptomatic of the other?"

"How do you mean?" Hunter asked. "Is the bombing a response to Wyer's murder?"

Caslin shook his head indicating he didn't know, "I'm thinking aloud. Wyer is watching MacEwan, perhaps even Bradley for some reason. These two figured in a massive case that Wyer's father worked on. The very case that saw Pete Fuller sent down for a thirty-year stretch."

"And somewhere along the line someone within Fuller's organisation sets a bomb off. Why?" Hunter asked.

"Let's not forget either that the Fullers were not targeted directly," Caslin said. "If you were trying to take them out there are any number of opportunities where you could get to Ashton or Carl but they didn't. They hit the minicab office. Are they sending a message or maybe a warning?" Caslin asked rhetorically.

"If they are then who is it aimed at, Pete… the boys?" Hunter asked. "They could have hit Pete himself in prison," she suggested. "It wouldn't be the first time."

"You're right. No one is untouchable," he said, glancing back towards the prison. "As hard as it is to get in or out, behind those walls anyone is fair game for the right price."

"Lots of questions but not many answers."

"That's what makes this job so interesting," Caslin said with a broad grin, unlocking the car.

CHAPTER SEVENTEEN

"WHERE ARE we with the raid on the clearing house, Terry?" Caslin asked, pulling out a chair and briefly scanning the noticeboard for updates he may have missed while sitting down.

"The raid took place in 1986," Holt said, referring to his notes as he spoke. "The clearing house was outsourced and run by a private contractor. The subsequent investigation was ongoing for nearly four years and resulted in twenty-six convictions. Pete Fuller was identified as one of the lieutenants on the ground largely because of his links to those with the skill set and muscle to pull off such an operation. However, it took several years to bring him in."

"How was he identified?"

"The case was quite an embarrassment for the police and the government of the day who were at that time preaching a tougher attitude towards crime. The rewards being offered for information dragged many a low-life out of their pits to throw names at us," Holt explained. "Although Fuller wasn't considered to be big time in the 80s, he was on the rise and intel had him working on and off with several of the players in and around York. Arguably, both North Yorkshire and Greater Manchester Police underestimated just how advanced some of these guys were. Fuller's organisation was in reality already a large cog in a far greater machine."

"Who was he working with?" Caslin asked, looking at Fuller's mugshot taken upon his arrest in 1990. His features were different now. The eyes sunken, the skin tauter. Prison life – prison food – certainly took its toll after several decades.

"The leaders of the operation were named as Harry Bates and Thomas Maguire. Both were old hands at armed robberies starting out in their youth knocking off post offices and progressing to armoured cars and the like. This was seen as their last shot at the big prize. A chance to cement their name in history… as well as a pension of sorts," Holt said, passing images of the two men across the table to both Caslin and Hunter.

"What do we know about them?" Hunter asked, checking out the photos.

"Maguire died in Pentonville Prison fifteen years ago from a heart attack. The guy was already in his seventies when he was sent down."

"And Bates?" Caslin asked.

"Still serving time. He's currently in Belmarsh," Holt said, naming one of London's toughest prisons. "But interestingly, neither of them was considered to be the orchestrator of the raid."

"Who was?" Caslin asked.

Holt shook his head, "Never identified. The file has the architect listed as a man called *Alfred* but that's only a codename used in reference to him. Despite the team's best efforts no one was either willing or able to name him. Even the offer of a reduced sentence to the convicted hadn't tempted them to reveal who he was."

"Perhaps they didn't know?" Hunter suggested.

"Or perhaps thirty years inside was preferable to grassing," Caslin said. "We all know this *honour among thieves'* line that gets bandied about is absolute rubbish. These guys would sell their own mother if they thought it worth their while. Either they were scared of him or you're right, they genuinely didn't know his name. I recall you saying not everything stolen was recovered. Is that right?"

"Correct, sir," Holt confirmed. "As I said on the phone, the estimated haul they escaped with was £22 million in a mixture of cash, gold and gems and we're talking in excess of £120 million in today's values and that's a conservative estimate. Only around £13 million has been recovered and much of that took over a decade of investigation to locate. That was achieved through tracing the flow of money between the known figures and using legislation for seizing monies derived from illegal sources rather than actually finding what was taken. That's why we can say with confidence that this Alfred character remains at large. The organisation of the raid was so meticulous that the fencing of what was stolen was so sophisticated as to render it almost invisible."

"It went somewhere," Caslin said, casting his gaze across Bradley's photograph. "What about Chief Superintendent Ford? I'll bet he slots in somewhere to all of this."

"You'd be right, sir. He was Bradley's supervising officer on the investigation. He did quite well off the back of that case," Holt said, handing over a brief listing Ford's career history. Both Caslin and Hunter began reading as he continued, "Despite not getting everyone involved, the number of those eluding arrest and the true value that went unrecovered was largely kept out of the media. The case was far from a failure but perhaps not the success it was painted as at the time."

"Which all brings us back to Bradley and his untimely demise," Caslin said, putting the document on the table before him. "Tony Mason, Wyer's business partner, was he in on this investigation?"

"No, sir," Holt said. "I checked but he did work with Bradley for a number of years. They certainly knew each other."

"Fair to assume Bradley would know of Mason's habits?"

"I would say so, sir," Holt said, as did Hunter, making her agreement visible with a nod. "It still leaves us without a definite thread to bring all of this together."

"MacEwan," Caslin began, wracking his brain to try and put the pieces together, "what is he known for?"

"In the early 80s, he was considered a low-level member of the criminal fraternity," Holt said, leafing back through his notes. "A few convictions for receiving stolen goods but nothing prolific. After his death in 1985, MacEwan took over his father's scrap metal business and it was suspected he ran an outfit ringing stolen cars using the scrap yard as the legitimate front. A few months after being interviewed about the raid on the customs house, he relocated to Spain. Although he kept his business going, he doesn't resurface in the UK until the late 1990s. By which time he's a millionaire, a pretty flamboyant one by all accounts having made a fortune in time-share investments and other property ventures."

"The same area of Spain as Bradley?" Hunter asked, seeking the connection.

"That, I can't say at the moment," Holt said. "I have a call into Europol and I'm waiting to hear back."

"Okay, keep digging," Caslin said, standing and crossing the room to come before the board. Raising his hand, he pointed at the picture of Jody Wyer. "Wyer's father worked this case and now, thirty years on, his son is investigating the very same group of people only it now encompasses some of his father's former colleagues. What brought Jody into this? Was it something his father told him or that he stumbled onto? The fact his business partner is somehow linked leads me to think it was the latter for no other reason than he agreed to go into business with him in the first place. If you couldn't trust your partner, you wouldn't leave yourself open, would you? Or am I missing something?"

"Keith Wyer, Jody's father," Hunter said. "What was his career like?"

"Nondescript," Holt said. "I'd register him as a journeyman officer. There are no marks against his file. He was adequate."

"I would hope my career highlights read better when the time comes," Caslin replied.

"Seeing as MacEwan's place is the only centre point we have for these faces, I downloaded a couple of data dumps from the cell towers around the scrap yard," Holt said. "Wyer's wallet litter – the receipts and scraps of stuff inside it – had him in a nearby petrol station a few days before he died, so I ran the mobile we have registered to him against the data from the cell towers. He was in and around the area on numerous occasions recently. Sometimes for hours on end."

"Sounds like he was staking the place out," Hunter offered.

"My thoughts exactly," Holt agreed.

"Have you got anywhere with the photographs that you took the other day?" Caslin asked Hunter, referencing their time spent at the vantage point in the business opposite MacEwan's yard. She nodded opening her own file on the desk before her.

"This is the only figure we have outstanding," she said, taking out copies of the frames she had taken. Spreading them out before her on the table so everyone could see, she pointed to the young man who had retrieved Bradley's car for him that day at the yard.

"Now he looks familiar," Caslin said, tapping one of the images with his forefinger. "Where do I know him from?"

"I thought so too," Hunter said. "While we were there the other day, I took shots of as many of the cars as I could see and then ran the indexes through the system just to see who pops up. I figured we could get a list going of MacEwan's people. From that list I cross-referenced the owner's data with the DVLA as well as our own files."

"Anyone interesting?" Caslin asked.

"Your standard who's who in the thug's database..." she said with sarcasm, "and then there's this guy." Hunter took out an arrest record of the man Caslin had pointed to. Turning it ninety degrees, both Holt and Caslin leaned over to see. It was the same man, although his hair was cut shorter with none of the wavy, surfer-style locks as he carried now. The record listed arrests for drug possession, affray and common assault to name but a few. Most of the crimes were low-level, habitual lifestyle arrests rather than for organised criminality.

"Oliver Bridger," Caslin read the name aloud. "It doesn't ring any bells."

"Ollie Bridger," Hunter confirmed. "Evidently working for MacEwan and well settled into his inner circle judging from what we saw. I think the reason he looks familiar is this," she said, taking out another arrest record. Placing it on the table alongside the first, Caslin frowned. "Similar, aren't they?" Caslin eyed the new sheet. He could have been looking at the same person. Again, the hair was shorter but a darker colour and the expression of resentment in the mugshot was almost identical.

"Twins?" Caslin asked, flicking his eyes to Hunter.

"No, but they were born only ten months apart," she stated. "They were in the same school year and could easily be mistaken for twins."

"I don't know them," Holt said.

"We came across Mark," Hunter said, pointing to the second sheet, "on our visit to Clinton Dade's office which is probably why Ollie caught your eye, sir. Both have popped up on our radar on and off throughout their juvenile and adult lives but not in a senior capacity. They are bottom of the food chain, really. But their presence here is interesting."

"How so?" Caslin asked, comparing their respective records.

"Well, first off, Ollie Bridger was picked up for his participation in an assault last year along with two others. They trashed a business and put the owner in hospital."

"Why is that significant?"

"Intel has it recorded as being related to the Fullers' business interests. They were believed to be acting on Ashton's instructions."

"Pressuring a client?"

"Suspicion of debt collection or racketeering is listed on the file but nothing stuck. The victim chose not to press charges and refused to identify them. That puts Ollie as an associate of the Fullers or at least he was at the time."

"And now he's working for MacEwan."

"Where it gets really interesting is that their father was Neville Bridger," Hunter continued. "He came through the ranks as an enforcer for a local money lender and had a criminal record as long as your arm."

"You said, *had*?" Caslin queried.

"Neville Bridger died in prison in 2004 during a riot," Hunter said. "I looked it up. His wing erupted and the inmates barricaded themselves inside taking three prison officers hostage. The standoff lasted four days until the authorities retook the wing and restored order. They found his body in the shower block. He'd been stabbed to death with a makeshift shank."

"Did they catch who did it?" Caslin asked.

"No. There wasn't any indication of who carried out the attack nor a motive for it. Most likely it was someone using the disturbance to settle a score. Let's face it, it could have been anyone."

"Sorry to ask the stupid question but is this relevant?" Holt asked. Caslin met his eye, inclining his head.

Looking to Hunter, he asked, "Is it relevant?"

"He was sentenced to eighteen years for his part in..." she held her breath, building the anticipation and watching Caslin's interest grow, "the 1986 Manchester Airport raid."

"Well, that's relevant," Caslin said smiling. "The ever-expanding circle."

"He was one of the last to be picked up hence why he received a lesser sentence than many of the others. The case had dropped from the public consciousness and I guess the judge wasn't looking to set such an example as a deterrent."

"Was Neville linked to either MacEwan, Dade or Fuller in a professional capacity prior to the customs house job?" Holt asked.

Hunter shook her head, "There isn't really enough information to make a judgement on that. Fuller and Dade were close in age and were moving in the same circles and so it would be reasonable to assume they knew each other but whether that stretched to criminal enterprise is a leap. Regarding MacEwan... the man's still a bit of an enigma. We just don't know enough about him."

"Okay, changing tack," Caslin said, returning his focus to the noticeboard. "Any lead on the mysterious redhead occupying Jody Wyer's life?"

"None at all," Hunter said. "We've been through his personal effects, the house, car... we've got nothing apart from a toothbrush, toiletries and some red hair in a brush."

Caslin sucked air through his teeth, "I can't help but think she ties in to all of this."

"Why?" Hunter asked.

"Well, for one thing because he kept her a secret from everyone else and secondly, he was working from home and keeping that a secret too. If she was spending so much time there, she might know what he was working on. It doesn't look like he was trying to hide it from her," Caslin explained, "which at most makes her a part of it or at least, a confidant. Either way, I want to find her and let's not forget, he's been murdered and she hasn't come forward. That tells me she knows something, or she's scared of someone."

"Could she also have played a part in killing him?" Holt asked.

"We certainly can't rule it out."

The sound of the doors opening behind them saw them turn. DCI Matheson entered purposefully. Caslin read the look of consternation on her face.

"Ma'am," he said in greeting.

"You've been making enquiries around Clinton Dade's operation," she said.

Caslin nodded, "Yes, we have. Why, what's up?"

"Uniform have just come across Dade," she replied, "and you're going to want to see it."

CHAPTER EIGHTEEN

THE PITCH of the engine increased noticeably as Hunter dropped a gear and pulled out from behind the slow-moving lorry. She was itching to reach the scene just as much as he was and Caslin could feel the anticipation growing inside him. The A166 towards Stamford Bridge was a busy road, east of York, the most direct route to the coast if not the fastest. They weren't going that far. Hunter slowed as the sat nav indicated an approaching left turn. Seeing the sign for the village of Holtby she eased off and left the highway.

"Through the village, wasn't it?" she asked, flicking her eyes at the screen set into the dashboard.

"Yes. Should be a right turn as we come up on Brockfield," Caslin advised her. Hunter nodded, focussing on the road ahead. Holtby came and went in a flash. One of the many tiny villages peppering the rural Yorkshire landscape, Caslin couldn't help but wonder how they came to be out here. Their route cut back to the west before turning north again, navigating the patchwork of farmland delineated by hedgerows and tree lines. Hunter turned on the indicators to signal they were turning onto Rudcarr Lane although Caslin didn't know why she bothered. There was no one out here to inform of the manoeuvre. Here, the road narrowed to such an extent that should they meet a vehicle coming in the other direction there would be the distinct possibility one or the other would need to pull off the road to give way.

Winter crops were visible in fields to either side of them and the road was interspersed with barren oak trees, their leaves shed in late autumn.

"There," Caslin said, pointing ahead to a liveried police car, its nose visible at the next turn in the road. Reaching the bend, Hunter pulled the car to the verge. They were alongside an opening to the field beyond with a small patch of flat ground between them and a gate. The gate itself was wooden and in a poor state of repair, hanging from one of the hinges. It had clearly been some time since it was opened, the hedgerow bordering the field now spreading across the posts. Alongside the gate was a stile, allowing access to the public path over the fields. This was in a far better condition. The landowner must have found a better access point for his machinery and abandoned this one years ago.

Caslin found his attention drawn to why they were there. A dark blue Mercedes was parked up, facing the highway, underneath a giant oak tree. Iain Robertson noted their arrival and beckoned them over.

"One of yours, I believe?" he said, approaching them and tilting his head in the direction of the car.

"Is it Dade?" Caslin asked, falling into step alongside the forensics officer.

"Identification in his wallet says so," Robertson confirmed. "But you're going to need a few tests to be sure."

"That bad?" Hunter asked.

"Aye," Robertson said under his breath, leading them down the passenger side of the car towards the rear.

The car doors were all closed. The rear passenger window was shattered with much of the glass falling inwards into the interior. The remainder was fractured in every direction but held precariously in place despite the driving wind rattling across the flat lands surrounding them. Caslin noted the drainage ditch running alongside the road, assisting to keep the farmland from flooding. Robertson noticed the glance. "We'll be dredging the ditch just in case they dumped the weapon or anyone else for that matter, in there before leaving."

"What do you think?" Caslin asked, returning his attention to the car and its passenger.

"Shotgun," Robertson said with a frown. "Most likely a sawn-off. The nature of the tissue damage is indicative of a wide directional spray from both barrel and cartridge."

Caslin peered through the window into the cabin, exhaling deeply as he registered the state of the interior. Immediately, he knew Alison Taylor would need a DNA sample to confirm the identity of the victim. Even a cursory inspection of the body slumped across the rear seat reinforced that view. In no way would a facial verification be suitable and he guessed a dental match would be equally unsuccessful. The rear window, roof, along with the upholstery were all coated in blood spatter, skin tissue and what Caslin assumed were skull and brain fragments.

"Point blank," he muttered under his breath.

"And several shots, I should imagine," Robertson stated. Caslin looked up at him. "We found two spent cartridges over there," he said, pointing to a patch of ground a few feet away. "I think the killer, or killers, put in two blasts before reloading and doing the same again. That's why you see what you see. They wanted to make absolutely certain."

Caslin shook his head, "No. That's not it."

"Then what?" Robertson asked.

"This was personal."

"Or they wanted it to appear so. Either way, I think the victim was almost certainly known to his killer," Robertson said. Caslin was intrigued.

"How do you know?"

"The window," Robertson said, pointing to the glass. Caslin

looked but didn't see what he was supposed to. He raised an eyebrow in a query. "It's on its way down... or up. The victim had lowered it. The top of the glass is down four inches. If he was a smoker, then I can imagine he might want it open in this weather but there's no butt dropped either inside or out. I'd wager it's more likely he was conversing with someone, probably the killer. Liver temperature sets the time of death at around midnight."

"Who could have got Clinton Dade to come all the way out here at that time of night?" Hunter asked.

"Someone he knew," Caslin said quietly, following Robertson's hypothesis. "The end result suggests someone who held a grudge. That might be a reason why they came out here – to be on neutral ground."

"But for such a lethal threat to get this close unchallenged..." Hunter left the thought unfinished, looking to Robertson to answer the unasked question.

"No, there are no other victims as far as we can tell," Robertson confirmed. "We'll carry out a full fingertip search of the surrounding area but there are no blood trails or evidence anyone else was attacked."

"What about up front?" Caslin asked, stepping to his left and peering through the front passenger window, assessing where the driver would have been sitting. Despite a significant amount of blood in the interior, he saw nothing leading him to believe the driver was also hit.

"The spray and subsequent spatter passing from the rear to the front of the cabin is consistent with a high-velocity impact," Robertson said, bending over and following Caslin's sightlines. "Judging from where it struck," he indicated the front windscreen as well as the inside of the driver's window, "I reckon there was no one sitting there when the gun went off."

"Which gives us a further couple of questions," Caslin said, "presuming you're correct about no other victims being present. Either the driver got out of the car to speak with, challenge, or greet the gunman and then made a run for it when everything hit the fan or…" he left the thought hanging as he looked around the immediate vicinity, playing the various scenarios out in his head. "He was complicit in some way."

"He could have been the gunman?" Hunter said, clarifying the thought.

"I'm not convinced of that but it would explain how he managed to get so close," Caslin said. "And one thing's for certain, if this is Clinton Dade, he didn't drive himself out here. We need to find the person who did. If the driver's running, we'll have to find him before the killer does. Likewise, if it was the same person, Dade's crew will also be looking for him and if they get there first, he won't be telling us anything. Knowing the names of those in this circle, we're on the clock. I reckon if he survives twenty-four hours, then he'll be doing well."

"I know it's an obvious thought but you've got to put the Fullers in the frame," Hunter said. "This kind of thing is right up Carl's street, wouldn't you say?"

Caslin had to admit the thought had already occurred to him. There was every chance one or the other faction sought a meeting in order to calm the situation down, particularly as Dade was so insistent that he wasn't to blame for the bombing. A neutral location away from prying eyes was logical. Caslin looked around for the nearest sign of habitation. There were two farmhouses, each surrounded by agricultural buildings, and both were at least three hundred metres away in opposite directions across the fields. This location was nigh on perfect for carrying out such a hit. No witnesses. No cameras. No one to see either party arrive or depart. Minimal chances of being seen, let alone caught. Something didn't sit right with him though. An instinctive feeling that had almost always served him well in the past.

"I can't see Ashton going for it though. Can you?" he replied to Hunter.

"Ashton got the brains of the family but Carl runs the

muscle. Perhaps he didn't know," she countered. Caslin inclined his head at the suggestion.

"Any sign of other vehicles?" Caslin asked, turning his attention back to Robertson.

"The ground is frozen solid, I'm afraid," he replied. "Very little chance of pulling tyre impressions but we'll do our best."

"I'll arrange to have the local properties canvassed," Hunter said, seeking Caslin's permission with an inquiring glance. He nodded. "We might get lucky."

The sound of an approaching vehicle came to ear and Caslin turned, looking down the road in the direction of Brockfield. The car was moving at pace and it seemed to be out of the ordinary somehow. The driver eased off as he came upon the police cordon, coming to a stop in the middle of the road. Caslin watched as two men got out. Recognising the driver, he indicated for Robertson to carry on with his work and made his way towards the new arrivals. A uniformed constable was already stepping across to block their advance. A movement that was not well received. The driver of the car chose to disregard the officer's instructions and attempted to bypass him. The officer placed a firm hand on the man's shoulder and issued a direct instruction to stop but was ignored.

"It's okay," Caslin called as he approached. The uniformed officer had a firm grasp on the man's clothing and he was about to make an arrest before Caslin intervened. The second man stood a few steps behind and held his ground, watching to see what was about to happen. "Alli, isn't it?" Caslin asked. The man glared first at the constable, despite being released, and then at Caslin.

"Is it him?" Alli asked, almost spitting venom as the words passed his lips and looked beyond Caslin towards the blue Mercedes.

"We think so," Caslin confirmed. At confirmation of Dade's apparent demise, Alli visibly appeared to shrink in stature before him. He looked to the ground at his feet, drawing deep breaths and Caslin realised he was trying not to break down. "How did you know he was out here?" he asked. The bitter anger in Alli's eyes dissipated to be replaced by a somewhat lost expression. Tears welled and Caslin saw at that moment the true nature of their relationship.

"Word travels," Alli said as if that answered the question.

"Was Clinton out here to meet someone last night?" Caslin asked. All of a sudden, Alli's expression changed from grief stricken to guarded. He shrugged.

"How would I know?"

"Word travels," Caslin replied with no hint of sarcasm. "Of all people, you should know what his plans were."

"He didn't say," Alli stated. "I want to see him."

"I'm afraid that's not possible at the moment," Caslin said before adding, "and inadvisable." Alli looked past him, once again, in the direction of the car and the forensic team crawling all over it.

"They'll pay for this."

"Who will, Alli?"

"Mark my words," he reiterated.

"Remember you're talking to a police officer," Caslin warned him. "I'm not your priest." Alli met his eye. He said nothing further but the fire of revenge flared in his eyes. "Any idea who he was out here with? Who was driving?" Caslin asked, glancing first to Alli and then his associate off to his right. Again, Alli declined to answer, his gaze drifting across the scene. The second man shook his head almost imperceptibly when Caslin lifted a casual finger in his direction.

"You're going to be a busy man, Inspector Caslin," Alli stated, turning his gaze back to him.

"Leave this to us," Caslin said, as sternly as he could. For his part, Alli smiled but it was tight-lipped and cold. "The best thing you can do is tell me what Clinton was doing out here before anybody else gets killed."

The smile faded and Alli took a deep breath, drawing himself upright. In doing so he more than matched Caslin for height and his stature returned to the imposing figure of their first meeting.

"Don't worry, Inspector," he said with menacing undertones. "It'll be over soon enough."

"You'll be starting a war," Caslin warned.

"They came at us," Alli hissed.

"This is one you might not be able to win."

"We'll see about that," he said, taking a couple of steps back before turning on his heel. He snapped his fingers towards the other man who fell into step alongside him. They strode back to their car. Caslin watched and as they reached it, Alli glanced back at him while opening the driver's door. He stopped, his gaze lingering for a few moments on Caslin and then back to the crime scene beyond. Caslin remained impassive as Hunter came to stand with him. Alli got into the car, slamming the door shut. He started the engine and crunched the gears as he set the car into reverse, moving off at speed. Alli manoeuvred the vehicle into a passing area and swiftly turned the car around. With one last angry look in Caslin's direction, he accelerated away, the tyres squealing momentarily as they sought traction.

"That didn't appear to go well," Hunter said.

"No. You're quite right about that," Caslin replied. "This is going to escalate quickly."

"What do you want to do?"

"Get us a search warrant for the Fullers," he said, turning to her. "It might be best if we can take them off the streets for a while."

"Is that wise?" she asked, looking concerned. "I mean, I know they'll be targets but we don't have a lot to go on that will hold them for a second longer than it takes for their brief to turn up."

"Let's see where the warrant gets us."

"Okay, where will we search?"

"Everywhere," Caslin said. "I want every business and

residential premises tied to them turned over. Oh… and I want it done today."

"That'll take some doing," Hunter stated.

"You sort out the paperwork and I'll have a word with DCI Matheson about drawing the bodies. She offered to help and this," he said, indicating over his shoulder with a flick of the hand, "should be motivation enough. If we don't put a lid on it, then Dade will just be the beginning."

CHAPTER NINETEEN

PULLING into the forecourt of the disused petrol station they found it deserted. The handful of men operating the car wash were nowhere to be seen. The cabin they operated out of was securely closed and there was no sign of recent activity. Hunter pulled their car to the side and parked up. Four liveried police vehicles pulled in behind them, fanning out and blocking both entrance and exit from the site. Getting out of the car, Caslin looked around. There were no sounds carrying from the building site to the rear either. He looked at his watch to check the time. It was a quarter after two and except for New Year's Eve, he couldn't imagine a construction site shutting down this early. Indicating to the waiting officers, they headed over to the site entrance. This too, was closed off by a length of Herras fencing. Looking beyond it and into the compound, Caslin could clearly see several vehicles parked outside the portacabin.

"Someone's here," Caslin said, grasping the padlock securing the makeshift gate in place. He shook it. The padlock was solid and held firm.

"It's almost as if they were expecting us," Hunter said.

"There's a shock," Caslin replied with a wry grin. Looking to the portacabin he could see the lights were on inside. He beckoned one of the team over. The officer approached with a set of bolt croppers in hand. "They just don't want to make it easy, that's all. Heads up everyone," Caslin said, addressing all of those present. "They'll do everything they can to get in our way. Don't let them distract you and watch your backs… and each other's."

The officer struggled for a few moments before a reassuring snap was heard and the padlock dropped away, clattering to the ground. The sound of metal on metal followed as the chain was dragged clear. Two officers lifted one end of the fence and levered it away and to the left allowing them access to the compound. The moment Caslin took a step inside the perimeter he heard a whistle, shrill and high-pitched but he didn't know where it originated from. Something seen in the corner of his eye made him turn, looking towards the rear of the site. From behind the scaffolding, roughly sixty feet away, he saw a blur of movement as several figures flashed past open sections of the building.

"What have we got here?" he heard Hunter say from behind. Everyone stopped as three dogs came into view. Caslin wasn't a fan of dogs, particularly Dobermans approaching at great speed. Instinctively, he took a step back. Looking to his left he didn't need to give the instruction as both officers who'd cleared their route were rapidly setting the barrier back into place. They managed to do so just in time as the animals arrived. They were clearly well trained as they came to a stop a few yards from them. Their ears were pricked and two of them stood their ground, eyeing the visitors intently. The third edged closer, walking the length of the fence as if assessing them. There was no growling, snarling or even a bark. They were there to deter people from entering the compound. Caslin admired their efficiency.

In the background, the door to the portacabin open and a figure emerged. It was Carl Fuller. He didn't approach them, merely folded his arms across his chest and leaned his shoulder against the building. Caslin held a fold of paper in his hands. Realising Carl had zero intention of coming over, he unfurled it. Holding it aloft against the fence, he called out.

"We are here to execute a search warrant!"

Carl shrugged, "I'm not stopping you."

"You've got twenty seconds to call your dogs off…" Caslin called, pointing at the animals. One of which was now standing before him with its head cocked.

"Or what?"

"Or I'll bloody shoot them," Caslin shouted. He didn't have an armed officer present and, in reality, he would never carry out such a drastic action but nonetheless, he made his point. Carl Fuller watched him for a few moments longer before stepping away from the wall. He poked his head back inside the portacabin, conversing with someone. Caslin saw him nod in response to something that was said and he turned. Putting two fingers in his mouth, he whistled and two of the three dogs visibly appeared to relax and turn away, trotting off in Carl's direction. The one staring at Caslin held its gaze for the briefest of moments before it, too, turned away and ran to join the others.

"I don't think it likes you," Hunter said dryly. Caslin smiled.

"It must be the reincarnation of my mother-in-law."

"Is she dead?" Hunter asked.

"We can but dream," Caslin replied as the fence was removed for the second time and they made to pass through. The guard dogs didn't react to their presence although every officer cast a wary eye in their direction. Hunter took care of issuing instructions to the search team while Caslin made his way towards Carl Fuller.

Walking up the short ramp to the entrance of the portacabin, he offered over the search warrant. Carl Fuller glanced at it but had no intention of taking it from him.

"Nah," he said dismissing the gesture. "I don't do paperwork."

"No, of course not," Caslin replied with a smile. "You'd need to be able to read," he added, slapping it forcefully against the younger man's chest. Carl accepted it under protest, glaring at him as he did so. Caslin brushed past him and made his way into the office. Inside, he found Ashton Fuller seated behind a desk, two associates clustered around him. He sat back in his chair, drawing a deep breath and exaggerating his exhalation as he took in Caslin's measure.

"Inspector Caslin," he said, smiling. "Back so soon?"

"You can't have heard me knocking," Caslin replied. "You two," he pointed to the men either side of Ashton, "move." The two men looked to Ashton who didn't respond. They held their position. Hunter came alongside Caslin, two uniformed constables accompanying her.

"You heard the man, *shift yersel*," she stated firmly in her best native Yorkshire accent, indicating the search team wanted access to the filing cabinets behind them. Begrudgingly, the two men stepped aside. Hunter encouraged her officers forward before looking to Caslin. "Everything's underway."

"Good," Caslin replied with a nod but his eyes never left Ashton.

"This might go better if you tell me what you're looking for?" Ashton said, sitting forward, resting his elbows on the desk before him and making a tent with his fingers. "What's all this about?"

"Terry?" Caslin asked, looking to Hunter.

"Has access to their apartments as we speak," she confirmed. Both of the Fullers lived in the city centre in adjoining apartments, prestigious addresses that saw them rub shoulders with the wealthiest residents the city of York could provide.

"I do hope you will be paying for any damage," Ashton said in an icy tone. It was the first time since their arrival that he'd exhibited anything but a smug attitude.

"Standard issue boots do tend to traipse in a lot of dirt," Caslin said. "I hope you don't have pastel carpets."

"*What is it that you want?*" Ashton said, the novelty of the situation departing him as his office was systematically ransacked by the assembled officers.

"Clinton Dade is dead."

"What's that got to do with us?"

"You're not out to settle the account?" Caslin asked. Carl appeared to his left, fixing him with a stare and passing the copy of the search warrant over to his brother.

"Maybe he got depressed," Carl suggested. "Couldn't take it anymore."

"And blew his own face off with a shotgun?" Hunter asked.

"It's been done," Carl countered.

"I'd suggest it's hard to do the last three... after the first, though," Hunter said.

"Maybe he picked up the wrong boy?" Carl said, grinning.

"Where were you last night?" Caslin asked, cutting in and breaking the hostile exchange between the two. Carl glanced in his direction.

"I was at home, watching the telly."

"And you?" Caslin asked, looking to his brother. Ashton smiled, his eyes revealing what Caslin took as a glimmer of amusement.

"Watching telly," he said, flicking his eyes towards his brother. "With him."

"Anything good?" Hunter asked.

"Don't remember," Ashton replied. "Do you, Carl?"

"No, I think I fell asleep."

Caslin expected nothing more imaginative from the pair of them. They conveyed a level of confidence in their position which he found unnerving. Neither were strangers to police procedure and despite being mildly irritated by their presence, they weren't thrown by the search. That was a bad sign.

"Sir," a voice came from behind. Caslin turned to see a constable standing at the entrance trying to get his attention. He glanced back at Ashton, the smile faded but the air of confidence remained. Crossing the office, he acknowledged the officer.

"What do you have?"

"There's something you need to see," he replied, gesturing for him to step outside. Caslin beckoned Hunter over and she made to follow but Carl was in her way. She locked eyes with him, her expression one of stern authority. He didn't move.

"Carl," Ashton said from behind Hunter. The corners of Carl's mouth turned up in a slight smile and he rotated his body sideways, granting her just enough space to slip by. She did so, never removing her eyes from his. She reached Caslin as he was leaving the portacabin. Together they went outside, Hunter noting Ashton standing up and falling into step alongside his brother as both of them followed.

The constable led them down the side of the portacabin and across the building site towards the rear. In this corner of the compound they found the daily site materials were stored, ranging from concrete blocks to shrink-wrapped pallets of unopened cement sacks. Piled against the outer perimeter fence were bulk bags of sand, each easily approaching a tonne in weight, awaiting the bricklaying crew. A uniformed constable stood to the left of one of the bags, holding a rod that reached from the ground to just above his waist. He had been using it to probe the contents of the bags.

"We found something," he said in response, pointing to the first bag. Caslin looked down and saw a package jutting out from the top of the sand. Whatever was buried it was wrapped in heavy-gauge polythene and well taped up, presumably to avoid the ingress of sand to the contents. Donning a pair of latex gloves, Caslin uncovered more of the sand from around the object, sweeping it away from the edges with his hands. The package was still wedged and, in the end, he used brute strength to draw it clear from the bag.

"Well, well, well," he said, holding it before him in both hands. He turned and angled it so that Hunter could see. She smiled. The package was a little under two foot long and despite the multiple layers of the polythene encompassing it, the opacity was such that the shape of a sawn-off shotgun was clearly visible.

"That's a fit up!" Carl barked from behind Hunter. "You've stashed that there!"

Two officers moved to stand behind him just in case he made a break for it.

"We've got better things to be doing with our time," Caslin countered, handing the gun to the constable alongside him who had made the discovery.

"You bastard," Carl said, almost spitting the words at him. Caslin looked at Ashton, who in stark contrast to his brother, remained calm and emotionless.

"Anything from you?" Caslin asked. Ashton bit his lower lip and sucked air through his teeth. His nose twitched involuntarily but he held his anger or frustration, Caslin couldn't tell which, in check.

"You'll never make this stick," he said quietly, tilting his head to one side and narrowing his eyes.

"Oh, I don't know, perhaps not," Caslin countered. "But it's going to be a lot of fun trying. DS Hunter, if you please," he said, turning to her.

"With pleasure, sir," she replied, beckoning the nearest officers forward. They took out their handcuffs as she began to read the Fuller brothers their rights.

"This is *such* bullshit," Carl stated, shaking his head and resisting the attentions of the officers who were trying to draw his arms behind his back. A brief glance in his direction from Ashton saw those efforts cease and both were taken into custody without incident.

"We'll be out before sundown," Ashton said to Caslin.

"We'll see. Separate cars for transit, please," Caslin said as they were led away. The last thing he wanted was for the two of them to concoct a story en route to the station. Turning to the officer holding the gun, Caslin eyed it. "Have that documented, photographed and then send it over to ballistics. I want to get it confirmed as the murder weapon as soon as possible."

"Will do, sir," the constable said.

Caslin turned away and headed back towards the office. Despite the find, the remaining members of the search team were still diligently going through the contents of the office. With a bit of luck, Caslin hoped they might find other incriminating evidence. He wanted to make the best use of this search as he could for if Ashton was right and they couldn't build a case that would hold up, the chances of being granted further warrants would be less likely. Magistrates didn't like to look foolish any more than anyone else did. Hunter met him halfway.

"That's a stroke of luck," she said. Caslin knew her well enough to read past the obvious.

"Meaning?"

"That the Fullers would be stupid enough to leave the murder weapon where we could find it," she said.

"Bollocks," Caslin replied with a grin. "You know as well as I do, they aren't that daft."

"Agreed."

"Someone's playing us," Caslin stated, staring into the distance and watching as Ashton and Carl were placed into the rear seats of waiting cars.

"If you think so, why did we arrest them?"

"The streets will be a little safer with them out of the way for a day or two," Caslin said. "For them as well as us."

"Someone has an interesting strategy," Hunter said, thinking aloud.

"Aye," Caslin agreed. "I'd put money on it they don't think we'll be able to pin this on the Fullers. I expect that gun is wiped clean of fingerprints and missing its serial number."

"So, what's the point?"

"At the very least it will piss them off... the Fullers, I mean," Caslin explained, "and will certainly disrupt their operations for a bit."

"There has to be more to it than that," Hunter countered.

"Without a doubt," Caslin said. "The thing is we're always one step behind. We need to get ahead of them somehow."

"If we knew who *they* were, it would help."

"We're coming at this all wrong," Caslin said. He didn't necessarily disagree with her but they had to change their approach. He was tired of another orchestrating their actions.

"I'm open to suggestions," Hunter said.

"We've been going through the old case histories and trying to link everyone together and there's only one candidate for that."

"The raid on the clearing house, back in 86."

"Exactly," Caslin agreed. "But we're no closer to knowing how this is related to the present and I don't think we're going to find the answer in the archives."

"Okay," Hunter said, following his thread. "So, what do we do?"

"Start with today and work backwards, rather than carry on with what we have been doing," Caslin explained. "There's too much information to go through from thirty years ago and Holt hasn't even been able to get hold of all the files yet. Out of the current names in the picture who do we have tying them together?"

Hunter thought on it before answering, "You've got me. Who?"

"Answer that... and I reckon we'll be getting somewhere," Caslin said, watching Hunter's irritation with him manifest itself. "I want to put some pressure on our sources and see what comes out. Rumours will be flying around and maybe one of them will be close to what's actually going on here."

"Shall we head back to Fulford Road?"

"You go," Caslin said. "I need to run an errand first. I'll see you back at the station later."

CHAPTER TWENTY

ARRIVING at the house around midday, Caslin pulled the car to the side of the road. Switching off the engine, he looked towards his father's property. Lights were visible inside and the curtains weren't drawn. Glancing at his watch, he thought that was a good sign. His father was up and about before lunchtime. No matter how often he visited, his relationship with his father in his mind, he still struggled with their dynamic. Somehow, they just couldn't seem to get along for more than an hour... on a good day.

Taking a deep breath, he picked up his keys and cracked open the door. A gust of cold air hit him and he fastened his coat as soon as he was able. After constant badgering, his father now agreed to lock the rear gate and force people to the front of the house. Too often, Caslin had been able to just walk in unannounced – a situation that left his father vulnerable as he'd found out to his cost a couple of years ago, ending up with the old man fighting for his life in hospital. Although Selby was a town of some size and population, where his father lived was in the established part and some way from the urban sprawl of modern development. His house was one built for the agricultural workers in the middle of the last century, one of several set apart from most of the neighbouring properties.

Approaching the door, Caslin pressed the buzzer, hearing it ring inside. There was a flicker of movement inside, a shadow passing in the hall beyond the door and Caslin waited. The noise of an engine carried to him and Caslin looked to his left, back down the road and saw an unmarked transit van pull up to the kerb on the opposite side of the street. The driver got out and walked out of sight, behind the vehicle. Caslin silently lamented the number of independent couriers he saw knocking around these days. The gig economy was roaring in Yorkshire. The sound of a chain being released from the other side of the door snapped his attention back to his father and the door opened. Caslin was surprised to find his son, Sean, standing before him in the entrance hall.

"Hey, Dad," he said with a smile.

"Sean…" Caslin replied, unable to mask the surprise. "What are you…?"

"Daddy!" his question remained unfinished as another voice came from within the house. His daughter, Lizzie, came running from the living room to greet him. He knelt as she threw herself into his arms knocking him off balance. He managed not to topple over and hugged her fiercely.

"What are you two doing…"

"Karen asked if I could babysit—"

"Have us visit!" Sean said, casting a frown over his shoulder at his grandfather who held his hands up in supplication.

"Sorry, sorry," he said. "Their mother asked if they could visit for the weekend."

"Did she now?" Caslin said, exhaling through his nose.

"Apparently, her other arrangements fell through," his father said, inclining his head forward and fixing a stern gaze on his son.

"Hmm…" Caslin replied, releasing Lizzie who took off back into the living room.

"Daddy, come and see what we're watching," she said excitedly.

"Okay," he called after her, standing and stepping inside. Sean backed away to make room and Caslin went to close the door behind him. The van was still outside and Caslin thought the driver was taking his time with the delivery. "It had better not be something made on *Elm Street*," he said pointedly to his father as he walked past him placing an affectionate hand on his shoulder as he did so. The older man chuckled.

"I've never been in to anything like that," his father said, following on. "Real life is horrific enough."

"True," Caslin agreed. "You were married to mum."

"Cheeky sod," his father countered, giving him a gentle tap to the back of the head as they entered the living room. Caslin was drawn to the television, pleased to see it was an animated film of some description but not one he recognised.

"There's a singing shark," Lizzie said excitedly, glancing in his direction briefly before focussing on the screen once again.

"It's awful," Sean chipped in without looking up from his position draped across an armchair and staring at his tablet. He looked like he'd been slumped there for hours but, in reality, it was probably only a couple of minutes. Caslin wondered if whatever held his attention was as equally stimulating as a musical shark or possibly more disturbing.

"Coffee?" his father asked.

"Please," Caslin replied. The characters on the television screen burst into song and he hurried after the departing form of his father and joined him in the kitchen. "They seem settled."

"Yes, they are good kids," his father said, taking two cups down from a shelf above the coffee machine and setting them on the work surface. "It's great to have them here, I have to say," he added, taking on a far-away look and suddenly appearing lost in thought.

"What is it, Dad?" Caslin asked.

His father glanced over to him shaking his head. "No, no, it's nothing," he stuttered as he spoke. Caslin didn't believe him but he let it go. "So, why wouldn't you have them this weekend?"

Caslin frowned, "Karen told you about that?"

"Yes, she did," his father replied, placing the filter head into the coffee grinder and running it for ten seconds, filling it and returning to the coffee machine. "She's not best pleased with you, your ex, I must say."

"Must you?" Caslin said playfully. His father smiled.

"Of all the times to drop your responsibilities this probably wasn't the best."

"*Drop?*" Caslin said. "I'm hardly dropping them."

"Work?" his father asked with an enquiring look. Caslin nodded. "I think she's past accepting that excuse."

"It was barely acceptable when we were married."

"Is it true?"

"What do you mean by that?" Caslin said, offended.

"Is it work or are you trying to mess things up between Karen and her new man?"

"Do you think I'm that petty?" Caslin asked. His father turned away from him. "And he's hardly new, is he?"

"Black?"

"What?" Caslin asked.

"Your coffee. Do you want it black?"

"Yes, thank you," Caslin replied. His father turned and passed him a cup. Caslin accepted it noting his father's stern gaze. "I really am very busy."

"What are you working on in this task force of yours?"

"It's not a task force as such," Caslin explained, not wishing to go into too much detail.

"It's Major Crimes, though, isn't it?"

"It should be," Caslin said, "but I've stripped Fulford Road of some of the best resources in CID and so we're still helping them out until they can re-balance the team."

"So, what is it that's keeping you away from your kids?"

"Nothing much," Caslin said. He hated discussing his work

with his father. There was always a better method that things used to be done by, often now illegal, that his father would feel needed to be explained to him in great detail.

"*Nothing much* is keeping you from spending time with your kids? Karen was right then?"

Caslin sighed before sipping at his coffee, "It's complicated."

"Try me," his father said. "I like complicated."

"To start with, I've got someone fermenting a turf war between rival gangs that may or may not be instigating tit-for-tat murders," Caslin said, frowning. "Right now, we have a group of names who are all quite capable of bringing this on but nothing to explain why they would choose to do so."

"You're right. That does sound complicated," his father replied, smiling.

"Add to that a decorated policeman consorting with known criminals from beyond the grave and I have a pretty big headache right now," Caslin said. "Any ideas?" His father turned back to the machine and went to set the filter head in place to make his own cup but struggled to do so, leading to him cursing under his breath. "Having trouble?" Caslin asked.

"Bloody machine," his father said as he finally drove the head into place. He silently went about making his drink. Caslin was happy the third degree appeared to be over without him receiving the customary lecture that usually accompanied such a conversation. His father crossed to the fridge and returned with the milk, not bothering to heat it first, he added some to his freshly made coffee. "From beyond the grave, you say?"

Caslin had gotten ahead of himself, "Yeah. We all thought he was dead. Turns out we were wrong."

"I see," his father said, staring into his coffee cup and stirring a spoon in a very deliberate way. "What's that all about then?"

"If I knew, I'd be spending the weekend with my children," Caslin said.

"What's he got to say for himself?"

"Who?"

"This policeman you're talking about. What did you say his name was?"

"I didn't say," Caslin said, drinking his coffee. "Bradley. A former DCI in Greater Manchester."

"Right," his father said, putting his cup down and crossing is arms. "And what's he got to say?"

"Not a lot... certainly without a Ouija board, anyway," Caslin said, shaking his head. "He's dead."

"Dead?" his father said, watching him intently. Caslin was slightly unnerved.

"Yeah, he died in a car crash the other day."

"I see," his father said, expressionless. Caslin was surprised at how serious the tone of the conversation was becoming.

"Relax, Dad," he said with a smile. "It's nothing for you to get into. I'll sort it out. Like I said, it's complicated."

"Of course, you will," his father said, breaking into a smile. "You always do. It's just a pity it comes at the cost of seeing your kids."

"That's a bit harsh."

"Is it?" his father countered. "You always manage to find something..."

"I don't *manage* to find anything."

"Come off it, Nathaniel. You've always been willing to pass your parental responsibilities off onto someone else. Usually it was your wife but now it's coming my way."

"You're a little out of order," Caslin said, feeling a flash of anger at the personal attack.

"*I'm out of order?* Take a look at those kids in there. How long has it been since they spent more than a couple of hours with you?"

"You, of all people, should know what this job's like!"

"I knew when to call time and come home. Maybe you should take a look at yourself."

"I can't believe I'm hearing this."

"That's just it, Nathaniel. No one tells you like it is anymore. You just listen to yourself and do as you please."

Caslin finished his coffee and put the cup down on the kitchen table shaking his head, "Coming from you, that's a bit rich."

"What do you mean by that?"

"You set the example that I followed—"

"Are you two arguing?" a voice came from behind. Caslin turned to see both Sean and Lizzie standing in the kitchen doorway. Sean stood behind his sister with both hands placed reassuringly on her shoulders. He was biting his lower lip while Lizzie sought an answer to her question.

"No, we're not," Caslin explained. "Just a mild disagreement... which I'm not entirely sure how it came about."

"You and mum used to have those," Lizzie replied, taking the events in her stride as usual.

"And still do..." Sean added.

"Thank you for helping, Sean," Caslin said tilting his head and making no attempt to hide the sarcasm. "Everything's all right, nothing for either of you to worry about. Right, Dad?" he said, looking to his father.

"Of course," he replied under his breath, looking out of the window and into the garden beyond.

"You see," Caslin said, forcing a smile. It fooled no one.

"Oh right," Sean said, nudging his little sister in the back. "It's all good."

"If you say so," Lizzie replied. Stepping forward, she threw her arms around her father's legs and hugged him momentarily. He looked down and tussled her hair. Then she was gone skipping back into the living room and bumping her brother, who rolled his eyes, as she passed by him. He turned and followed. Caslin chuckled.

"Sometimes I think they're more grown up than I give them credit for," he said.

"They certainly are. More than their father, at least."

Caslin faked a smile, "And on that note I think I'll head off."

"If you like," his father grumbled, turning his back on him.

"I'll give you a call over the weekend, see how you're getting on?" Caslin said, lightening his tone and trying to appease whatever anger his father was currently fostering towards him. The only response was an almost inaudible grunt.

Caslin chose not to pursue it further and left the kitchen. He went into the living room and scooped Lizzie up in his arms. Turning her upside down, he tickled her stomach. The action was accompanied by shrieks of delight as her long blonde curls dangled down across her face. Dumping her carefully onto the sofa, he leant down and kissed her forehead. She gave him another fierce hug.

"You two have fun this weekend," he said, "and try not to give your granddad too hard a time."

"We won't," Lizzie said with a devious smile that indicated quite the opposite. Caslin crossed to Sean and was begrudgingly given a farewell hug. Soon, Caslin felt he'd be lucky to be offered a handshake as his eldest was reaching an age where any physical contact with his father would be deemed suicidal for his social credibility. Glancing over his shoulder there was no apparent movement from within the kitchen. His father was clattering around out of sight taking out his frustrations on his utensils. Somehow, they were butting heads again and not for the first time, Caslin was at a loss to explain why.

Closing the front door behind him, he stepped onto the path and headed for his car. His phone rang and he took it out noting it was Hunter as he answered the call. Continuing on down the path, he glanced back over his shoulder at his father's house feeling disheartened at how the visit turned out but pleased to have seen his children.

"Sarah, what do you have?" he asked.

"Hang on, sir. I'll put you on speaker. Terry's here as well," she said. Caslin waited patiently. The sound of her slightly disembodied voice came to him indicating she had opened the call to the room. "Can you hear us?" she asked.

"I can. Go ahead," Caslin replied, reaching his car. Opening the door, he saw the delivery van was still parked across the street but he gave it no more attention as he clambered into his seat. Placing the phone on the dash, he hit the engine start button and dabbed the accelerator. The car fired into life and his call was transferred to the internal speakers via the car's bluetooth connection.

"We've been digging around in Pete Fuller's background, sir," Hunter said. "It's more than interesting."

"Go on," Caslin replied.

"Apparently, Fuller and Neville Bridger go back a long way," Hunter said.

"How so?"

"They were as thick as thieves growing up well before they came onto our radar," Holt continued, reading through his notes. "They came through the system together growing up in the same care home. They were both considered problem children and, unlike Fuller's sister, neither lasted very long at foster homes. Once kids hit a certain age the odds of getting a permanent place drop rapidly. They must have been the only constant in each other's lives."

"What's the significance of the sister?" Caslin asked. Holt wouldn't have mentioned her without reason.

"Their parents were estranged with no father listed on file. The mother was an alcoholic, suffered from schizophrenia and was prone to violent outbursts hence why social services were involved. Bridger's background was pretty similar. Pete Fuller's sister, Emilia, was rehoused with a foster family and stayed with them until adulthood but their relationship remained strong despite growing up apart."

"Still waiting on the significance," Caslin said.

Hunter picked up the story. "Well, this is where it gets

intriguing. Neville Bridger was married to Emilia Fuller. Which makes Ollie and Mark..."

"Pete Fuller's nephews," Caslin finished for her.

"Strange bedfellows for the two of them to be keeping under the circumstances," Holt said. "Particularly as we have Ollie still linked to the Fullers' organisation recently."

"Isn't it just," Caslin said under his breath. "If we know this, I reckon it's fair to say Dade and MacEwan know who they are as well."

"I'd be surprised if they didn't," Hunter said.

"I'd like to explore Fuller's family angle a little more," Caslin said, thinking aloud. "If Fuller and Neville Bridger were so tight, how come Bridger's children are working for the opposition. Which one was it?"

"Mark is a part of Dade's crew," Hunter confirmed.

"And Ollie is alongside MacEwan?" Caslin asked rhetorically. "For Mark to be welcomed into Clinton Dade's inner circle something must have gone on. Find out what it is."

"There's always another possibility," Holt added.

"What's that?" Caslin asked.

"Mark got as close as he could to enable him to make the hit," Holt suggested, "on Fuller's behalf. He's been inside a long time and I checked on the dates, he's due out in what... eighteen months to two years? Maybe he's been planning it for ages and wanted it done before his release knowing he'd be the prime suspect."

"That's a thought," Caslin said. "But where does the bombing of Fuller's business come in to that theory? Remember, that came first. Keep it in mind, Terry, but find out if something went down between Fuller and Neville Bridger or his sons. Where are we with our own resources?"

"People have gone to ground, sir," Hunter said. "It's almost like everyone is expecting this to get worse and no one wants to get caught in the crossfire."

"Someone has to know something," Caslin stated. "Shake

down every informant we have on the books. Don't worry about being polite. Do whatever you have to. This is too big for this level of silence. We're missing something... and it's really starting to piss me off."

"Will do," they both replied in unison and Caslin ended the call.

CHAPTER TWENTY-ONE

"Ashton and Carl's brief is kicking off downstairs," Hunter said, ducking her head into Caslin's office. "Threatening to sue us for wrongful arrest, harassment and anything else she can come up with." Caslin glanced up from reading the folder before him with an expression that almost indicated he hadn't heard a word she'd said.

"We found the likely murder weapon in a homicide on their property," he countered with a frown which quickly transferred to a smile. "What does she expect?"

"The custody sergeant wants to know what we plan to do with them."

"In what way?"

"Are we going to interview them further?"

Caslin shook his head, "No point. They've not given us anything and I don't see that changing. Usually, I'd look to play one off against the other but that approach won't work with these two."

"They're pretty arrogant too," Hunter said.

"Much as I hate to disagree with you... because they are arrogant... but I'd argue their attitude is more to do with confidence," Caslin said. "They know we won't be able to make a case without a witness, or forensics, to tie them to the weapon. Where are we with that?"

"As you said, the shotgun was wiped clean. No serial number and although we can tie the shotgun cartridges to Dade's hit, there are no ballistics matches with any prior cases," Hunter explained.

"So, there's no previous case that can link them to ownership even circumstantially."

"That's right. All we have is their enmity towards Dade and the fact the gun was found on their building site. It's barely enough to hold them for the initial detention period let alone get an extension."

"You're right," Caslin said, sucking air through his teeth.

"Do we bail them?"

"No. Let's keep them here for the full twenty-four hours," Caslin said. "Let them sweat for a little while."

"Their brief will go mental," Hunter said.

Caslin shrugged, "If she's on an hourly rate it will be a nice earner although she'll give the custody suite a group headache. Who's the sergeant today?"

"Steve Owen."

"Tell him I'll buy him a pint."

Looking beyond his office, Caslin saw Terry Holt enter. He took off his coat and threw it in the general direction of the coat rack but missed by some margin. He failed to notice as he made a beeline for them scooping up a folder from his desk as he passed; determined expression on his face. Appearing alongside Hunter, he was almost breathless as he spoke.

"Sir, I've just met with an informant and I think you'll be interested to hear what he had to say." Caslin beckoned him in and Holt pulled up a chair, sitting down and catching his breath.

"About the Fullers?" Caslin asked. Holt shook his head. Evidently, he'd run through the station to get back and was feeling the effects of the exertion.

"Neville Bridger," Holt said. "The word is that someone

grassed Neville up for his role in the Manchester raid. Did anyone else find it odd that in the months following the raid multiple members of the gang were picked up, often in quick bursts, but then there was nothing until Neville Bridger was collared well over a decade later?"

"Associations come to light and you only need a couple at a time for them to lead to others," Hunter argued. Holt agreed.

"Yes, but the case was cold... not even being investigated at the time of Bridger's arrest," Holt said, opening the folder in his hands and leafing through the contents. He couldn't find what he was looking for and gave up, placing the documents down on Caslin's desk. "Officially, the case was never closed but there were no active officers assigned to the investigation but then, all of a sudden, Neville gets fingered for it and goes down for a stretch soon after."

"I don't remember anything in the file relating to an informant in his arrest," Caslin said, spinning Holt's file one-hundred-and-eighty degrees and scanning the contents himself.

"You won't have, sir," Holt said. "I checked. But that's not the only thing that bothers me. I can't see where they got the information from about his involvement. If you look at the evidence, the Crown Prosecution Service had – locations, dates, times, bank accounts – it was all there."

"I didn't see any of that," Hunter said.

"You wouldn't have," Holt said. "Bridger pleaded guilty at the time so there was no trial. I imagine the evidence was so well stacked against him he realised his best option was to do so and go for the reduced sentence in return."

"So, who gave us Bridger?" Caslin asked.

"The honest answer to that is *we have no idea*," Holt said. "However, my informant reckons it came from Fuller."

"Pete grassed on his brother-in-law?" Hunter said, sounding incredulous.

"And his childhood friend," Caslin added.

"Not buying it." Hunter shook her head.

"My guy says that when Pete was sent down, it was Neville who laid claim to his business interests. Which is logical bearing in mind their history and family ties," Holt said. "However, his wife, Emilia, died in 1991 and then things began to change. Whether Neville liked having the power or his temporary position as head of the organisation didn't garner the respect needed to maintain control, I don't know but he started to make changes. Many of Pete's most trusted allies dropped from view. A couple of them were subject to enquiries by our colleagues but nothing ever came of the investigations."

"Neville was disposing of his competition..." Caslin said aloud.

"That was the talk of the day," Holt confirmed.

"Why wouldn't Fuller just take care of it himself?" Hunter asked. "From what I know of him, he doesn't look the sort to roll over on his associates and let's face it, he's more than capable."

"It might not be true," Caslin said. "But people talk and the rumour mill can get a lie halfway around the world before the truth has got its pants on."

"Bridger was killed inside, wasn't he?" Hunter asked.

Holt nodded. "May have been connected, might not," he said. "It could just as easily be the settling of a score on the inside as much as being a hit orchestrated by Fuller."

"I'm with Sarah on this," Caslin said, indicating Hunter. "I don't think it's Fuller's style but if that became common knowledge, or even the spoken rumour, that might explain why the Bridger boys lined up with the opposition."

"Exactly," Holt said emphatically. "Whether Fuller had Neville killed or not is irrelevant. Both Mark and Ollie held Fuller responsible for their father's death. As a result, there's no love lost between the cousins either. Mark had a major falling out with Carl Fuller a couple of years back. He shows up amongst Dade's business interests shortly after."

"What about the other one...?" Caslin momentarily forgot the name.

"Ollie," Hunter reminded him.

"Yes, Ollie. What about his relationship with the Fullers? What do we know about it?"

Holt shook his head, "There's no intel to suggest he piled in with his brother on the Fullers. As you said, he was arrested recently when apparently still working for them. By all accounts, Ollie is the calmer one of the two and far more calculating."

"Like Ashton Fuller is to his brother, Carl," Hunter said.

"I would say so," Holt confirmed. "Looking at his history, Ollie was still popping up in relation to the Fullers long after Carl and Mark came to blows, which I found interesting. Perhaps, he didn't hear the old rumours or buy into them."

"Or there was something else going on?"

"Such as?" Hunter asked. Caslin's brow furrowed in response but he didn't elaborate further. His mobile phone vibrated on the desk in front of him. Glancing at the screen the call originated from a number he didn't recognise. Picking it up, he answered.

"Caslin," he said flatly.

"I see you've not refrained from only bothering me," the voice said at the other end of the line. Caslin was thrown for a brief moment. He recognised the controlled aggression of the bearer and shouldn't have been surprised. The fortified walls and strict regime meant nothing if you were the right person with the requisite resources. Caslin glanced to both Hunter and Terry Holt, indicating for them to make themselves scarce. Neither of them questioned the request although both noted the change in his demeanour. Hunter closed the door behind them, glancing back in his direction through the glass. Caslin looked away and sank back in his chair.

"Well, this is unexpected," he said, flashes of what might be motivating the caller passing through his mind.

"You appear to be taking a great deal of interest in my affairs as well as those of my family," Pete Fuller said, keeping his voice low and commanding.

"There is much to see," Caslin said.

"Why are you holding my boys?" Caslin thought about his response for a few seconds catching Hunter's eye as she looked on from a distance.

"They are suspects in a murder inquiry."

"That's bullshit..." Fuller replied, "and you know it."

"What I do know," Caslin said, drawing a deep breath, "is that a lot of people in and around your circle are very active all of a sudden. Some of whom haven't been seen in years and as soon as they surfaced, people started dying."

"Very tragic," Fuller replied.

"And somehow it all seems to be revolving around you."

"Is that a fact?"

"Now, why might that be, Pete?" Caslin asked. He then fell silent allowing a pause in the conversation and waited patiently. The sound of Fuller's breathing carried down the line. There was more to be said. Caslin knew it. "This situation is escalating rapidly, Pete. If we don't get a handle on it more people are going to be killed. You know this."

"You sound sure of yourself," Fuller said, after a few moments.

"I can't help but think Neville Bridger has something to do with it."

"You've been doing your homework, Mr Caslin."

"Staying up late, that's true."

"Neville's been a long time dead."

"And yet, his shadow casts itself some way into the future, does it not?"

"Neville Bridger didn't bomb my business," Fuller said.

"Nor did he shoot Clinton Dade in the face," Caslin added. "But someone did both."

"And someone is trying to put my boys in the frame."

"So, it would appear."

"You know this and you're still keeping them in a cell?"

"Where they belong," Caslin said. "Either for this or for everything else they have done."

"Now, you listen to me, Inspector," Fuller said, his voice lowering and taking on a new level of malevolence, Caslin hadn't heard previously. "If you pin this on my two, you'll be fitting them up for something they haven't done. You mark my words if you take down my family for this then the gloves are off."

"That sounds like a threat."

"It is," Fuller stated. "You've come after my family and that brings yours into play."

Caslin heard the words and didn't need time for them to sink in. The intent was obvious. "Be careful with your threats, Pete. You're in the home stretch now. Six months from now you'll be moved to a D-Cat," Caslin said, referring to when a prisoner is approaching parole and not considered a flight risk, they are often moved to an open prison ahead of release. "Are you willing to jeopardise that and risk seeing out the rest of your sentence inside?"

"I'd take it twice over for the sake of my children," Fuller said. Caslin assessed his tone and didn't doubt his commitment. "You're standing in a glass house, Caslin. *Let he who is without sin cast the first stone.*"

Caslin knew Fuller hadn't found God from within the prison walls and felt somewhat baffled by the reference. "Now what are you talking about?"

"Instead of wasting time trying to hang my boys out to dry maybe you should be focussing on the real players in this game."

"And they are?" Caslin asked, noting Terry Holt attempting to catch his eye from his seat. The DC had a phone pressed to his ear and an open-mouthed expression on his face. He waved in Caslin's direction drawing Hunter to him in doing so. He said something to her and she immediately looked to Caslin. Something was wrong.

"You seem distracted, Inspector Caslin," Fuller said.

"I'm still here," he replied. "Waiting for you to give me a steer... like you did my colleagues a few years ago regarding Neville."

Fuller chuckled. "I've heard that one too. I didn't give him up no matter what you've heard to the contrary."

"Then tell me who's throwing Ashton and Carl to the wolves?"

"You're asking the wrong man the wrong questions," Fuller said. Caslin watched as Terry Holt slowly replaced the receiver of his phone down on the desk. He glanced again at Hunter who stepped aside giving him enough room to stand. Holt looked to Caslin with an expression that could only be described as one of nervous apprehension. Both of them came towards his office. Hunter cracked open the door and Holt shifted his weight nervously between his feet alongside her. Caslin frowned. "Soon enough, you'll find the right man," Fuller continued, "and only then will you get the answers you're after."

The phone line went silent and Caslin glanced at the screen to see if the call had disconnected. It hadn't. He was more than a little perplexed at the cryptic direction the call was taking. He turned his attention to the two officers before him putting his hand across the microphone. "What's up?" he mouthed, flicking his eyes between them. "One of you?" he whispered.

Holt cast a fleeting glance sideways to Hunter who bit her lower lip and looked away. It was Holt who spoke, "Uniform responded to what they thought was a domestic a little over half an hour ago. They arrived at the property to find an elderly male unconscious and blue-lighted him to hospital."

"And?"

"They also found two children at the scene." Caslin's blood ran cold. "They're okay," Holt stressed. "Your kids were unharmed but the male is in a bad way. We think... we think it's your father, sir. They've really done a job on him."

Caslin felt his body go light. A strange sensation coursed through him and he could feel his heartbeat increasing as it thudded inside his chest. Lowering the mobile, he looked at the screen whilst attempting to process the information. It was a few moments before he realised, he was holding his breath and almost had to tell himself to stop. Returning the handset to his ear, once again, he focussed on Fuller and him alone disregarding the presence of his team.

"If you've hurt my family..." he said in a menacing tone borne out of the white-hot anger building inside him, "I will *dedicate my life* to destroying everything... and everyone you hold dear."

"You should be careful with *your threats*, Mr Caslin," Fuller said, not missing a beat. "Sometimes the answers you seek are far closer to home than you can ever imagine."

"My family are innocent in all of this."

"Innocence was lost long ago, Inspector Caslin. Everyone must pay for their sins and sometimes it is our children who bear the brunt."

"I will come for you," Caslin said in a whisper.

"I don't doubt it," Fuller replied, and the phone line went dead.

CHAPTER TWENTY-TWO

THE THIRTEEN-MILE JOURNEY from Fulford Road to Caslin's father's house in Selby usually took half an hour but in a liveried police car, with the lights and sirens in action, they shaved a third off of that. The car screeched to a halt at the kerb side and Caslin was out of the passenger seat before it stopped moving. A handful of neighbours were huddled on the footpath offering a mixture of concern and ghoulish voyeurism. Caslin ignored them and was directed towards an ambulance parked a short distance away by a uniformed constable standing at the entrance to the house. The rear doors were open and rounding the corner of the vehicle to the back, he found both his children being attended to by a paramedic.

Lizzie stood up and launched herself into his arms. His daughter clung to him as if to let go would risk falling to her death such was the tightness of her grip.

"I've got you," he said. Looking through the tangled curls of her hair, Caslin saw his son, Sean, sitting on a gurney with a red blanket around his shoulders. He was huddled beneath it, his face pale even in the darkened rear of the ambulance. He smiled in response to Caslin's unasked question to his well being. It was weak and Caslin could see signs of bruising to the side of his cheek. Anger flared but he suppressed it. "Are you okay?" he asked.

"I'm all right, Dad," Sean replied.

"Your son's taken a blow to the side of the face," the paramedic said, glancing at Caslin but maintaining his focus on Sean. "I'm sure it's nothing serious but we want to take him in just as a precaution."

"I understand," Caslin replied, nodding appreciatively. Footsteps behind him marked the arrival of DS Hunter. She had followed on in her car. Coming alongside, she placed an affectionate hand on Lizzie's arm to show her support and smiled at Sean.

"Have you been inside?" she asked. Caslin shook his head gently.

"You have a few minutes, if you like?" the paramedic said. "We're not ready to leave yet."

Caslin used his free hand to push the bundle of blonde curls away from Lizzie's face, she leaned back and he made eye contact.

"Stay here with your brother. You're quite safe now. I'll be back in a minute and we'll go to the hospital together. Okay?"

"Okay," Lizzie replied. "How is Granddad?"

Caslin looked to the paramedic who flicked his eyebrows up and returned his gaze to Sean. "I'm sure he'll be fine," he replied, smiling. "He's tough like your old dad." Placing her carefully back down, she resumed her place alongside her brother who extended his blanket and put an arm around her. "I'll be back," Caslin said to his son who nodded.

The two of them made their way up the path to the front door where they were greeted by the constable who stepped aside to allow them to pass. Caslin entered first. The usual anticipation that he experienced when entering a crime scene was tinged by anxiety on this occasion. Seldom did work crossover into his personal life but when it did, the gut-wrenching feeling and the associated guilt hit Caslin hard.

"Three men," the voice of the constable on the door came from behind them as they entered the living room. The scene was chaotic. The coffee table, with its glass top, was smashed and whatever once rested upon it lay in pieces across the floor. His father's sideboard and drinks cabinet had suffered a similar fate and the room stank of alcohol from all the broken bottles of wine and spirits. "They forced entry at the front door," the officer continued as Caslin surveyed the room, "pushing back here where… I'm sorry, sir… where they attacked your father."

"Did they say anything?" Caslin asked, ignoring the sentiment not because he was unfeeling or didn't care but because he needed to keep his emotions in check.

"No, sir. They didn't speak," the officer explained. "Your children were incredibly brave, sir."

"Thank you."

"Your eldest tried to intervene which is when he was struck, over there," the constable said, pointing to the entrance to the kitchen.

"Did they go for my kids?" Caslin asked, his voice cracking and briefly betraying his emotional state. If the officer noticed, he didn't show it.

"No, sir. It would appear they were targeting your father alone. You'll probably know better than us but it doesn't appear as if anything was taken."

Caslin scanned the room afresh passing over the bloodstains on the carpet and walls, looking for a sign of anything missing. Of course, there were none. Caslin knew why they were there and it wasn't with robbery in mind. "No. Looks clean," he said, eyeing Hunter. "Any descriptions to go on?"

"Three men. Probably white," the constable said, "but they wore ski-masks and overalls."

"Overalls?" Caslin asked.

"Yeah, like uniforms. I spoke with a couple of neighbours, the ones who called in the report of a domestic, and they said they saw the men leaving in a transit van."

Caslin cursed himself under his breath. "A delivery van?"

"Yes, that's right. It was dark brown or black. They weren't sure which."

"I saw it," he explained to Hunter. "They were outside when I bloody left earlier."

"There's no way you could have known. You can't blame yourself."

"That's funny because I'm doing exactly that," he said, running a hand through his hair pain evident in his expression. "Get onto Broadfoot, would you? I want an armed presence at the hospital just in case they want to try and finish the job."

"I will. How is your father?" Hunter asked.

"I don't know," Caslin said, feeling the guilt magnify for not having already asked that very question.

"He was unconscious when we arrived," the constable said. "The paramedics were on scene within five minutes. They took great care with him."

"Thank you," Caslin said, turning to Hunter. "I'm going to the hospital with the kids. I'll find out and let you know. Can you stay here, canvas the neighbours and find out as much as you can about what anyone saw?"

"What do you want to do about Fuller? He orchestrated this."

Caslin was silent for a moment, his anger worn visibly on his sleeve. "Nothing, yet."

"But, sir. With the phone call and all..."

"Nothing," Caslin snapped. "He's not going anywhere and we all know he's crossed a line. I'll make sure he gets what's due to him."

"Yes, but why did he do it? He has so much to lose."

"He also knows we'll struggle to link this to him directly, it's all circumstantial. We'll take him... but when I choose to and not before."

"Okay, sir. Your call," Hunter said.

Whether she agreed was irrelevant to him. Fuller was

sending him a direct message and there had to be more to it than merely protecting the interests of his children. Their telephone conversation played over and over in his mind. It seemed far more significant now than he had given it credit at the time. Fuller's words were out of character somehow, his choice of phrase, his tone... something, but Caslin couldn't quite comprehend the inference. Not yet, at least. Perhaps once his anger subsided. *If* his anger subsided.

"WE WILL TAKE your brother through and once we have him settled, we'll come back for you," the nurse said to Lizzie, smiling affectionately and instantly placing the little girl in a comfortable state of mind. Caslin squeezed her shoulder gently, his arm already around her as Sean was led out of the cubicle for a precautionary examination. The initial assessment in Accident and Emergency from both the triage nurse and the doctor indicated he'd probably suffered a small concussion but they were being thorough and following up with a scan. Caslin appreciated it. For her part, Lizzie had stumbled and fallen in the melee at his father's house and was complaining of her arm being painful. She would be taken for an x-ray as soon as the department could make room to fit her in.

"Thank you," Caslin said to the departing nurse.

"No problem," she replied, offering both of them another wide smile, friendly and reassuring.

Caslin turned to his daughter. "It's nothing to worry about, I promise."

"When will Mummy be here?"

"I called her before I got to Granddad's house, so any—"

"I'm here," Karen said, appearing through the closed curtain to the cubicle. Lizzie leapt up from her seat and her mother dropped to her haunches and embraced her tightly. Too tightly as it turned out with Lizzie wincing as her bruised arm was pressed. "I'm so sorry, darling," Karen said, releasing her grip and pulling back so she could look into the little girl's face. "Mummy's here now," she said, drawing the girl close to her chest again.

Karen was out of breath and sweating, clearly having rushed to get there as quickly as she could. Now her daughter couldn't see, the compassion exhibited in her expression was abandoned as she turned her gaze towards Caslin.

"Sean's been taken for a scan," he said. The visible anger subsided and was replaced by concern. "It's purely precautionary."

"And Lizzie?" she asked, stroking her daughter's head which appeared fixed to her mother's chest.

"She'll be going for an x-ray soon. Again, just as a precaution."

"What about… your father?" Karen said, hesitating and fearful of the answer. Caslin pursed his lips and stood up.

"I have to go and see. By the time we got here, he'd already passed through A and E. He needed surgery," Caslin said. Looking to Lizzie, he indicated he didn't want to say further at the risk of scaring the child. The truth was his father was admitted unconscious and rushed to theatre for emergency surgery. The extent of the injury was unknown to him and he was agitated at the thought of the severity of his condition. "I'll let you know as soon as I do."

Karen nodded, "Please do."

Caslin knelt down and Lizzie turned her head to the side so she could see him. "Mummy's going to stay with you while I go and see your granddad, okay?" She nodded and he reached across cupping her cheek with the palm of his hand. He smiled and she returned it. Standing up, he pulled the curtain aside and stepped out looking around for a sign to get his bearings. For the life of him, he couldn't remember which direction he'd entered from. Thinking he'd approached from his left, he set off in that direction. Within a few steps he heard the sound of the curtain being drawn behind him and footfalls.

"Nate," Karen called after him. Caslin stopped and turned as she trotted towards him. Looking past her, he could see the curtain was closed. There was no sign of Lizzie. "Just one thing," she said catching up to him.

"Yes?" he asked as Karen slapped him across the face. The blow stung his cheek. It was the last thing he'd expected.

"You promised me you'd keep your job away from this family." She waved an extended finger in front of his face.

"You're blaming me for this?"

"After what happened to Sean… *you promised me!*" she hissed. A sudden, fresh pang of guilt stabbed at his chest upon hearing those words. They tore through him. After nearly losing Sean when he was caught up in a case along with the subsequent years of trying to repair the mental damage, Caslin swore he would never let his children come to harm again as a result of his job. Karen was right. He hadn't seen this coming. The rational response would be to deny his culpability but the emotional one was damning.

"I… I'm…" he stammered as she turned her back on him and stalked back towards the cubicle. "Sorry," he said to himself, watching as she disappeared from view and back to comfort their daughter. Taking a deep breath, he resumed his course. A handful of people were present either waiting to be seen or relocated to their respective wards. They saw the exchange and he read their shocked expressions as a further indictment of his failure.

Ten minutes later, Caslin had given up on wandering aimlessly and sought help from a passing member of the medical staff. An internal phone call followed and he was directed to a specialist diagnostic ward, a temporary placing where his father could be assessed as to his medical needs before being found a permanent place on the respective ward. Confident of his route through the maze that was York Hospital, he finally arrived.

The entrance was secured with access only granted via use of a programmed key card or by a member of staff unlocking it from within. The days of wandering onto any ward without permission were rapidly becoming a distant memory. He pressed the intercom set alongside the entrance door and glanced up at the security camera overhead. The speaker crackled and he leaned in as the voice greeted him.

"Detective Inspector Caslin," he said into the microphone. "I believe you have my father on the ward."

There was an audible click as the lock was released and Caslin entered. There were doors off the corridor to either side giving access to storage, offices and what he guessed were treatment rooms of some sort but the main hive of activity was further along. Here, he came across the nurse's station where he identified himself once again. Looking along the corridor to his right, he saw the unmistakable figure of an armed policeman standing outside a room. He realised then that his father was inside and he could have saved himself a bit of time by contacting Fulford Road and seeing where the protection had been placed rather than wandering the corridors aimlessly.

"The doctors are with your father now," the nurse said, pointing to the room.

"How is he?" Caslin asked, apprehension edging into his tone.

"I believe the surgery went well," she told him, "but the doctors will be able to tell you more."

He thanked her and headed for the room. Not recognising the protection officer, he took out his warrant card and brandished it as he approached. The officer nodded approval and Caslin rapped his knuckles lightly on the door and entered. His father was in a private room. There were two windows off it facing the outside and a third internal one with a view to what appeared to be a staff room. Two doctors were standing at the foot of his father's bed, deep in discussion. Both acknowledged his arrival and he identified himself. Taking in his father's appearance, he was struck by how pale and gaunt he was, far more so than normal. A clear indication of the trauma he'd been through. His left arm was connected to a drip and the right-hand side of his face was red and swollen, the skin already darkening as the bruising developed. His head was heavily bandaged, wrapped around his crown and down across his left eyebrow. The eye itself was covered with a large gauze pad and taped in place. Oxygen was being fed to him via a tube to his nostrils.

"Your father has taken quite some damage, I am afraid to say," the consultant explained. "The emergency surgery was to repair tissue damage around the eye."

"Is he… will he be all right?"

"It will take some time but we are very confident about his prognosis," the doctor stated with a smile. "Mainly, he has sustained bruising and trauma that is largely superficial. It will take time to heal but it looks far worse than it is. Obviously, your father's age will determine how long it takes regarding recovery time but he is in no immediate danger. When he wakes up, we will know more about how the trauma has affected him."

"And the eye?" Caslin asked.

"We will have to wait and see," he replied, tilting his head slightly. "Once the swelling goes down, we will be able to run some tests. In the meantime, please be positive."

Caslin looked at his father. Without the medical paraphernalia and the obvious wounds, he could be forgiven for thinking he was at peace, asleep and resting comfortably. "Has he woken?"

"He came around in the ambulance on his way to the hospital and remained so until we took him into theatre. Usually, with the possibility of a concussion we don't do so, but in this case, he was given a general anaesthetic to allow for the procedure. His CAT scan didn't give us any concerns around his head injury so we pressed ahead. I should imagine he will be asleep for the next hour or so. When he comes around, he will most likely be groggy and a little disorientated."

"That sounds like good news, Doctor," Caslin said, feeling the anxiety dissipate slightly.

"It is good news, Mr Caslin. Your father has come through this ordeal remarkably well for a man of his years, at least physically."

"Thank you," Caslin said.

"You're welcome. Please excuse us," the consultant said and the two men left Caslin alone with his father.

Approaching the side of the bed, he reached out and placed his hands onto the old man's. Suddenly, his father – the fierce, embittered, aggressive man who held such sway over him – looked every bit as fragile as his seventy-plus years might dictate. The man who was always the strongest, most prominent character in his life reduced to this state was troubling to see. If he needed a reminder that everyone was mortal, then this certainly qualified. Caslin's phone rang.

"Sir, it's Terry Holt. How is the family?"

"They'll be okay, thanks, Terry," Caslin replied quietly, looking at his father and hoping the doctors were right. "What do you have for me?"

"I had a thought… after you left the office earlier," Holt said, and Caslin could infer from his tone the DC was somewhat pensive.

"What is it, Terry?"

"I don't think Fuller was trying to hurt you."

CHAPTER TWENTY-THREE

"I REVISITED the telematics data we took from Bradley's wrecked Mercedes and came at it from a different angle. Now, we didn't know why he was making the stops that he did but figured there had to be a reason, right?" Holt said.

"As in when he took a drive out to the lighthouse at Flamborough Head?"

"Exactly. He's resurfaced from his secret life in obscurity with a goal in mind. Therefore, it follows logically that every stop he made and every visit to a location had a purpose. I doubt he came back for the weather. At the time, I only plotted his course over the main roads he used and the places where he frequented the most," Holt said, standing and crossing to one of the several noticeboards they were utilising to display case information. "So, I went back and added everywhere he travelled to documenting where the engine was turned off, presumably where he stopped, as well as for the length of time in each location. We had him making two stops in Selby on two separate occasions."

"Selby," Caslin repeated. Holt met his eye. Hunter flicked hers between the two of them grasping the significance.

"Your father?" Hunter asked. Caslin frowned and looked to Holt encouraging him to continue.

"We can't be sure of why he was in Selby but the day after he arrived in the country and then again two days before he died, Bradley's car was stationary in the town. Not only *in the town* but on the outskirts."

Caslin sat back in his seat. "Presumably, you have more?"

"I do," Holt said, returning to the table they were seated at and picking up a folder. From this, he withdrew the copy of a map and passed it across to them. Routes were marked out, highlighted in different colours representing separate days. Caslin scanned them. "We still don't know what Jody Wyer's interest was in this case. We know from his mobile phone records that he was paying attention to MacEwan and his operations. What we didn't do was take a look at the telematics data from his car."

"And you have?" Hunter asked.

Holt nodded enthusiastically, "I cross-referenced the information I got from Wyer's BMW with that of Bradley and I got a hit."

"They crossed paths?" Caslin asked, looking up from the map he held in both hands in front of him. Holt nodded. "Where?"

"Selby," Holt stated. "The signal from both cars was relayed via the same cell tower on that first date. The day after Bradley arrived from Spain."

"Are you saying they met?" Hunter asked, trying to put the pieces together. Holt turned the corners of his mouth downwards and opened his palms in a gesture of uncertainty.

"We've no idea, really. But what we can say with certainty is they were in the same location at the same time. Wyer could have been following Bradley or they could have been setting up a meeting. We've no way of knowing."

"And why Selby?" Caslin asked before casting his mind back to the phone call at the hospital that'd brought him back to Fulford from his father's bedside. "You said on the phone you didn't think Fuller was targeting me?"

Holt pulled out his chair and sat down reaching into his folder. "I've got an answer for both," he said, looking at Caslin, "but... I don't think you're going to like it."

"That's certainly my reality today, Terry. What do you have?"

Holt took a deep breath gathering his thoughts. Holding both hands out in front of him, he presented his palms up splaying his fingers wide and raising his eyebrows, "Just hear me out. I haven't followed it all the way through yet but..."

"We're listening, Terry."

"All right. Cast your mind back to the 80s. The customs clearing house is hit at Manchester Airport. It's a massive job, bold, high profile, caught everyone by surprise and is an embarrassment for both the police and the government. The authorities of the day tried to keep a lid on the details by not releasing what was taken, but in today's money, we're looking at one hundred and twenty to thirty-million pounds. You can imagine the resources that were thrown at the investigation. Greater Manchester immediately put fifty officers on the case but once the scale was fully established, they knew they needed more."

"They would have sought help from surrounding forces particularly those with connections to anyone who potentially could be in the frame," Caslin said, following Holt's logic.

"That's what I thought," Holt said, raising a finger in the air and smiling. "So, I went back to the case files I brought out of the archive, those I have anyway as the remaining ones still haven't materialised despite repeated assurances..."

"Terry... focus," Caslin said, masking thinly-veiled irritation. He knew Holt was going somewhere and he was eager to join him.

"I totted up the number of officers from the initial assignation right through to when the case was in full swing. Over three hundred officers in one form or another plus more on top when it came down to raiding addresses around the country. One name caught my eye," Holt said, spinning a sheet of paper on the table before him and sliding it in Caslin's direction. Both Caslin and Hunter looked at it. It was a list of names. Holt had highlighted one with a yellow marker pen.

Caslin had to read it twice before he could fully process the information. He glanced at Hunter and then back to Holt. Hunter spoke first, "Your father?"

"There must be a mistake," Caslin said, briefly shaking his head. "He was uniform all of his life. He never went into CID."

"I thought so too," Holt said. "But I checked and then I checked again. He was seconded from North Yorkshire onto the investigation team almost as soon as it was expanded. He remained there for a little over a year."

Caslin's eyes narrowed, his expression accompanied by a deep frown. "He never told me that. Are you sure?" Holt nodded. "Where does he fit in... I mean... why would he be the target? I presume that's where you're going with this?"

"If he wasn't... then, it's incredibly coincidental," Holt explained. "My initial thought, as was yours I imagine, was Fuller was retaliating against you personally for targeting Carl and Ashton. Maybe that's still the case. Perhaps Jody Wyer thought your father had some information he could use and went to see him or maybe his father knew yours. Did he ever mention Keith Wyer to you either in passing as an acquaintance or as a colleague?"

"Not that I recall," Caslin said. "This is all news to me."

"Regarding your father's participation in the Manchester investigation, I've no information on that. I tried to find out what the scope of his role in the team was if he was desk-based or in the field. Who he reported to... that kind of thing but I've not had any joy? At the moment, he's just a name on that paper in front of you."

Caslin slapped both hands down on top of the very sheet of paper, Holt was referring to. "Let's keep it like that for now. This information doesn't leave this room. Understood?" he asked, meeting eyes with both of them in turn. Holt nodded without speaking. Hunter appeared pensive. "If you have a problem with it, say so," Caslin said.

"No, sir," she replied, "but we need to get this clarified as soon as possible. Otherwise…"

"All right," Caslin said quietly, covering his mouth and nose with his hands. "All right… I know."

"How do you want to proceed?" Hunter asked.

Caslin thought on it, casting an eye across the information boards erected all around them. "I want the two of you to stay here. Terry, you carry on trying to find out where my old man fits into the securities raid but… do so quietly. The key figures in this seem to be a step ahead of us at every turn, so let's not tip our hand. Sarah," he turned to Hunter, "Jody Wyer was deeper into this than we are and I'm finding it hard to believe the all-consuming passion he had for this case was kept secret from his lover. I should imagine the nameless redhead is either linked or related to someone in and around his investigation. He wouldn't be dragging an innocent person into all of this, not someone he cared about. He knew how dangerous it was. That's why he kept everyone in the dark… but not her. She's involved somehow, I'm positive, and she'll have information we can use. Find her!"

"If they were onto Wyer, then it's logical they may have been onto her as well," Hunter suggested. "That might be why we can't find her. She could be dead already."

"Then where's the body?" Caslin said. "They weren't too fussed about where they dumped Jody."

"She may have killed him," Holt said, almost apologetically. "Would have been able to get close enough and knew what he was up to."

"Find her and we'll ask," Caslin replied.

"Where will you be, sir?" Hunter asked him.

Caslin took a deep breath, his expression one of thoughtful introspection. "I'll be at the hospital."

SOMETHING CAUSED him to wake with a start. Blinking furiously, he looked around trying to get his bearings. It was dark outside but the sky was changing. The night replaced by the brooding slate-grey of an overcast morning. His vision adjusted to the surroundings. His father slept six feet away, his breathing shallow and steady. He'd had a good night. Although not waking from his surgery, the staff seemed unconcerned and that was reassuring. The time to worry was when the medical team did so. Looking to the door, Caslin saw the outline of a figure standing on the other side. Sitting forward, he stretched out, feeling a twinge in his lower back. He winced. These chairs weren't designed for sleeping in. Standing up, he went to the door and cracked it open. The armed officer turned to him offering a smile and a nod in greeting. Caslin mirrored the gesture and closed the door, returning to his father's bedside.

The old man was stirring. Perhaps that was what had woken him, he didn't know. Caslin helped himself to a cup of water from the jug placed on his father's table alongside the bed. He wouldn't need it for a while. The water had an aftertaste of plastic. It had been sitting there since the previous day. Looking at his watch, he wondered whether the visitor's restaurant would be open yet. He'd kill for a cup of coffee.

"You look dreadful."

Caslin realised his father's unbandaged eye was open, watching him. For how long, he didn't know. "You don't look in great shape yourself, Dad," Caslin replied, putting the cup down beside the bed. His father smiled faintly.

"That's good because I feel awful."

"You're going to be okay," Caslin said, bestowing as much confidence in the prediction as he could.

"Then why does your face look like I've already died?"

Caslin shook his head, "It's complicated."

"There's that word again," his father whispered. "You're a terrible liar, Son."

"I'm not lying."

"Then what? *Lizzie and Sean!*" he said, trying to sit upright.

Caslin reached over and placed a firm but reassuring hand on his chest easing him back down on the bed. "They're all right. I promise. No harm done."

"I couldn't stop them..." his father said. "Damn it, I tried but..."

"It's okay. You did your best," Caslin said calmly. "No one can ask anymore of you than that. Can you tell me about them?"

His father sighed, rolling his head to the right and looking out of the window. "Three men... maybe four... I'm not too sure. It all happened so fast. They wore balaclavas. I couldn't see their faces."

"Did they say anything?"

His father shook his head. "Not that I recall. There was a knock on the door and I answered it. As soon as I cracked it open, they forced their way in. I tried to push back but... he was too strong. I shouted at the kids to run but... it all happened so fast. I'm so sorry, Son."

Caslin pressed his hand into his father's, seeing tears welling in the old man's eyes. He couldn't recollect his father ever apologising to him for anything in his entire life. "It's okay. Don't be too hard on yourself."

"What did they want? What did they take, do you know?"

Caslin loosened his grip and turned sideways allowing himself to perch on the side of the bed alongside his father. "I need to ask you a few questions, Dad. Is that okay?"

"Yes, of course."

"And I need you to be honest with me."

"That sounds ominous."

"You were seconded to a case back in the 80s. The raid on the Customs House at Manchester Airport, outsourced and run by a company called Manchester Securities. Do you remember? What can you tell me about it?"

"That was a long time ago, Nathaniel. Why on earth are you asking me about it now?"

"After I left yours yesterday, I couldn't understand why we'd argued as we did. It felt like it came out of nowhere."

"Usually does when you're involved," his father said, turning his head and facing away. If he'd been able, Caslin figured he'd have left the room by now.

"And today, that's got me thinking. The mood change happened after I mentioned DCI Phil Bradley, didn't it?"

"What are you talking about?"

"You knew him," Caslin said quietly. "More than that, you worked with him. Perhaps, even for him."

"So, what if I did?"

"People are dying, Dad," Caslin said, maintaining his composure for if he were to try and force the conversation, he knew his father would throw up the barriers and not allow him in. That was a trait they shared. "Sean and Lizzie were there." At the mention of his grandchildren, his father broke down. The façade of indignation slipping away as quickly as it had been conjured.

"I'm so sorry… so, so sorry," his father repeated as the tears fell.

"Did Bradley come to see you?" Caslin asked. His father wiped his cheek with the back of his free hand, the other was constrained by the drip. He shook his head.

"I… I can't…"

"I'm going to get to the bottom of it, Dad. Whatever this is all about it is going to come out, I assure you. You have to talk to me. The time for burying your head in the sand and hoping it will all go away has passed."

His father took a deep breath, closing his one good eye as he did so. Opening it, he fixed his gaze on his son. Suddenly, he appeared frail again, much as when Caslin first set eyes on him in the hospital bed. "Okay," he whispered softly, bobbing his head almost imperceptibly in agreement. "Bradley did come to see me but… he wasn't the first."

CHAPTER TWENTY-FOUR

"You have to realise what was going on at the time," his father said, glancing nervously towards the corridor as the shadow of his armed guard crossed the threshold under the door and momentarily broke the shaft of light.

"I'm listening," Caslin said. "Take as long as you need."

"I was having a tough time," his father explained. "A few months prior your mother had packed her bags and left taking both you and Stefan with her. No word. No discussion. You'll not remember, or not realise, but I came home after a night shift to find you were all gone. Just a letter on the table telling me it was over."

Caslin shook his head. His memories of that day were very different. He wasn't even a teenager at the time, barely into double figures. Their mother took both boys aside and told them they were going to miss school and head off on an adventure with her that day. Neither his brother Stefan nor himself had a clue that their mother never planned on them coming back. She had packed most of their clothes while they'd slept, rousing them early and ushering them out to the car where her friend waited. He was a decent man. One they grew to love in a strange sort of way despite his elevation into their mother's affections, displacing their father and themselves along the way. Eventually, they would marry and live happily. Stefan and himself found their placement in the boarding house of the independent school quite challenging. It was far from what they were used to in York but they managed.

As for his father, they'd never discussed the impact of his mother's actions nor the causes that led her to do what she did. From a distance, however, it was clear how detrimental the break-up had been for him. His descent into alcoholism was fuelled by it but often his mother had hinted, over the years, that the drinking came first. The truth wasn't known to him much like huge swathes of his father's life.

"I don't remember much," Caslin said, not wishing to revisit those days for they held pain he himself had never processed.

"I kept going as you do but I struggled. I'm not ashamed to admit it. Anyway, I was drinking too much. I knew it. Everyone knew it," his father said, his face contorting with the anguish of revisiting those feelings. "Until one day, I went into work... I was still hammered from the night before... and it wasn't the first time."

"What happened?"

"I was sent home on sick leave. I guess it'd be different now. I'd have been out on my ear," his father said. Caslin didn't comment. They had more in common than he'd thought for he, too, had rocked up at work in an unfit state on occasion. "Two days later, my superintendent paid me a visit at home. He suggested that I try something fresh. Get out of uniform for a while. He figured it might help bring me back. Anyway, they were assembling a task force to try and tackle the Manchester raid and some of the names being touted had associations with Yorkshire, York specifically, and that's how I got involved."

"What were you focussed on?" Caslin asked.

"We knew a job like that took a lot of planning and needed a sizeable network in order to pull it off. The raid itself was carried out by a group of ten... and they were professional about it too.

These weren't DIY homeowner specials, they were skilled. But that was the easy part. To be able to fence that much cash, jewellery and gold bullion in particular, they needed expertise that just weren't commonplace back then if ever."

"If you have a large organisation or businesses with a high turnover of cash, then the money can be dropped back into circulation relatively quickly," Caslin argued, "but on the scale of what they took you're right. The speed necessary to keep that number of people happy by paying them off quickly would've been challenging."

"And that's just the money. When it came to fencing the remainder there aren't too many people with the resources and know how to shift that volume. We knew they needed to call on countless others to process it and that's where we figured we'd be able to pick them off. In many cases it worked too."

"You worked for Bradley?" Caslin asked.

"I was assigned to his team and paired with another officer from Greater Manchester under the umbrella of a detective sergeant."

"Keith Wyer?" Caslin asked, putting two and two together.

"Yes. How did you know?"

"Keith's son was taking an interest in Bradley... and perhaps you as well."

"Jody," his father said quietly. "A good kid."

"A dead kid," Caslin replied. His father looked at him, nodding solemnly. "You met him?"

"I did. After Jody paid me a visit, Bradley showed up shortly after."

"Had you met him before?"

"No, not at all," his father said, shaking his head. "But he was Keith's son and apparently, his father spoke highly of me."

"Did you remain friends, you and Keith?"

"Not really. I didn't know he had died until Jody called."

"What did he want?"

"To ask questions... get answers."

"About what? Bradley?"

"Among other things. Neither of them knew what they were getting into. They thought they did. They thought they had it all figured out but they didn't realise who they were dealing with. Is the girl okay?"

"Which girl?"

"Jody's girlfriend. She is such a pretty little thing. I'd hate to think of her caught up in all of this."

"Redhead?" Caslin clarified. His father nodded. "I don't suppose you caught her name, did you?"

"Lovely young lady, very sweet. Louise, I think he introduced her as but I didn't catch her last name."

"Okay, thanks," Caslin said, making a mental note. "Can you go back a bit? Back to where you got involved in the investigation."

His father drew a breath. "It didn't take us long before we began to focus on a second-generation scrap merchant here in York."

"MacEwan," Caslin confirmed.

"Yes. You've heard of him?" he asked. Caslin nodded that he had but didn't want to reveal everything he knew. It was an odd sensation, speaking to a relative as one would a potential suspect in a criminal investigation but these were rapidly becoming strange days. "A few of us had the long-held belief that he was part of the crew using his businesses to both store and ship the proceeds of the raid out of the country in his boats. He owned a boatyard up the coast in Whitby."

"I read in the case files that MacEwan was interviewed but released without charge and no further investigation was undertaken," Caslin said, a little confused.

"Yeah, that sounds about right. That was Bradley. At least, I think it was."

"Go on."

"This is when things started to go a little awry, Son," his father said, eyes flitting around nervously, anywhere but

meeting Caslin's. "You have to realise I was a mess...
vulnerable."

"What happened, Dad?"

"I'm not sure how it came about. Genuinely, I don't," his
father said. "We paid MacEwan a visit at his yard. It was just
myself and Keith Wyer at this point. It wasn't a raid. We didn't
have a search warrant or anything. At that moment, MacEwan
wasn't considered to be a key suspect. We were on a fishing
expedition, running down the names we'd come up with as
possibles. Imagine our surprise when we stumbled across the
smelting operation."

"The gold?" Caslin asked.

"Damn right!" his father said, sounding excited as he recalled
it. "Turns out we were right in that MacEwan was fencing some
of the proceeds but we had no idea he was one of those smelting
down the bullion. Rendering it untraceable, he was then
shipping it to his network of associates on the continent via his
boats up the coast."

"None of this is in the files."

"It wouldn't be. Keith and I managed to detain those present,
there weren't many, and called it in to the DCI."

"Bradley?"

"The very same. He came down to the yard to see us. I
couldn't believe it. A few months into my first CID investigation
and it was going to make my career. Some guys work their entire
lives without a collar like that."

"I know."

"Bradley's eyes nearly popped out when he arrived. We'd
rumbled the largest part of the operation pretty much by
stumbling across it. A pure fluke. But he didn't react as I
expected."

"I don't think I'm going to like this, am I?" Caslin said.

"I'll not insult you by asking you not to think less of me, Son.
I know that'll be impossible. Not a day passes where I don't
question what we did back then. *What I did.*"

"What did you do... cut a deal?" Caslin asked, failing to keep the disdain from his tone. It was far from a leap to realise the upshot of what occurred that day bearing in mind the absence of detail in the files and how MacEwan didn't see time inside for his role.

"Bradley negotiated it," his father said, staring down and refusing to meet Caslin's eye. "We hadn't made it common knowledge where we were going and so... no one knew. Bradley and Wyer went back a way and... I think they weren't strangers to helping themselves to things they came across if you know what I mean?"

"I know the type."

"Anyway, Bradley wasn't sure about me. He didn't know if I was one of them."

"Whether you'd be willing to take a cut?"

His father nodded. "I felt intimidated. Threatened. Not that I'm diminishing my role in any way. I was there and just as culpable as the others. As it turned out, Keith Wyer vouched for me and it sort of... happened."

"Dad... for the love of..." the words tailed off as Caslin's head sank into his hands.

"Like I said... I was a mess. Most of the time I could barely hold it together and... I figured I had nothing to lose. Your mother was gone. You boys..."

"I'm not letting you pin the guilt of this one on me, Dad. Not this time!" Caslin snapped. The silhouette of the armed guard, visible through the opaque glass, turned at the door at the sound of the raised voice. Seconds later he turned away again. Caslin lowered his voice. "What were you thinking?" he whispered.

"That's just it, Nathaniel," his father said quietly. "I wasn't really thinking at all."

"How much?"

"Did we take?"

"Forty pieces of silver?"

"If you think I'm proud of what I did... what we did, then

you are mistaken," his father said, reaching out and gripping Caslin's forearm.

"How much?"

"An even split. An even split of everything MacEwan had in his possession."

"How the hell did you make that fly?" Caslin said. "I mean, you're talking millions of pounds."

"Well, it wasn't all MacEwan's. Obviously, he couldn't give away the share of everyone else. These people were serious criminals. MacEwan took the arrangement further up the chain and smoothed things over. Their network was already in place and having us onboard gave them a shield from the investigation. MacEwan himself was also highly motivated to avoid some serious jail time. It was not the millions you're talking of but still a lot by anyone's standards."

"The people further up the chain, did you ever meet them... get to know their names?"

"No, not at all. We all figured that was for the best."

"But how did you manage to keep it quiet?" Caslin asked, profoundly impressed whilst disgusted in equal measure.

"That would have been impossible, so we took precautions. Each of us agreed not to touch our share for the foreseeable future. Not until we were out of the job. All of us. That way, we could move on with our lives, distancing ourselves from our past and no one would notice."

"No one would notice? You mean, you'd bypass friendships... even family so your change in circumstances would go unnoticed?"

"Exactly. Out of sight, out of mind," his father said. "How many of your friends do you still speak to since you left the Yard? Not many, I'll bet. It wouldn't take much. Move to a new location, retire abroad." Caslin could see the logic. He could count the people on one hand – two fingers if he was honest about it. "Time would pass. The money would be there. We just had to bide our time before we could lay our hands on it."

Caslin let out a deep sigh, "And MacEwan, how did he feel about this?"

"Once he was in the clear, he went to Spain. That was the last dealing I had with him. I only found out he was back on the scene recently."

"What about the others? I can't see how the rest of the gang benefitted from this little arrangement."

"They didn't," his father told him. "MacEwan handed them to us on a plate. After all, he was in the clear and the more of them who went down the greater his share became."

"I still don't see how you managed to keep this quiet. Who else was in on it?"

His father shrugged, "Besides Bradley, Keith and myself... I've no idea but there could have been others. With hindsight, there almost certainly were but remember most of the officers around the investigation were from another patch. I didn't know them and I never asked. Didn't want to know."

"For Bradley to get such a massive career break and never to rank higher than DCI, there must have been something else going on. Did anyone wonder how you guys got the breakthroughs you did?"

"None of us took the credit. We did it through a series of anonymous tip offs. It was a slow and roundabout way of going about it but eventually the information would land on the right desks and arrests were made. For us to take the credit would have drawn too much attention to us. We couldn't allow that and nor could MacEwan. If we'd hooked them all at the same time but left MacEwan out, then it would have been obvious. We all had to be invisible."

Caslin got off the edge of the bed his legs felt unsteady and he pulled over a chair. Sitting down, he rubbed at his cheeks with the palms of his hands before locking eyes with his father.

"Where's the money?"

"It's safe. I never touched it, not once and it's been a long time since I had any intention of ever doing so. I want you to believe that. It's important to me that you do. If I could change what I did back then… believe me, I would."

"It's offshore?"

"In various bank accounts, yes."

"Did everyone do the same?"

"For the most part," he explained. "Despite our best efforts at removing MacEwan from the focus of the investigation, he couldn't continue the smelting operations. It's quite a slow process and there was so much to do. So, he had to put all of that on hold."

"Are you saying there's still gold bullion leftover from that raid sitting somewhere, out of circulation?"

"Maybe. I don't really know. Bradley promised to keep an eye on him: MacEwan. Once the deal was made with whoever was in charge, the remainder would be split between us, MacEwan and the lower elements of the gang. Bradley thought there was no way MacEwan could have moved what was ours on to the market without making waves. Bradley was wise to it. Besides, much of what was taken had already been shipped and without needing to pay back those who were sent down, MacEwan was sorted. He didn't need to run the risk of double crossing us. We could all wait it out."

"What did Bradley want when he came to see you?"

"He felt it was time to cash in."

"Apparently, he was suffering from cancer. From what we've found out about his secret life he was probably already living off of dodgy funds and it stands to reason he wanted to make the most of what time he may have left."

"Was it terminal?"

Caslin shook his head, "I've no idea but even if not, maybe it gave him the motivation to move things along. You said the arrangement was to wait until you were all retired."

"Yes. That was what we agreed."

"Keith Wyer's dead. You've been out of the job for years. Bradley faked his death a couple of years back so why now?"

"I don't know," his father said. "I know he was back here with MacEwan. He said as much when he came to see me. I should imagine they were hatching some kind of plan for the remainder but I wanted no part of it."

"No part of what?"

"I didn't ask. I didn't want to know and I told him as much too."

Caslin thought about it allowing the information to sink in. It was going to take time. Of all the eventualities he'd considered in this case, this particular outcome would never have crossed his mind as plausible. How should he feel about it – about his father – he had no idea?

"What did Jody Wyer ask of you?"

His father fell quiet, appearing pensive. A few moments passed where the silence weighed heavily on both of them. "I think he was hoping his father would live up to the memories he still held of him."

"What did you tell him?" Caslin asked.

"Nothing. I couldn't destroy the lad's memories, so I sent them away. I thought we could bury it forever," his father said, his gaze drifting down to meet Caslin's eye. "No son should ever have to face his father's demons."

"It looks to me as if someone else has figured out what was going on," Caslin replied flatly, folding his arms before him. His father realised the inference of those words.

"What happens now?"

Caslin stood up and crossed the short distance to stand next to his father. Placing a reassuring hand on his arm, he smiled weakly and gently shook his head. "I honestly don't know."

"It had to come out eventually, I suppose."

"I'll figure something out," Caslin replied, and not for the first time those words sounded hollow. He had no idea how to resolve the situation.

CHAPTER TWENTY-FIVE

BACK AT FULFORD ROAD, Caslin reached the door to their investigation room but held off from entering. Looking through the inset window, he eyed both Hunter and Holt busying themselves. They were working hard, especially so since his family had come under threat. The nagging question, one he'd wrestled with from the moment his father had broken his silence right up to this point, was still churning through his mind. His duty as a police officer was clear, his duty to his family equally so. The problem was the two roles were not necessarily compatible with each other in this situation. A uniformed constable appeared at the end of the corridor catching his eye. Forced into action, he spun and walked confidently into the room. Greeted by both of them, he beckoned them to come together.

"I've got a lead on our mysterious redhead," he said, sounding upbeat. "She was introduced as Louise but I've not got a surname. Terry, can you run it through the information we have and see if that name comes up associated with, or related to, anyone we already know?"

"Will do, sir," Holt replied, setting to work.

"How did you come by the name?" Hunter asked, coming alongside Caslin.

"I met with a source," he replied, meeting her eye briefly and looking away immediately concerned she would see straight through him. Glancing back up, he raised his eyebrows and explained, "Jody Wyer introduced them."

"That's great. It gives us something," she said.

"Better than that it would appear MacEwan is back in the frame for fencing the proceeds of the Manchester raid back in the 80s. My source fingers him as the ringleader who smelted the stolen gold and also arranged for it to be shipped out of the country. The word is there is still more to be had and that's where we need to focus."

"Your source," Hunter asked. "How credible is it?"

Caslin took a deep breath unsure of what to say. "If you'd asked me that last month, I would have said impeccable but right now I'd say it's worth serious consideration. Good enough?"

"Of course."

"It looks very much as if MacEwan not only ripped off his co-conspirators when it came to the laundering of what was stolen, but he is also implicated in giving them up to us over a period of time following the robbery."

"So, it wasn't Fuller who grassed on Neville Bridger?" Hunter said, open-mouthed.

Caslin shook his head. "Doesn't look like it, no."

"And Fuller himself?" Holt asked, glancing up from the paperwork he was sifting through. "Did MacEwan sell him out too?"

"I'm pretty certain, yes," Caslin confirmed. "What's more, I think Fuller might have worked it out."

"After all this time? How?"

"That… I haven't figured out yet but I'm confident that's the case. He may not know it all but he's getting there."

"What makes you so sure of that?"

"MacEwan is still alive," Caslin said. "Perhaps Fuller wants his money seeing as he'll be getting out soon or he doesn't have all the facts yet. It'll only be a matter of time though. I want us to focus on how and where MacEwan would be likely to store stolen bullion for the last thirty years and how he's planning on taking it out of the country under these circumstances. He's savvy enough to know where the heat will be coming from, both us and Fuller's crew, and he'll want to move it to where he feels safe and that's not here."

"Spain?" Hunter suggested.

"My thoughts exactly. With Fuller nipping at his heels, MacEwan will no doubt want to make the move soon so let's get on it."

"We had to release both Ashton and Carl this morning," Hunter advised him. "We had no grounds to hold them for any longer."

"That'll expedite things a little. More motivation for MacEwan," Caslin said before heading for the sanctuary of his office and breathing a sigh of relief that he'd managed the briefing without giving too much away. How long he could keep it up for, he didn't know.

"Sir," Hunter called after him as he reached the doorway. He turned to face her. "All of this started with the bombing of the Fullers' premises."

"Yes."

"What sparked that?"

Caslin had already formulated a theory but would admit the details were sketchy. "I think Bradley and MacEwan were working together to launder the proceeds of the robbery. Bradley's faked death plays into it nicely. Who would look for a bent copper when he's already dead? Both of them came back here at the same time for a reason. Whether that was triggered by Fuller's forthcoming release or not, I don't know, but that's what they're here for. And if you're looking to pick someone's pocket… again, it would be best if that person was looking in the other direction when you do."

"A distraction," Hunter said. "Have Fuller and his entire organisation geared up against the likes of Clinton Dade."

"Exactly. I wouldn't rule out them having put a hit out on Dade just to stoke the fires further," Caslin said. "If two rival gangs are looking to tear the other apart, what better smokescreen to use in order to slip out with a lot of their money?"

"It follows," Hunter said, "but it's thin."

Caslin nodded, "I know but I want us to run with it."

"And where do the Bridger boys fit in to all of this? I mean, if they thought Fuller had got their father sent down but in reality, it was MacEwan… how come one of them is working for him?"

"MacEwan's been playing one side off against another for decades giving them and us the run around. Do you reckon he would think twice about the manipulation of two young lads with an axe to grind? Think about it."

Hunter frowned, seemingly unconvinced. "If Fuller knew about Bradley, assuming your source is correct, why would he tip off MacEwan by eliminating Bradley? Surely, he would be better off following them to where they've been keeping it and taking retribution then. It would make more sense, wouldn't it?"

Caslin had to admit the logic was sound. "Maybe he wants MacEwan to make his move."

"To flush him out?"

"Makes sense too."

"In which case, when we take down MacEwan we'll probably have to contend with Fuller's goons at the same time," Hunter concluded. "What makes you so sure Fuller is on to this? Your source, who is it?"

"I'd prefer not to say at the moment," Caslin replied. Hunter's eyes narrowed but she said nothing. He turned and walked into his office. With his back to them both, he let out a sigh and closed his eyes attempting to settle his breathing. The less the team knew about his father's role in this the better, for the time being at least. There would come a time when that would no longer be possible and he feared that wasn't too far away.

It was Fuller's own words that implied he knew the score. When he told Caslin to look closer to home he was referring to far more than the safety of his family. Fuller knew. Caslin was sure of it but he had chosen not to say. Nothing would have him removed from this case faster than having his father implicated right at the heart of it. The gangster was playing the game by his rules and Caslin had to work out what his next move was likely to be as well as how to counter it. He felt a sharp stab of pain in the back of his head – a well-recognised symptom that manifested when he was under times of significant stress. Pressing a thumb and forefinger into both his eyes, he sought to relieve it.

"I've got it," an excited shout carried from the other room. Caslin turned to see the animated form of Terry Holt celebrating his eureka moment. He saw Caslin looking through the window. Hunter went to him, looking over his shoulder. "I've found Louise!"

Caslin came out of his office and joined them, eager to put a face to the ghost they'd been searching for. Looking at the screen, he noticed Holt had a social media page up.

"Do I pay you for surfing this?" he asked playfully. Holt laughed.

"Quickest way to find a picture," he explained.

Caslin spied the name – Louise Bennett. "Do we know her?"

Holt shook his head. "No. She's not known to the police."

"Who is she?"

"I cross checked the names of everyone involved in the case starting with the most recent – those we're investigating now or have spoken with in the past week – and it didn't take long. She's divorced but kept her married name. You'd know her better by her maiden," Holt said, opening another tab on the screen and displaying a gallery of photos she had uploaded to her page. Scrolling down, he found what he was looking for and double-clicked on it. The computer took a few seconds to process the request before enlarging the image in the middle of the screen. A picture of an attractive, redheaded woman appeared, seated on what looked like a sea wall and taken on a bright and warm day judging by their clothing. She was with an older man and woman, both standing behind her, the man with a hand on her shoulder. It was a family picture but was unlikely to be recent. Caslin recognised the man and knew his current appearance resembled someone far more aged, if not haggard, than he was depicted here.

"Scott Tarbet," Caslin confirmed, naming DCI Bradley's cousin and witness to his apparent death.

"She's his daughter?" Hunter asked, looking at Holt.

"The one and only," the DC confirmed. "The only child of Scott and Margaret Tarbet."

"You thought he was holding out on us when we spoke to him, didn't you?" Hunter asked Caslin. "How did she end up with Jody Wyer?"

"I don't know," Caslin said, mulling it over. "Did Jody even know who she was?"

"I'll wager her father has something to do with it," Hunter said. "Shall we pay him another visit?"

"Hold fire on that," Caslin said, turning to Holt. "Do you know where she is?"

Holt shook his head, "No. She was an avid poster on social media, doing so daily until about a month ago and then she dropped off the site and hasn't posted since."

"She was dating Wyer by then. Any sign of him on her feed?" Hunter asked.

"Nope. Scanning through it, she was a pretty upbeat character espousing the virtues of democracy, vegetarianism and… *dancing cats*…"

"*Cats?*" Caslin asked. Holt shook his head.

"Never mind. The point is, pretty usual stuff until about five months ago. Then the general mood of her posts changed and I think I know why," Holt said, closing down that particular image and scrolling across to another. He opened that up. It was a shot at a cemetery. "The anniversary of her mother's death. Looks like it hit her hard."

"How did she die?" Hunter asked.

"Cancer. But, judging from the details Louise has been sharing, she put down underfunding of the NHS alongside stress as a major contributory factor. She posted several times about how she wished she could have taken her mother abroad for treatment."

"Stress? Caused by what?" Caslin asked, intrigued.

Holt shrugged. "No idea but I'll see what else I can find. Needless to say, she's not been active recently, so I've no lead on where she is."

"Any indication of Bradley visiting Tarbet since he returned to the UK?" Caslin asked, looking up at the noticeboards and casting his mind back to the telematics data that Holt had acquired.

"He didn't go anywhere near Whitby," Holt said. Caslin walked over to the boards and began tracing the routes they knew Bradley had taken revisiting them in his mind as he did so.

"He went out to Flamborough Point though. That's on the east coast but nowhere near Whitby," Caslin said, looking over his shoulder. Hunter came alongside.

"But if you're looking for a safe place to meet a dead man..." Hunter suggested. "Pretty much guaranteed to ensure there's no chance of their meeting being witnessed by anyone who knows them."

"But to what end?" Caslin said aloud. His father thought Jody was looking for confirmation that Keith Wyer wasn't involved in anything untoward but now Caslin wasn't so sure. There was another possibility opening up before him. Bearing in mind the co-conspirators' agreement, Keith died well before he would have had the opportunity to claim his share of the proceeds. Similarly, if Scott Tarbet's account were to be believed, he was substantially out of pocket when his vessel was burnt out and the insurance payment was withheld. "What if... they are all working towards the same goal?"

"Money?"

"The money or the gold," Caslin confirmed. "There are those who lost out such as Tarbet and Wyer senior. Then there're those who are greedy like Bradley and MacEwan. Our next task besides figuring out when and where MacEwan will make his move is to nail down their motivations. If we can do that, then we'll know where those people," he pointed to the key individuals listed on the board, "fit with one another."

"And let's not forget those who have been robbed?" Hunter added, thinking of Fuller and the other gang members currently serving time.

"Of both wealth... and liberty," Caslin said, glancing at her with a knowing look.

"So, whose door do we lay Jody Wyer's murder at?" Holt asked.

Caslin's gaze drifted across the noticeboards, the pictures of the dead, the likely suspects and the links between them. There was a case that could be made against any number of them if the truth were known. It was frustrating.

"We're close," he said, in answer to the question. "This is all going to shake down in the coming days, I can feel it. We need to be ready to move as and when they do."

CHAPTER TWENTY-SIX

THERE WAS the unmistakable sound of metal keys coming together as Caslin waited. The door creaked open on its hinges, reinforced metal and the better part of two inches thick. The prison officer appeared, beckoning him to pass through. Caslin thanked his escort and joined the newcomer in the adjoining room. Following the attack on his father, Caslin left nothing to chance. Pete Fuller was placed within HMP Full Sutton's *Close Supervision Centre*. As they walked, Caslin could feel the difference within moments. Full Sutton was a maximum-security prison but here, within the centre, those procedures were elevated to another level entirely. For the majority of the day the prisoners were often kept in isolation from one another. Many of them had extreme personality disorders to go along with their criminal convictions and couldn't be trusted to interact with others and therefore when given their exercise time they did so alone.

"Any famous names in here at the moment?" Caslin asked his escort casually.

The officer glanced at him over his shoulder. "Plenty who are notorious. Don't know about famous. Did you have anyone in mind?" he asked as an inmate began shouting somewhere nearby. Caslin couldn't tell from where. A number of other voices picked up the baton and soon the jeering reverberated all around them.

"Didn't you have that guy the papers called the UK's Hannibal?" Caslin asked, referencing a murderer sentenced to a full-life term back in the 1970s.

"Used to," the officer said as they reached yet another security door. He looked up at the camera mounted above the door, itself securely fixed behind a protective screen. There was an audible buzz and the lock clicked to signal the door was unlocked. The escort pushed it open. "He was moved to the *Monster Mansion* last year and they're welcome to him."

"The Monster Mansion?" Caslin asked, following. Once they were through the door was closed and this time the securing of the locks sounded as a deadened thud. They were well into the bowels of the prison here. Metaphorically speaking, Caslin felt the sun didn't shine anymore.

"Wakefield's equivalent," the officer explained. "They get most of the big-time psychos, sociopaths and nutters who like to eat people."

"You must miss him," Caslin replied with a dry sense of humour. There was a grunt in response that Caslin took as unappreciative of his sarcasm. They came to another locked door at the end of a short corridor. The officer opened it and they entered the room. Inside was a table and two chairs. Caslin noted all three were bolted to the ground. That alone was mildly unsettling. He was ushered through.

"You know the procedure?" the officer asked. Caslin indicated he did but the rules were explained to him once more. He was advised to keep his distance, not to interact in any physical way and that they were under constant surveillance from a camera mounted in the ceiling. He had already surrendered his personal effects, mobile phone, wallet and even his belt was considered unacceptable to take with him. "Wait here and we'll bring him to you," the officer said once he was happy the protocols were fully understood. Caslin wasn't too concerned about Fuller. His request to place him inside the centre was considered reasonable under the circumstances. He sold it as a way to ensure Fuller could no longer direct his associates beyond the walls.

However, if he was honest, his motivation had been less about that and more an act of spite in retaliation for the attack on his family. Holt's revelation about his father's involvement in this case left Caslin in something of a dilemma. Was Fuller sending him a message that his family were touchable or was the attack aimed squarely at his father? Perhaps it was both. Either way, Caslin chose to respond in kind.

He didn't have long to wait. Within a few minutes, the door to the room opened and Pete Fuller shuffled in. His feet and hands were manacled between ankle and wrists, minimising the length of the steps he could take. He looked older than at their last meeting, arguably suffering from the stricter regime and lack of creature comforts the prison's black-market could provide. Within the centre such luxuries were far harder to come by even for someone as adept as Fuller. He was deposited into his chair and he sank back drawing breath as he eyed Caslin, standing on the other side of the room with his back to the wall. His lips parted in a thin smile, the eyes gleaming with satisfaction.

"Lovely to see you, Inspector Caslin," Pete Fuller said, the smile broadening. He clasped his hands together in front, interlocking the fingers. Caslin looked to the accompanying prison officer.

"You can leave us," he said. The officer cast a glance in his direction and then another at Fuller but didn't question the request.

"Behave yourself, Fuller," he said as he approached the door in an authoritative tone. The prisoner tilted his head slightly to the left but his eyes never left Caslin nor did the smile leave his face. The door slammed shut and Caslin heard the key turn in the lock.

"Alone at last," Fuller said. His eyes scanned the room drifting around the plain walls and back to the table in front of him. He attempted to look beneath it but couldn't angle his body shape to do so because the chair was fixed in place.

"Lost something?" Caslin asked.

"I don't see a recorder," Fuller stated. "And you haven't brought one of your colleagues with you."

"Your point?"

"This an unofficial visit, is it?" he asked, grinning. "How's the family?"

Caslin took a slow deliberate step forward and then launched himself across the room catching the inmate totally by surprise. He grasped Fuller's shirt firmly, first pushing him backwards before pulling him forward and slamming his face against the table. "My kids were there!" Caslin snarled, wrenching Fuller back upright and leaning in with fury written across his face. For his part, Fuller, red faced and wide eyed attempted to throw himself toward Caslin and land a blow with his forehead but Caslin was wise to it and retreated just out of reach. Caslin sent an open-handed slap with the palm of his hand against the side of Fuller's head. The inmate wrestled with his restraints but was powerless to respond.

"You're a *big man*, aren't you, Caslin?" Fuller hissed at him, spittle dropping from his mouth as he spoke. "You think you can walk over me just as yer old man once did, huh? Is that it? Bent coppers run in the family..." Fuller's breathing was ragged, the adrenalin rushing.

Caslin took a step back seeking to calm himself. He hadn't known how he would approach the discussion and was shocked by his own level of aggression. He was astonished at the speed with which he lost control. The realisation struck him that such outbursts were no longer confined to his past. That unnerved him.

"They were my kids," Caslin said, placing clenched fists on the table opposite the chained prisoner. "If you so much as look at my children again, I will bury you."

Fuller glared at him still breathing heavily but the anger dissipating as the seconds passed. "Your father robbed me of nearly thirty years."

"No. He took from you what you stole from others. He's not why you're in here."

"He put me here while he's out there spending *my money*."

"David MacEwan put you in here."

"*MacEwan?*" His eyes narrowed. Not for the first time, Caslin took pause. Fuller watched him intently as if he was assessing the validity of the statement. "He hasn't got the balls."

"You didn't know," Caslin said. Now it was his turn to smile. "All this time here was me thinking you were ahead of the curve and I was playing catch-up and... *you had no idea?*"

"You're messing with me," Fuller said but his expression belied the assumption. The final pieces were fitting into the jigsaw puzzle in his mind and the scale of the deceit was coalescing.

"How frustrating it must be for you," Caslin said, glancing around the room, "to learn of this whilst you are stuck in here."

"How do you figure?"

"By the time you get out of the centre, let alone your jail cell, MacEwan will be in the wind. Taking all your money... and your gold... with him. He's been playing you for nearly three decades. I'm willing to wager you thought he was safeguarding your share whilst all the time he's been setting you up. You and everyone else."

Fuller kept his counsel, Caslin watching as the fury steadily built within him. Finally, he spoke, "There's always a way."

"If you can find him. He's been planning this for months if not years."

"I'll find him," Fuller replied in an icy tone.

"There is another way."

"And that is?"

"You give him to me."

"Fuck off, Caslin."

"Think about it. There's no way I'm going to let MacEwan leave the country. He's making arrangements to do so as we speak. The only way you can be sure of getting to him is to help me."

"And what would that do for me?" Fuller asked.

"You'll know where to find him."

"He'll be inside," Fuller said. Caslin nodded.

"And a man with your connections can always get to him within a prison. Where could he run to?"

"Aiding and abetting, Inspector Caslin?" Fuller asked.

Caslin shrugged, "Once he's jailed that's my job done. MacEwan becomes the responsibility of the prison service. What do I care?" Fuller sat back thinking it over. "Of course, you could take your chances. Perhaps MacEwan will slip past us, get out of the country and disappear. Perhaps you're right and you will be able to find him. He'll only have an eighteen-month head start."

"I won't have to wait."

"Oh… right," Caslin said, leaning against the wall and folding his arms in front of him. "You can rely on Carl and Ashton to step up. The only problem with that plan is that I have them locked up at Fulford Road. Due to the overwhelming evidence amassed against them for Clinton Dade's murder, I was able to extend their custody to the thirty-six-hour mark and they'll be officially charged this afternoon."

"You bastard! They didn't do it. They've been fitted up and you bloody know it."

"Yes. You're right, I do. But that's the thing about the law. It doesn't matter what I know, only what I can prove and I can place your boys at the scene. It's not too big a leap for a jury to put the gun in their hands and thanks to joint enterprise it won't matter who pulled the trigger. They'll both go down for it.

Maybe we can arrange a family reunion here at Full Sutton, what do you think?"

"I'll see your father in here too," Fuller bit back.

"He made his choice and he'll have to live with the consequences," Caslin stated coldly. Allowing the conversation to drop, he waited. The isolation of Fuller's incarceration played into his hands. Caslin was banking on Fuller being ignorant of his sons' release. Although confident it still remained to be seen if he could get this one over the line. After what felt like an age, Fuller sat forward. Placing his elbows on the table and bringing his hands together, he made a tent with his fingers.

"And what makes you so sure I know where MacEwan will be?"

Caslin came to the table and sat down on the free chair directly opposite him. "Because you know MacEwan and he will have found a way to let you know what he was doing with the gold. Otherwise you would have suspected him long ago. Clearly you didn't, which means you trust him. Misplaced trust as it happens. The money's gone, Pete," Caslin argued. "What you can do now is ensure MacEwan gets what he deserves."

Fuller met Caslin's eye, "I can always earn more money."

"Earn is an interesting choice of words but… yes, you can."

"Know this, Caslin," Fuller said, leaning forward and lowering his voice, delivering the words with menace. "This may well allow you to get your hands on MacEwan… but it sure as hell isn't going to keep me from your father."

Caslin felt his blood run cold. "I know you've got everyone who wronged you in your sights but… I'm sure there's a compromise to be had." Fuller flinched almost imperceptibly but the movement was there, nonetheless. He was curious. "There must be something we can do to… alleviate the situation."

Fuller sat back glancing up at the camera in the ceiling and then back to Caslin. "What do you have in mind?"

"My father never touched his share of the money. Everything

he had is safe. None of it is traceable as far as I know and sitting in various accounts on the continent."

"Just what are you offering, Inspector Caslin?" Fuller asked, the reappearance of the thin smile crossing his lips once again.

"You know what I'm offering."

"*I want to hear you say the words,*" Fuller said in a whisper.

Caslin took a deep breath. "The money he took… in exchange for his life."

"There… that wasn't so hard," Fuller replied, grinning. "One more thing, Inspector."

"And what's that?"

"Don't think that this settles everything and leaves us even. If you make this deal, you should know that it means more than just your father's safety."

"Yeah, and what does that *mean*?"

"After this you will be my man now," Fuller said quietly, ensuring with his expression that Caslin knew exactly what he was implying. He lowered his right hand extending it across the table, palm up. Caslin looked at it and then into the eyes of the man offering it. Tentatively, he reached out and accepted the handshake. Immediately, Fuller took a firm grip and dragged Caslin towards him. At the same time, he threw himself forward and head butted Caslin square in the face. Caslin's vision momentarily went dark as a searing pain shot upwards and into his brain, all awareness overcome by a wave of nausea that swept over him.

Caslin struggled to break free from Fuller's grip but the hold was too strong. No matter how much he tried to pull away, he couldn't. Seconds passed that felt like minutes as he strained against Fuller's iron grip. There was movement around them as the door burst open and two prison officers entered.

Grunts and raised voices came to Caslin's ear as his senses reasserted themselves. The officers were attempting to free him. Just as he thought he would never break loose, the hold was broken and Caslin's momentum carried him backwards and he almost fell, recoiling from his attacker. Throwing out his arms, he braced against the wall to stop himself from slumping to the floor. Blinking furiously, lights danced before his eyes and something wet was running across his mouth. Steadying himself with one hand against the wall, he probed the area of his face with the other. Taking his hand away, he saw the fingers were covered in blood. It was pouring from his nose and further inspection made him think it might be broken. His mouth was wet and Caslin swallowed hard.

The unmistakable taste of his own blood made him feel sick. Looking back across to the other side of the room, Fuller was grappling with the two prison officers as they unceremoniously attempted to drag him from the room.

"Wait!" Caslin yelled and both men stopped. Fuller ceased his resistance. The bottom half of his body lay on the ground with his legs behind him, his torso supported in the air. Each officer had a firm grip under Fuller's armpits. The inmate made their task harder by holding his manacled hands aloft, extending his arms fully to ensure they had as little purchase on his body as possible. His shirt was half pulled over his head. The struggle was certainly not over, not unless Fuller wanted it to be. Caslin stumbled over holding one hand against his nose in an attempt to stem the flow of blood.

Fuller stared up at him. His face was flushed with all the exertion of the moment but his eyes shone with satisfaction.

"Where will I find MacEwan?" Caslin asked, taking his hand away from his face and snorting up blood that threatened to flow. Fuller's breath came in short ragged gasps.

"White Hart Farm," Fuller whispered in between breaths. "Just south of Reighton. You'll never tie it to him... but that's where it should be."

"Reighton," Caslin repeated.

Fuller nodded. "It's a good deal, Inspector Caslin. You remember that."

"Get him out of here," Caslin said and both the officers

resumed their efforts. The prisoner offered no further resistance but did nothing to assist. Fuller was dragged from the room. All the while his eyes never diverted from Caslin.

Watching on, Caslin felt a sense of shame that he had never previously experienced.

CHAPTER TWENTY-SEVEN

THE VILLAGE of Reighton sat on the cusp of the border between north Yorkshire and the East Riding, on the coast. With a population of fewer than five-hundred residents the assembling of an armed assault team would be sure to make waves amongst the locals. To that end, Caslin addressed his team in the relative obscurity of a yard owned by a small haulage firm in the nearby village of Grindale. The premises were located on the site of a former agricultural facility used for storing and processing grain. The silos were long gone and the concrete hard standing was being utilised by the current owners for trailer parking. There were no permanent offices on site and the route to the entrance along the access road took them far from the main highway. A line of trees was a bonus providing them with an extra screen to shield them from curious eyes.

Caslin walked to the head of the group, each member was busy checking and rechecking their equipment was in order. They arrived under the cover of darkness several hours before sunrise and would soon decamp in order to carry out their objective. The radio crackled and Caslin brought it up. Hunter was in situ several hundred metres away from the gated entrance to White Hart Farm where Pete Fuller had told them to expect to find MacEwan. A surveillance operation on MacEwan's scrap metal business rewarded them with little information. There had been no activity there in the previous couple of days. Likewise, a check with the border force delivered no hits on his passport recording him leaving the UK. It would appear he was prepping for his departure. Either that or he was already gone.

"Go ahead," Caslin said, depressing the talk button.

"It's quiet," Hunter told him in a calm and authoritative tone. "There's been no movement since we've been here."

"Okay, keep me posted."

Caslin surveyed the men and women readying themselves to raid the farm. Twenty officers, specially trained in weapons and tactics, were preparing to advance on MacEwan's location. The anticipation was building and so was the anxiety. The officer with operational control, Chas Freeman, approached alongside Assistant Chief Constable Broadfoot. Caslin knew the former quite well, a highly skilled and competent specialist. Caslin greeted both of them.

"Any further word on the numbers we're expecting to encounter?" Freeman asked.

Caslin shook his head. "Not yet. There's no sign of movement in or out according to my people on the ground.

"So, we might encounter no resistance at all?"

"Unlikely... If our source is correct then I would expect a handful but no more than ten. MacEwan has never been seen with a massive entourage. Besides, in this case, it'll draw too much attention to them and he wants to leave unnoticed."

"Fair enough."

"You still want to take them at the farm and not wait for them to leave?" Broadfoot asked. "They would be constrained by their vehicles."

"Once they're on the move we'll be into *hard stop protocols,*" Freeman explained. "Although my people can most likely control it, multiple targets will add to the risk for both them and us. Not forgetting the members of the public. I'd rather strike at the farm where we can keep those risks to a minimum. Our surveillance of the site yesterday showed that the farmhouse itself is in such a state of disrepair that it's unlikely they will be using it. In all likelihood, they will be housed in one of the outbuildings. We will take them there."

"Understood," Broadfoot said.

"My team are ready to deploy," Freeman stated, adjusting his earpiece.

"Let's do it," Caslin replied, glancing at Broadfoot who nodded. Freeman called out the order and en masse they clambered into vehicles, a mixture of unmarked saloons and SUVs.

Caslin indicated in the direction of his car and Broadfoot fell into step alongside him. Caslin cast an eye skywards as they walked. Dawn was breaking and for the first time in days it promised to be a bright start. There were few clouds overhead. Today, he would have gladly embraced the darkness. The overcast mornings they'd been getting used to would have given them the added advantage of masking their approach. With a bit of luck, MacEwan would be caught completely unawares. Reaching the car and opening his door, he got in. Broadfoot went to the passenger side and joined him. The senior officer was nervous, too, Caslin could tell, but his ability to hide his emotion was far superior to his own. Lifting the radio, he contacted Hunter.

"Any change?"

"None," came the reply.

"We're inbound," Caslin stated. "ETA is about five minutes."

"Roger that," Hunter confirmed.

Caslin felt his stomach churn. The last-minute doubts that always struck him whenever he rolled the dice, were clear and present. If this proved to be an impulsive act based on poor intelligence, then he would be at fault. The responsibility lay with him and his assessment of Fuller's credibility. As the minutes ticked past, he couldn't help but wonder whether or not this was a gamble he should have initiated. If MacEwan evaded capture in this raid, then they would have shown their hand and alerted him to their interest. He hadn't been seen in days and the fear that he'd already left the country was also chipping away at Caslin's confidence. The only way they could tie him to any of this was to catch him in the act. There was no other material evidence. Should this day end empty handed then, in all likelihood, their shot at MacEwan would have passed. Going along with it would be Caslin's chances of protecting his father.

Starting the car, he selected first gear and accelerated away in pursuit of the strike team. They would carry out the raid and once the suspects were in custody and the scene secured, Caslin could then move in. Catching up to the rear of the convoy, he slowed the car down. They were less than two miles from the farm and the operation was expected to be over within minutes of them entering.

"How confident are you with the accuracy of Fuller's information?" Broadfoot asked for what must have been the fourth or fifth time.

"As confident as I can be," Caslin replied, following the lead of the cars in front as they were forced up onto the grass verge in order to pass a tractor they'd come upon on the narrow lane. "We searched the ownership of White Hart Farm and what Fuller told us certainly checked out. MacEwan is the proprietor. He purchased the farmhouse and all the ancillary buildings twenty-five years ago but has never run it as a going concern or listed it against any of his other businesses. The ownership is via a series of shell companies, all of which are registered outside of Europe. Without Fuller's information, we would never have come across it. It stands to reason he has kept it off the books for a purpose we're not aware of."

"If Fuller's on the level, then we're in for a big day," Broadfoot said.

"Yes, sir."

"Tell me," Broadfoot began, changing tone. "Where are we with identifying Jody's killer?"

Caslin didn't doubt his commanding officer's commitment to breaking this case but his personal angle was equally important to him if not more so. The murder of his godson was an open wound that he wanted to close. "We are still unsure as to why he was killed, sir. By all accounts, he was following up on the inquiry his father worked in the 80s but as to why, or to what depth he reached in doing so, we still don't know. We think we've identified his girlfriend and once we've tracked her down, she may be able to provide some answers."

"Yes, Louise. Scott Tarbet's daughter. Hunter filled me in," Broadfoot said. "You've had no joy in locating her?"

"No, sir. Not so far. Because of the obvious association with her father, the lead witness in Bradley's faked death, I'm reluctant to descend on her network with all of our resources. She's disappeared from sight and is probably using friends or relatives to help keep her head down. We could pick her up at one of their addresses but equally we could miss her. If so, she might be spooked and take off. So far, she's been quite adept at staying under the radar and when we have the chance, I don't want her to slip past us."

"Hmm…" Broadfoot murmured, an indication tantamount to disagreement. Caslin glanced across at him.

"She will be my next priority after we take down MacEwan, sir. You have my word."

Broadfoot remained silent for a few moments before cracking a thin smile. "I don't doubt it. Thank you, Nathaniel."

They crossed over the main Scarborough Road bringing them to a point just south of the village of Reighton and within direct view of the sea. An orange glow spread as far as the eye could see as the sun crested the horizon.

Caslin brought his radio up to his mouth, "You should be seeing us any moment." The convoy took the next right and soon came upon Hunter sitting in her car in a layby screened from the main road by overgrown foliage. As they passed, she started the engine and pulled out behind Caslin picking up the rear. "We'll hang back and let Freeman lead the assault. Once we have the all-clear, we'll go in and bring out our guy."

"Can't wait," Hunter replied.

The target area had been reconnoitred in great detail on the previous evening but no one managed to get close enough to observe any movement on the site. Vehicles were present parked under cover in one of the barns and light was visible from within another.

The convoy took the turn off the highway and onto the farm's approach road at speed. A more clandestine approach was proposed, considered, and roundly rejected due to the topography of the surrounding farmland. In every direction the terrain was flat giving rise to concerns that the assault team would be too exposed to mount a successful operation. The suspects would potentially have a three-hundred-and-sixty-degree view with which to spot their arrival. The access road to the farm was both the one way in and out. A high-speed assault along with the element of surprise was determined to yield the greatest chance of success.

They sped up the access road and into the complex of agricultural buildings, a horseshoe set up of brick barns behind the dilapidated farmhouse. The incumbents within each car were aware of their individual tasks and had their feet on the ground before any of the vehicles came to a full stop. The first team moved on the farmhouse and the remainder fanned out with the intention of sweeping the adjoining buildings. Caslin and Hunter pulled up outside of the yard, parking their cars horizontally across the access road in an attempt to cut off any escape route. Hunter got out of her car and joined Caslin and Broadfoot as they took cover behind their vehicles. The three of them waited patiently, listening to the discussion of the assault team as they relayed their progress via an open communication link. Caslin looked around, showing concern.

"What is it?" Broadfoot asked.

"I don't see their cars."

"No one left last night," Hunter said.

The first minute of the assault seemed to pass slowly as the team battered in doors to gain entry but with the passing of each subsequent one, Caslin felt his confidence ebb. The assault team were split into five groups of four and were proceeding to sweep the interior, shouts sporadically coming their way through the speaker to indicate another room was successfully cleared. There were no shots and no apparent sign of resistance. A quick glance towards Hunter revealed her thoughts were similar to his. Caslin rubbed at his forehead. Those who entered the farmhouse appeared outside once again, making for the ancillary buildings to support their colleagues. Despite the absence of an opposition they moved as a unit with weapons at the ready to respond at any given moment. Until they knew the scene was secure, they would proceed with caution.

"This isn't good," Caslin muttered under his breath. Broadfoot glanced at him but said nothing. The disappointment was etched into his face. Within moments their fears were realised as Chas Freeman's voice came across the radio.

"The scene is secure. Zero contact," he said quietly. "They're gone."

Caslin's heart sank and he let out a deep sigh. He was gutted. "Shit."

"How is that possible?" Broadfoot asked.

Caslin shook his head. "There must be another access to the farm that we missed. It was dark last night, a lot of cloud cover."

"There's nothing on the map," Hunter said, disappointed.

Caslin inclined his head in the direction of the yard indicating they should go in. "It might not even be on the map. These farms have been here for centuries. Who knows when the paths were last documented?"

They came out from behind the cars and headed for the yard. By the time the three of them entered, the assault team were already coming out. The built-up tension of the previous fourteen hours had now dissipated to be replaced by a deep sense of frustration. Freeman appeared from the cart entrance to one of the barns crossing the uneven cobbles to meet them.

"Well, someone's been inside," he said, looking to Broadfoot before Caslin and pointing to the building he'd just come from. "Someone's dropped a bollock though because they're definitely not here now."

"How long?" Caslin asked.

"I'd say recently. Very recent, if I had to guess."

"Thanks, Chas," Caslin said, walking past him. Freeman set about organising his team's withdrawal. "Come on. Let's take a look."

They entered the barn and looked around. There was nothing of note to set their eyes upon but in stark contrast to the attached farmhouse this section of the farm appeared to be better cared for. The floor was concrete, showing signs of cracking and breaking up in places but didn't appear prone to damp. In fact the closed shutters hid windows that were in good condition and a brief inspection of the locks to them and the doors revealed they were relatively new and in perfect working order. At one end of the barn were a couple of tables and some casual chairs. Hunter crossed to the table and examined some discarded wrapping and plastic bags.

"Interesting," she said, rummaging through one of the bags.

"What's that?" Caslin asked. He went to join her while Broadfoot walked around scanning the interior for something, anything, to assist the investigation.

"Takeaway containers," Hunter said, focussing on the contents. She brought out a slip of paper that was scrunched into a ball. As she unfurled it, Caslin could see it was a receipt. "Dated yesterday," she confirmed, passing it to him. Caslin took it and briefly read through what was listed on it.

"What do you think? Four, maybe five people?" he asked. Hunter nodded. "That's be my guess."

"It looks like Fuller sold you a pup," Broadfoot stated, coming to stand with them.

"Not necessarily, sir," Caslin replied, passing him the receipt. Broadfoot eyed it suspiciously but having checked the date, he looked to Caslin.

"Then we've missed them."

Caslin thought on it. Turning to Hunter, he asked, "You were in position from what… four o'clock yesterday?"

"A little after, yes."

"And no one came or went after that time?"

"A car came in a little after seven but no one left."

Caslin crossed to one of the windows and opened it pushing the shutter away. He looked to the rear of the complex. There was a dirt track heading across the field to the east. "So, that receipt was time and date stamped at seven o'clock when they bought it."

"Yes."

"It's a bit late in the day to make a big move, isn't it? They wouldn't decamp across there in the dark at that time. If they were going to they would have left earlier."

"Not gone to pick up a takeaway, you mean?" Hunter said.

"Exactly. Which means they were on the move early this morning. How was MacEwan shipping the gold out previously? Via his boatyard up the coast," Caslin said, remembering the details his father provided him with. "What if he's doing the same now?"

Hunter shook her head, "I went through his business interests with Holt. He offloaded that boatyard years ago."

Caslin's theory fell apart before he had even begun to flesh it out. He sighed. The sense of disappointment among them was palpable.

"Keep at it," Broadfoot demanded. "I'll head back with Freeman. Get back to me with your next steps by the close of play."

Their commanding officer walked away without another

word. Caslin closed his eyes and grimaced. "There goes an unhappy man," Hunter said softly, watching Broadfoot leave ensuring only Caslin could hear her words.

"Get on to Terry back at Fulford. Have him run down the businesses that we know MacEwan has a stake in along with any residences, land or assets within a fifty-mile radius of this location. We're due a bit of luck. We still have time. We know the area they're in which narrows down the search parameters," Caslin said, conveying confidence that Hunter didn't share.

They stepped outside into bright sunlight. The smell of the sea carried to them on the breeze. Freeman and his team were finishing the packing up of their gear into the lock boxes of their vehicles and were now preparing to leave. Caslin thrust his hands into his coat pockets. Despite the sun the day was still freezing.

"I had better move my car so they can get out," Hunter said, striding away. Caslin acknowledged Freeman's wave as he got into the passenger seat of his Range Rover. The car pulled away followed closely by the other four vehicles. Judging from the forlorn expressions on the departing faces the morning failed to match up to their expectations. Caslin's phone was vibrating in his pocket and he took it out. Glancing at the screen it showed a number he didn't recognise. His first thought was of Pete Fuller but he knew he was still being held in isolation at Full Sutton. He tapped the answer tab.

"DI Caslin," he said, watching the last of the vehicles drive out of the yard.

"Is that Inspector Caslin?" a man's voice asked. It seemed remotely familiar to him but he couldn't quite place where he recognised it from let alone assign a face or a name.

"Yes, it is. Who is this?"

"It's Geoff. Geoff Thomas."

"From…?" Caslin asked, straining to remember where they'd met.

"From Flamborough Head. I run the café, out at the…"

"Lighthouse," Caslin said. "Of course. What can I do for you, Geoff?"

"I'm sorry to bother you so early but there are some strange goings on out here this morning, Inspector. Not sure what to make of it to be honest."

CHAPTER TWENTY-EIGHT

THE COASTAL ROAD was set back barely half a mile from the sea, picking its way through farmland to either side. The main road, the A165, carried you inland down to Bridlington, south of Flamborough and further around the coast. The road Caslin took was more direct and less travelled but the trade-off was the increased journey time. Easing out of his lane to get a better view, he sought to pass the slow-moving car in front only to be forced back as the oncoming vehicle flashed its lights and sounded a warning blast of its horn. Even at this speed the journey itself should only take fifteen minutes. The dashboard lit up to signal he had an incoming call. He looked to the heads-up display and saw it was Terry Holt.

"What did you find out?" Caslin asked, dispensing with the customary greetings. Leaving Hunter back at White Hart Farm to secure the scene and await the forensic search team, the call from Flamborough Head had piqued his curiosity.

"A lot of historical info about when it was built…"

"Skip the history, Terry."

"Sorry," Holt replied. "Trinity still own, maintain and run the lighthouse although it's a fully automated system now so they haven't needed keepers for twenty-odd years. However, what is interesting to us is that once they took the lighthouse under remote operation, they retained the tower and fog warning station whilst selling off the attached real estate."

"Who bought it?" Caslin asked.

"That's what's taken me the time. It's another case of a company within a company. Well, more like several companies within several more," Holt continued. "Long story short – I don't know… yet. What I would say is the ownership is so vague that I wouldn't be surprised if it turns out we can tie it to one of MacEwan's shells. I always get suspicious when the answers aren't obvious. I wouldn't necessarily put money on it…"

"If you were playing the percentages?"

"Seeing as MacEwan is in the area and Bradley was recently as well. I'd say pretty high," Holt replied. "Is Hunter there with you?"

"No," Caslin replied, dropping through the gears, indicating and pulling out into oncoming traffic and forcing his way through much to the annoyance of other road users. "I left her back at the farm."

"That's not good," Holt stated, concern edging into his voice. "I think we may have just found…"

"Where MacEwan is. I know but let's not get carried away," Caslin said. "Call Hunter and tell her what's going on. I'll check it out."

"What about ACC Broadfoot?" Holt asked, thinking ahead.

Caslin was reticent, worried about raising the alarm on the back of a hunch. "Our local contact advised me there were a handful of them coming and going this morning. They were there when he arrived to unlock his business. If it is MacEwan, we have to assume they are moving what they have and using the lighthouse as a way station. If it's them, I'll try and slow them down."

"If they're there what were they keeping at White Hart Farm?" Holt asked. It was a good question. "Never mind. I'll get onto them."

"Thanks, Terry," Caslin said, hanging up. He swore loudly, frustrated at his lack of forethought.

In all likelihood, Bradley wasn't out at Flamborough to meet someone or not primarily in any event. If their theory was right, then he probably knew MacEwan owned the buildings and was observing them but to what end, he couldn't say. Caslin's mind was reeling as he made yet another unadvised passing manoeuvre. This time, he was forced to apply his brakes and swerve back into his lane to avoid a certain head-on collision with an oncoming van.

Moments later, he came upon the outskirts of Flamborough town itself. The route circumvented the centre and he reached a junction. Turning left and heading directly to the coast, Caslin was acutely aware there was only one road to or from Flamborough Head and he was driving along it. Keeping his eyes trained on the road, Caslin paid attention to the traffic passing in the opposite direction. Unsure of what MacEwan could have stashed out here, they could be using any type of vehicle. The location came to the forefront of his mind. No one would think to look out here but equally the nearby farm was just as remote and safe from prying eyes. There was a reason. There had to be. Perhaps MacEwan had several locations he was using to spread the risk of discovery.

There was little movement on the road and Caslin suddenly felt vulnerable as he approached the visitors' car park. The wide-open expanse in the run up to the lighthouse left him exposed. Caslin pulled in to Selwick Drive, the residential road set across from the lighthouse to the rear of the café. Should anyone be paying attention, he could be taken as visiting friends or returning home. He parked the car with his target still roughly one hundred yards distant and the café and gift shop between them. From his vantage point, he could see two cars and a van parked alongside the lighthouse's outer perimeter wall. There was another mini-van a short distance away and Caslin considered one of these must belong to the café's proprietor who had called him earlier. No one was visible and after a few moments, Caslin knew he would need to get closer. If he couldn't confirm the theory, then there was no point in his being there.

Getting out of the car, he shut the door and scanned the nearby vicinity. It was still early and there didn't appear to be many residents in and around the nearby assortment of bungalows. Those in employment had probably already left for work and the remainder were still behind drawn curtains. The wind coming in off the North Sea was strong with frequent gusts buffeting him as he set off across the open ground towards the lighthouse. Caslin used the café as a cover for his approach. The only part of the complex where he could be seen was from within the tower of the lighthouse itself.

Coming to the white buildings, Caslin slipped between a storage block and the café approaching the rear door to the kitchen. It was closed but he saw movement on the other side. He rapped his knuckles on the glass three times. Moments later, a figure appeared on the other side distorted by the obscured glass. The door cracked open and a face peered hesitantly through the gap.

"Geoff? It's DI Caslin," he said, needlessly lowering his voice for there was no way anyone would be able to overhear their conversation. The door opened wider and the familiar face of the café's owner appeared.

"Come in," he said, stepping back.

"You're on edge," Caslin stated. The man nodded.

"It's that lot, over there," Geoff said, indicating with a flick of his head in the direction of the lighthouse. "They were here when I arrived. One of them didn't take kindly to me looking at them."

"What did he say?"

"Nah… it was more the look he gave me. I called the wife – told her he was a wrong-un. Not someone I want to meet on a dark night for sure."

"What are they up to, do you think?" Caslin asked. "How many are in there?"

"Four or five, I reckon," Geoff confirmed. "And I've no idea what they're up to. Never seen them here before either. I probably wouldn't have given it much thought except Mary remembered your visit and suggested I give you a call. What do you think is going on?"

Caslin looked past him and out of the window towards the lighthouse. All was quiet. "I don't know but..." he said, addressing him directly, "it's best if you stay in the kitchen out of the way for the time being. Is it just you here?"

Geoff nodded. "But we have staff arriving in the next half-hour. Is that all right?"

Caslin looked at the clock. It was approaching 8 a.m. and he did a quick calculation in his head. He knew Hunter would be here soon enough but how long it might take for Broadfoot to arrive with the armed support was anyone's guess and he still needed confirmation. He didn't want to put any members of the public in danger but by the same token, he couldn't risk the word getting around to the residents there was a police operation underway. "Do your staff arrive by car?"

"Usually, yes."

"Where do they park?"

"At the back, behind the café."

"And they enter the same way I did?" Caslin asked. Geoff nodded, suddenly looking concerned. "That should be fine but do me a favour, would you? I want you to let me out of the front door but then close it behind me and keep it locked. No one in that way, no one out. Understood?" Geoff nodded vigorously.

Walking to the front entrance, Caslin peered out of the window but still didn't see any indication of movement. The perimeter wall was five foot high and curved around the building with the access to the visitors' car park passing alongside. The wall met a double-entry gate alongside the head of the coastal walking trail, itself a similar height, and offered access to both the lighthouse complex and the monitoring station on the nearby point. Nodding at Geoff, the owner stepped forward and turned the key in the lock before sliding back the bolts, located top and bottom, and pulled the door open. Caslin took his radio from his pocket and switched it off before setting his mobile to silent. The last thing he wanted was for either of them to give away his position at an inappropriate moment.

"Thanks," Caslin said, slipping out. He heard the bolts being slammed back in place and got the impression Geoff would be on the phone to his wife within seconds. He figured it didn't matter. Turning right as he left the café, he squeezed between the outside seating and hopped over the knee-high boundary wall of the outside dining area. Hugging the exterior wall of the gift shop, Caslin reached the corner of the building and eyed the fifty feet of open space between himself and the lighthouse's boundary wall. Breaking into a run, he covered the distance as quickly as he could and dropped to his haunches alongside the first of the parked vehicles.

Popping his head up, he looked for a reaction to his approach but everything remained quiet. This close to the wall, he had no chance of seeing over it so he crept forward keeping low until he reached the brick. The gate was further around and to his left. Caslin ignored it, instead choosing to move to his right. As the wall began to curve, he stopped. Level with the tower, Caslin turned and backed up a couple of steps in order to be able to get a run at the wall. Three quick steps forward and he leapt up throwing his arms over and gripping the edge of the wall on the other side. Scrambling up with confidence that the tower masked his efforts, Caslin hauled himself up onto the top. Keeping himself flat, he rolled over and dropped his legs down the other side. Carefully lowering himself to the ground, he stopped to listen to the sound of the waves crashing upon the rocks – the only sound.

Moving quickly and with purpose, Caslin made his way around the tower keeping as close to the wall as he could. With every step the attached building revealed itself and Caslin felt his vulnerability increase. Each window was an opportunity for those inside to see him. With no way of knowing the interior layout, he had no ability to mitigate the chance of discovery. That is if they were still inside. The building attached to the lighthouse was rectangular and double storey. As Caslin came around the side, he chanced a look through a small ground-floor window. The glass was dirty and smudged to such an extent that he couldn't make out much detail. It appeared to be a storeroom of some description and barely six feet square. Content that he wouldn't be seen at this point, he moved on, skirting the side of the building and passing to the rear.

Peering around the corner, he came upon a grassed area reasonably well maintained and encompassed entirely by the perimeter wall. From here, Caslin could see the access gates on the far side. Movement in the corner of his eye caused him to freeze in position pressing his back to the wall and attempting to become one with it. It was the form of a figure passing by the window next to him and once confident that he wouldn't be seen, Caslin slowly leaned over in order to see through it. He could make out three people standing together plus the one who'd originally caught his eye. Due to the build-up of muck and grime on the glass, he was unable to identify any of them. Scanning the interior, he sought an access point that might allow him to eavesdrop or at the very least give him a decent view of them. The interior was mostly open plan from what he could tell. The door to the storage room he had just walked past was ajar on the far side but apart from that the only other option appeared to be the main access door.

Easing himself away from the window, he made his way back around from where he had come. His confidence boosted, he made a more detailed assessment of the room. It appeared to be a large store cupboard, an offshoot from a kitchenette and probably converted at some point post construction. The window was secure appearing to have been painted shut years ago. In any event, it was probably too small for him to fit through. Caslin could see light coming into the room from above. There was a drainpipe running down the corner of the exterior where the building met the base of the tower and Caslin gave it a tug. It was cast iron and felt securely fastened to the wall. With great care, he reached up and then used the ninety-degree junction between the buildings to brace against as he began the short climb. The flat roof was only around seven feet above the ground and Caslin made the ascent with relative ease.

Once on the top, Caslin made his way to the skylight. It was single-glazed and in a poor state of repair. The frame was steel and the combination of the salt air and sea mist had corroded many of the fixings. Even a cursory attempt to prise it saw enough movement to indicate his efforts would bear fruit. Taking a firm grip with both hands, Caslin levered the frame from side to side and found he was able to lift it from its housing with minimal noise and exertion. Placing it down at his side, he looked into the room below. The sound of muffled voices came to him but they were too distorted to comprehend. The drop of seven feet wasn't going to be a problem because there was a table set almost directly beneath the skylight but the gap to squeeze through was only marginally wider than Caslin's upper body.

Lowering his feet through first, he braced both arms at either side and eased himself through the gap. Momentarily fearful he might fall, Caslin wondered whether he should retreat but realised he was already committed. Levering himself to one side, he put his left arm down, supporting himself with only his right. The strain was immense and he struggled to regulate his breathing as his chest was clamped to the sides of the opening, legs flailing as they sought to gain purchase on the table beneath. Ultimately, he reached the point where he had little choice but to have faith in his plan and make the drop.

Hitting the table with a thud saw him immediately off balance. His inability to look beneath him and therefore to properly assess the drop made his landing awkward. In trying to counter balance, Caslin overcompensated and fell backwards off the table. Despite managing to get his feet out from under him and break his fall, he still staggered into the opposing wall. Holding his breath, he waited for the shout to go up signifying his discovery but it didn't come. Breathing a silent sigh of relief, he crept to the doorway and peered into the next room through the gap between door and frame.

Three figures were in view although one, a woman, stood with her back to him. She was a brunette and her hair was cut short. She was dressed in hiking gear. Of the other two, Caslin recognised both Mark Bridger, who was similarly attired to the woman, and the man who was currently speaking, David MacEwan.

"You told me he would be here," MacEwan said. Despite being unable to see the entire room and anyone who might be out of view, Caslin guessed he was addressing the woman. A theory confirmed by her response.

"And he *will be*," she replied. MacEwan swore under his breath. "You just have to be patient. With this wind, the swell will be up…"

"We should have been out of here before sunrise," MacEwan snapped. Turning to someone out of view, he said, "It was your bloody plan. The longer we stay here the greater the chance of them finding us."

"They didn't see us leaving the farm this morning and they haven't tied this place to you in twenty years, so there's no reason they should now," a calm voice argued but Caslin couldn't see who it belonged to. He tried to improve his angle of vision but to no avail.

"He'll be here," the woman repeated.

"Well, he better be here soon," MacEwan said, looking to Mark Bridger beside him. Caslin was quite taken by how rattled he appeared to be. For all his perceived connections and criminal participation over the years, MacEwan struck him as a nervous individual quite far removed from the imposing figure of his imagination. The sound of the main entrance door opening and a burst of noise from the outside came along with it as another person entered. Caslin shifted position again and eyed the newcomer. He was athletically built and walked with the poise of a military man. Caslin assumed he was another of MacEwan's men.

"Is he here, Brad?" MacEwan asked the new arrival.

"He's here," the man confirmed. "He's dropped anchor and is bringing the boat in now."

"It's about bloody time."

"You see," Ollie Bridger said, striding into view from Caslin's right. "Nothing to worry about." He walked towards MacEwan and tapped Brad on the side of his arm in an overly friendly gesture. "Let's get things down there."

"Wait," MacEwan said. Ollie turned to face him with an inquiring look on his face. "It's too late. People might see. We should call it off today."

"No way," Ollie replied, shaking his head and coming back to stand before MacEwan. "We're too far advanced for that. I know I said they won't find us but tomorrow's another day."

"No. It's too risky now. We should have been gone under cover of darkness."

Ollie looked to his brother who met his eye. The two exchanged something unsaid between them. The significance of which only brothers as close as they were would comprehend. "Do you think?" Ollie asked.

Mark shrugged, "It was going to be later… but now is as good a time as any."

"Fair enough," Ollie said, drawing a concealed pistol from the rear of his waistband.

"What are you doing?" MacEwan barked. In one fluid motion, Ollie brought the gun to bear and shot MacEwan twice in quick succession, once in the upper thigh of each leg.

CHAPTER TWENTY-NINE

THE GANGSTER SCREAMED and collapsed as his legs gave out beneath him. Caslin jumped back in shock, overbalancing and stumbled, falling backwards. Reaching out and grasping a shelf he attempted to break his fall but it failed to support his weight, breaking away from the brackets holding it in place. Caslin hit the ground hard with the contents of the shelf coming down on top of him. A further two shots sounded coming almost on top of one another. Then silence descended for a few seconds before a final, solitary shot echoed around the building.

Caslin was momentarily frozen in place. *Had the shots and the screams masked the sound of his fall?* Listening carefully, the sound of MacEwan groaning carried through from the adjoining room.

"I can't believe the bastard shot me!" he heard Mark Bridger say. He sounded surprisingly calm. Tentatively, Caslin detached himself from the miscellaneous items in and around him, careful not to make any further noise.

"It wasn't supposed to go down like that, Ollie," the woman's voice said.

"Plans change, Babe," Ollie replied and footsteps could be heard echoing on the concrete floor.

Managing to get to his feet without drawing attention to

himself, Caslin shook his head. He had no idea what his next move should be. Listening in, the woman was talking about the swell. With a boat anchored off the coast they were planning to move their haul out of the country by sea after all. Caslin looked at his watch carrying out a mental calculation in his head. Returning to his vantage point, he peered through the crack once more. Something crossed his sightline completely obscuring his view. He flinched taking a step backwards vainly hoping not to be seen. It was already too late. The door opened fully and there she stood with a gun trained on him. Her hair was far shorter and by the look of it recently dyed but she was unmistakable. Louise Bennett looked him up and down, smiling.

"Inspector Caslin," she said. "Very nice of you to join us."

She gestured for him to come towards her with the barrel of the gun, walking backwards as she did so. Caslin raised his hands slightly, palms up in a gesture of subservience. Stepping through into the room beyond, Caslin got his first look at what just happened. MacEwan lay where he had fallen with blood pooling around his legs. He was breathing heavily, ashen-faced and most likely experiencing the onset of shock. To their left the man MacEwan identified as Brad lay prostrate on the ground with what appeared to be a gunshot wound to the chest and another to the head. The latter was dead centre in his forehead, execution style. A semi-automatic pistol lay to his right as if he'd lost his grip on it as he went down.

Mark Bridger was sitting on the ground nearby cradling a pistol in his lap. Ollie had placed his own weapon on the floor next to them and was tending to his brother. Neither man paid Caslin much attention. Ollie levered his brother's arm from the sleeve of his jacket rather unceremoniously which brought a howl of derision as a fresh wave of pain struck.

"Bloody hell, man," Mark said.

"Behave," Ollie replied, taking out a knife from his pocket and widening the opening in the sleeve of Mark's undershirt in order to inspect the wound. Checking both sides of the arm,

Ollie gently patted his sibling's cheek. "It went clean through, little brother. You're going to be fine."

"That's easy for you to say," Mark replied. "You're not sitting here with a hole in your arm."

Ollie took the knife and cut the remainder of the sleeve off. Using it as a makeshift dressing, he tied it around the wound, tightening it which brought forward yet another complaint. Glancing to Louise, he flicked his eyes towards a window overlooking the approach road.

"Take a look," Ollie instructed her before retrieving his gun, standing and coming over to Caslin. Louise backed up a couple of steps ensuring she kept her weapon fixed on Caslin and quickly looked around outside. Ollie Bridger used both of his hands to frisk Caslin, presumably hunting for either a weapon or technology to indicate he was in communication with the outside world. He took Caslin's mobile as well as his radio.

"It looks clear out there," Louise said, coming back.

"I fear I may have underestimated you," Ollie told him.

"People often do," Caslin replied.

"I didn't think you'd piece it together this quickly. Although," Ollie said, glancing around, "this probably wasn't your most intelligent move."

"You'll get no argument from me."

There was a flash of light in Ollie's hand as the screen lit up to display an incoming call. Ollie's eyes lowered to the mobile phone in his hand. Caslin flicked his eyes to Louise as she shifted position slightly. Any doubts he may have had around her ability with firearms were dismissed as Caslin realised she was ensuring Ollie was out of her firing line if he should make a move. He had no intention of doing so.

"I'm very sorry, Inspector but you're going to miss Hunter's call," Ollie declared, dropping the mobile onto the floor. The screen smashed and then he stamped on it with the heel of his boot. Caslin winced as he heard the crunch and saw the screen go blank.

"What are we going to do with him?" Louise said, indicating MacEwan with a tilt of the head. Ollie glanced at the gangster lying on the floor and then back at Caslin. With a slight shake of the head, he left his side and crossed to MacEwan. He beckoned his brother to come over and Mark laboured to his feet. The two brothers stood over the stricken man.

"You thought you were so clever, didn't you?" Mark said.

"You want it all. Is that it?" MacEwan said.

"This wasn't about money," Mark replied.

"Thought you could grass on our father and get away with it," Ollie said. "You've been around enough. You know what happens to the likes of you." The brothers brought up their guns and aimed them at MacEwan. Ollie cracked a smile whereas Mark remained stone-faced.

"Fuck you!" MacEwan hissed just before both brothers squeezed their triggers. Two shots sounded throughout the room as MacEwan's head fell backwards striking the floor. Ollie raised a hand and placed it on his brother's shoulder applying an affectionate squeeze.

"It's done," he said softly.

Mark met his brother's eye and nodded before looking at Caslin. "And him?"

"Yes, what are we going to do with Caslin Junior? You've got some balls coming in here by yourself," Ollie said.

Caslin shrugged. "I could say similar to you."

"How so?"

"You and your brother going up against Fuller, Dade…" Caslin said, glancing at MacEwan's dead body, "and him."

Ollie laughed. "Oh… that's one way of looking at it, yes."

"And now you're going up against the police as well. There's no end to the list of enemies that you're willing to rack up in pursuit of what… revenge, money?"

"It was never about the money!

"This was about justice," Mark said.

Now it was Caslin who laughed. "Justice. Is that what Jody

Wyer's death was all about? I've seen the result of your kind of justice. What a load of bullshit. People like you are all the same... take whatever you want regardless of who gets hurt and dress it up with some twisted code of honour."

"Our father did what he was supposed to do. He played by *all the rules*... loyalty... trust... and we had no better example," Ollie argued. "Look what happened to him: turned over by the very people who were supposed to be his friends."

"That's naïve," Caslin countered. "There are no friends in this business. I'm amazed you haven't learned that by now."

"You're right, Caslin. When it comes down to it, the only people you can count on is your family," Ollie said. "And we set our own rules, same as you."

"What the hell do you mean by that? The rest of us follow the law," Caslin stated.

"Is that so?" said Mark. "Can the same be said of your father? Where was his moral compass and your precious law when he was lining his pockets?"

"My father will have to answer for what he's done."

Ollie laughed. "And you will see to that, will you? You'll take down your old man? We both know you'll do everything you can to keep him out of prison because you're not so different to us. You put your family first and morality comes second. A distant second at that. We're not altogether different, you and me Mr Caslin. I'd argue we're the same."

Caslin looked at MacEwan's dead body. "Where is it going to end?" he asked. "You planted the bomb in the minicab office. You were family. *They trusted you.* Then you lured Clinton Dade out into the middle of nowhere and killed him. For what? To start a war between his people and Pete Fuller's. Where does Dade fit into your righteous indignation?"

"An unfortunate casualty but please don't try to convince me that you'll shed any tears over the loss of Clinton Dade. He was no better than Fuller or his two sociopathic children."

"Pete Fuller's figured this out. You know he's going to come for you?"

"He knows as much as we've allowed him to. If he manages to come for us," Ollie said, with no apparent concern for that eventuality, "we will be waiting."

"Fuller didn't grass on your father," Caslin said.

"But he failed to protect him," Ollie said. Caslin looked at Mark and then back at Ollie. "Our father was one of the last to be rounded up, you know that. When he went inside, Fuller was still trying to figure out where the heat had come from. He and Dad went back so far. He was married to his sister and kept his business afloat after good old Uncle Pete was sent down. And what thanks did he get? Pete shunned him. He may not have pointed the finger directly but by doing that word got around and people talked. Events took their own course as they were always likely to."

"He threw our father to the wolves," Mark said, venom in his tone. "Pete Fuller deserves everything coming to him and one day soon he'll be out. Then, he'll be ours."

"This is never going to end," Caslin said. "The bitterness. The hatred. It will keep growing. You'll have to take out Ashton and Carl, too, otherwise they'll come after you. Ultimately, this will consume you until at some point in the future someone will put you down. This is the reality. These are the people you have taken on with your vigilante crusade. You've done well so far but you cannot expect to get away with it forever."

"Funny," Mark said, "we're pretty good at it."

Caslin thought about their apparent confidence. They didn't strike him as fly-by-night. These two had proved quite adept at orchestrating their Machiavellian revenge mission perhaps with even more depth than he realised. If they were feeding information to Fuller, then they were arguably controlling his response in some way.

"Fuller didn't get to Bradley, did he?" Caslin asked. Mark looked to his brother and Ollie smiled.

"No. We took care of Bradley. It was too good an opportunity to miss. We might not have got a better chance. He doesn't come back to this country very often and once we realised, he was negotiating with MacEwan to be paid up then we knew he was going to disappear again. Just like he did two years ago. He had everybody fooled, even us. Not MacEwan, obviously but that was one fact he kept to himself."

"What about the police?" Caslin asked. "What about my father?"

"That wasn't us," Ollie stated. "That was all Fuller."

"Someone must have tipped him off. If not you, then who?"

"I'm not going to tell you where he got his information from," Ollie added, with a smile. There was a smug satisfaction conveyed in that expression. He was toying with him. Caslin knew it.

"You are a crafty little bastard," Caslin said.

"Taken as a compliment," Ollie said, the smile broadening into a grin.

Caslin glanced to his left in the direction of Louise. "And where do you fit into all of this?" he asked. "Did you have any feelings for Jody Wyer or were you just manipulating him for the benefit of these two clowns?" For the first time there was a chink in Ollie's demeanour. Perhaps he had hit something of a nerve there.

"Jody was a means to an end," Louise said.

"When he outlived his usefulness, these monkeys killed him. Is that about right?"

"You think Jody was on some personal crusade of his own?" Mark asked Caslin, before breaking out into a fit of genuine laughter. "He was looking for his father's share... his crooked father's share... so that he could get out of a job where he was sitting up all night watching married men banging their mistresses on the side. Wyer was no better than the rest of us."

"He wasn't a killer though, was he?"

Ollie shrugged. "He thought he could slip in and take a share of the money and then disappear. He fancied himself as a big-time player but he couldn't even get the better of his business partner."

"Mason dropped Jody right into your hands."

"Mason was useful for MacEwan. Gambling debts make for decent leverage. But, at the same time, he was prone to running his mouth which is most likely what put Wyer onto us in the first place."

"Wyer didn't know he'd let a fox into the hen house," Caslin said, flicking his eyes towards Louise.

"I watched my father lose everything because of what Phil Bradley did. His own blood," she said. "The police, the insurance company investigation and all the accompanying stress from the debt. Not to mention the guilt. My mother got sick and I watched as the doctors tried to save her but couldn't. Then I watched her give up. Watched her die and my father crumble in front of me. The man he once was destroyed... Fifty years of graft to end up where he is now. A bucket load of debt and a..." her voice cracked momentarily, "and a dead wife. All of that while living with the suspicion of having killed his cousin for an insurance scam."

"Ah... I see," Caslin said. "So, you've done all of this in order to give your dad a nice retirement? I didn't understand, I'm so sorry," Caslin said with emphasised sarcasm. "That's what the rest of us call life. It's not fair and you don't always get what you deserve but you persevere and make the best of it you can."

"Thanks for the advice, Inspector but I'll go about things my way," Louise bit back.

"You do that," Caslin said, "and then watch as your lover here gets tired of you. Then you'll be the next one floating in the sea." Caslin inclined his head in Ollie's direction. "How devoted to a woman do you think a man can be if he's willing to pimp her out to get his hands on some money. Albeit a lot of money, I'll grant you, but still makes him no better than your pimp and you... well, you know what that makes you. Come to think of it that's probably giving you too much credit. Some people sell themselves as it's the only way they can get by. You didn't just sell yourself for money but you cost Jody Wyer his life."

Ollie stepped forward and struck Caslin across the face with the butt of his pistol. Caslin staggered backwards grimacing at the sharpness of the pain from the blow. Blinking tears from his eyes, he felt blood running from his nose. Reaching up, he wiped it with the back of his hand. "That's enough," Ollie said, through thinly-veiled aggression.

"What are we going to do with him?" Mark asked.

"We're a little short of hands all of a sudden," Ollie said, pointing to the still forms of both dead men lying on the floor but his eyes never left Caslin. "We can always use some help to get stuff down to the boat."

"Speaking of which," Louise said, "we probably ought to get a move on. Dad will be waiting."

"So that's the plan, is it? Daddy brought his fishing boat down the coast and you're going to load it up and get across the channel."

Ollie laughed. "You're one hell of a detective."

"I expected something a little more sophisticated, I have to say. We'll be carrying it along the cliffs, will we?"

"Something like that," Ollie said, smiling. "You look like a man who could do with a workout."

Ollie gestured for Caslin to walk towards him at the point of a gun. Caslin held his hands up in supplication. Ollie shook his head.

"Put your hands down, Inspector, it looks embarrassing." Caslin did so as Ollie stepped to one side, indicating for him to continue. Caslin walked towards the main entrance door. "That will do," Ollie said. He stopped where he was, Ollie pointed to his right. "Open that door."

Caslin eyed the cabinet next to the main door. It was a standalone cabinet, nondescript with two doors. He pulled open the left-hand door and inside were a number of rucksacks stacked against each other. They looked full. Heavy. Casting an eye over them, he raised an eyebrow at Ollie.

"If they're full of gold, I've no chance of lifting it."

Ollie laughed. "They are full of cash, Inspector. We've been trading the gold a little at a time. It's not as profitable an exchange rate but cash is a lot easier to spread around."

"Any particular one?"

"Whichever takes your fancy."

CHAPTER THIRTY

REACHING FOR THE NEAREST RUCKSACK, Caslin took a hold and tested the weight. It was heavier than he'd thought. Looking at the others, he knew this couldn't be all of it. There were only four. As if reading his mind, Mark Bridger answered the unasked question.

"You didn't think it would all still be here, did you?" he said, grinning. "We've been shipping it out bit by bit over the last few months."

"I thought that's why Bradley came back from the dead," Caslin said over his shoulder. He'd dropped to his haunches and was awkwardly attempting to fit the straps over his shoulders.

"No. Bradley's been receiving it at the other end on the continent," Mark explained. "He figured he'd done his bit and wanted to be finished with it all."

"That's why we had to make a move," Ollie said. "Couldn't risk him doing another vanishing act which is exactly what I expect he was planning. Only this time, we would have had no idea where he was headed."

"Still figured you'd have more," Caslin said.

"MacEwan cut a deal with whoever masterminded that job

years ago. He probably didn't get to keep as much as you thought."

"I see," Caslin said, nodding and hefting the rucksack into the air and over his shoulders.

"While you're at it, you can help Mark to put one on."

Caslin looked at the younger of the Bridgers. Mark had managed to slide his coat back on but there was no way one of his arms could be used to bear the weight of the remaining rucksacks. Caslin looked down at them choosing a black one with yellow trim. He pointed to it.

Mark nodded. "Yeah, that's my colour."

With the weight of his own, Caslin struggled to pick up the rucksack. With a surge of effort, he managed to hoist it up just high enough for Mark to slip his arms through the straps and then onto his shoulders. The younger man grunted as he took the strain. It would certainly be an uncomfortable walk for him down to the shoreline. Ollie looked to Louise.

"I've got him," she confirmed, keeping an eye on Caslin. Putting his own gun back into his waistband, Ollie crossed over and picked up the next rucksack. Once he'd adjusted the straps, he assumed responsibility for Caslin again. Louise then picked up hers. The last one remaining.

"Let's go," Ollie said. "Mark, you take the lead, then Louise with our friend here and I'll bring up the rear."

Mark unlocked the front door. Poking his head out, he double checked that their route was clear before leading them out into the brilliant sunshine. The sudden change in light caused Caslin to put his hand up to shield his eyes from the glare. Following the first two, he walked to the gate. There was every chance that they would bump into Hunter. He prayed that they didn't. She should have been there by now and would almost certainly have come across his car. The real question would be whether Broadfoot, Freeman and his team would make it in time. Caslin doubted it.

Louise took hold of the gate and opened it fully, allowing the others to pass through all the while scanning the approach road for signs of trouble. If it weren't for the bloodstains on the sleeve of Mark's coat as well as his own bloody nose which thankfully had stopped flowing, they could have been forgiven for being out on a day's hike. Apart from Caslin that is, for he looked very much out of place, dressed in his suit but there was no one there to see them in any event.

"To the right," Ollie instructed, guiding Caslin towards the start of the walking path along the cliff top. He chanced a glance in the direction of the café, hoping to see a friendly face but he didn't. His heart sank.

The path was a well-known rambling trail that extended from Bridlington around the coast to the Flamborough Cliffs and on to North Landing. Subsequently, the going here was relatively easy with the path being well managed to accommodate the number of visitors throughout the year. After descending in single file for approximately a hundred yards, the path split with the left fork marked as the continuation of the coastal trail. The right-hand fork continued downwards in a steeper descent to the water's edge of Selwick Bay. The sea was crashing against the cliffs and on another day Caslin would have been uplifted by their beauty but from his vantage point as they walked, he could see a small boat anchored some distance off the coast. He assumed that was Scott Tarbet's. The water here was too shallow for him to bring the boat closer. However, an inflatable rib was beached beneath them with one solitary figure sitting at the stern watching the small party descend towards him.

The weight of the rucksacks was significant. Along with that fact the steep incline also forced them to take their time in order to reach the pebble beach safely. They were in a natural cove, hemmed in by vertical chalk cliffs on both sides. The bay was not large and was accessible by the rib until high tide. By then the approach would be far too treacherous. Had Scott Tarbet managed to arrive before dawn, as expected, there would have been every chance they could have been well clear before anybody knew that they had ever been there. As it was now, only the café's owner had noted their arrival. Without Caslin's previous visit, he would no doubt have made very little of the presence of the small group of hikers nor even seen the rib landing below.

Crossing the beach towards the boat, Caslin saw Scott Tarbet become increasingly agitated as he realised Caslin was with them. No sooner had they come within earshot, he jumped off the rib and marched purposefully towards them.

"What the bloody hell is he doing here?"

"Calm down, Scott," Ollie said, attempting to placate the older man.

"He's a bloody policeman."

"I know exactly who he is. And I will handle it."

"Handle it!" Tarbet barked, red faced. "How exactly are you going to do that?"

"I'll do what I have to do," Ollie replied calmly before adding, "same as always."

"Is that so?" Tarbet said in a condescending tone mocking the younger man.

"Dad," Louise cut in. "If Ollie says he'll deal with it, then he will okay?" Tarbet seemed to accept his daughter's word.

Caslin laughed. "That means they plan to kill me, Scott. Are you comfortable with that? You might be many things but not a killer."

"You know nothing about me, Carson."

"Caslin," he corrected him. "Although, you did turn a blind eye to these two killing your cousin."

Tarbet looked into Caslin's eyes and then at the Bridgers in turn. He made a show of not caring but he didn't fool anybody. The news was a shock to him. He shrugged. "Phil hung me out to dry. What kind of man does that to his own family? I guess he had it coming."

"I don't know. Perhaps the same kind of man who allows his daughter to get mixed up with the likes of this scum," Caslin said, looking directly at Ollie Bridger. If the latter was offended, he didn't show it. He merely grinned at the insult. "Just one more innocent life taken for your ridiculous moral crusade."

"Ridiculous?" Mark asked.

"Ridiculous," Caslin repeated. "Those people who died in the bombing. Clinton Dade. The carnage that is likely to follow his assassination. All of that so little Mark and Ollie can settle a score on Daddy's behalf… and earn themselves a fortune while they're at it."

"Too right," Mark said. Caslin looked to him. He was sweating but it was clearly more than just the result of the short hike down from the lighthouse. The bullet may well have passed clean through his arm but he was still bleeding and the last thing you really want to do with a gunshot wound was cart a heavy rucksack down a cliff face.

"I think your little brother is going to need to see a doctor quite soon," Caslin said, turning back to Ollie.

"He will be just fine," Ollie countered. "Won't you, Mark?"

"I'll be grand. Don't worry about me," Mark said, but his tone was edged with a touch of fear belying the bravado.

"Get in the boat," Ollie said to Caslin.

"He's not coming with us," Tarbet said, remonstrating with Ollie.

"What? You suggest we just leave him standing here on the beach?"

"We don't want him with us, do we?" Tarbet argued, the pitch of his voice raising to match his anxiety level.

"I don't know," Ollie said, thinking about it. "It'd be quite poetic for a son to face the sins of his father, don't you think?"

"Another angle for your revenge?" Caslin asked. He was acutely aware that every minute he gained on the shoreline offered his colleagues a better chance of reaching them before they put to sea, but he had no way of knowing how much extra time was required.

"We weren't intending to go after the bent coppers," Ollie

said. "From our point of view getting nicked is an occupational hazard even if the arresting officers are lining their own pockets at the same time. Sometimes, these types of people can prove to be quite useful.

"Yes, you found Bradley useful," Caslin said. Something in Ollie's reaction indicated that wasn't who he was referring to. If not Bradley, then who?

His mind was racing through the key elements of the case. The Bridgers managed to carry out their revenge attack on Bradley, running his car off the road, with or without MacEwan's knowledge. It was an act that Caslin had wrongly attributed to Pete Fuller. The attack on his father was initiated by Fuller no doubt as a result of the Bridger's intervention. Both Keith Wyer and Greg Tower were already dead and that left only one other, Chief Superintendent Toby Ford. A man who was at the heart of the original investigation commanding DCI Bradley, Keith Wyer and his own father. A man with the power to direct the inquiry. He was also the surviving witness to Bradley's apparent death at sea. Caslin's father implied there may well be others further up the chain, names he claimed not to know. Ford had the potential to orchestrate everything that had come to pass. The moment of their first meeting flashed through his mind, the recognition of Caslin's name when they were introduced. He picked up on it at the time but failed to realise the significance.

"I see the wheels turning, Inspector Caslin," Ollie said as he interpreted his facial expressions. "People say you need a little luck in this life. Personally though, I prefer to make my own. You're right. Mark and I couldn't have done all of this by ourselves. I mean, we're good… but we're not that good. Life becomes far easier with a benefactor, doesn't it?"

"Even the limit to your revenge has its price, eh?"

"We made our peace and we cut a deal."

"And I've figured out who with. I met him for the first time recently, you know, and I'll take great pleasure in bringing him down."

Ollie read Caslin's determination. He was unnerved. "The problem for you is if you were *somehow* able to get yourself out of your current predicament, then the only way you can take him down is to burn your own father. Are you prepared to do that, Mr Caslin? Or are you willing to trade those principles of yours to save him?"

"We do what we have to," Caslin said calmly, reiterating Ollie's own position. "But you are right about one thing?"

"What's that?"

"We do have our own choices to make." Caslin reached up and unhooked the straps of his rucksack, arching his shoulders back and allowing it to slide down his arms and on to the beach.

"Pick it up," Ollie instructed. Caslin smiled but remained as he was. "Pick… it… up!" he repeated. Caslin glanced down at the rucksack and then at the gun Ollie was waving at him, gesturing with it towards the rucksack. Caslin proceeded to fold his arms across his chest. "What do you think you're doing?"

"Making my own luck," Caslin argued. "There's no way you're getting me into that boat."

"Bloody hell!" Mark exclaimed, depositing his rucksack in the rib with Tarbet's assistance. Drawing his brother's attention, he pointed back up the path. Ollie turned and followed Mark's indication up the cliff face. A number of figures, all clad in black, were heading down the path at speed. Caslin felt a sense of relief but he knew he was far from out of danger. Knowing they were without a sharp shooter amongst them it would be minutes before they were in a position to aid him. Ollie looked back in his direction.

"Get his rucksack," he barked at no one in particular having given up on forcing Caslin into the rib but that didn't mean he wouldn't shoot him.

Louise ran past her boyfriend and came alongside Caslin. "You know, you're a massive pain in the arse," she said.

"You sound like my ex," he replied. She knelt and braced herself. Taking a hold of the rucksack, she made to lift it. As she rose, Caslin grabbed her shoulder and spun her so she was between himself and Ollie Bridger. The rucksack fell to the ground. Slipping both arms under hers, he brought his hands up behind her head interlocking his fingers at the base of her skull and clamped them in place. Louise struggled but no matter how much she attempted to wrestle herself free, Caslin held her in a vice-like grip.

Ollie stepped forward, raising his gun and aiming for Caslin's head. Ensuring Louise was in between them so Ollie couldn't get a clean shot, he leant into her making it harder still. A shout came from above. It was a warning from the armed police even though they were in no position to action an arrest. Caslin knew they were following their engagement protocols. Once a warning was given, they were legally allowed to open fire if they felt it necessary. Caslin appreciated their forethought.

"Get the bag," Ollie shouted. The police were closing in and Caslin recognised the growing panic in his voice. For all his cunning, the meticulous planning, everything was beginning to unravel.

"Just leave it," Mark shouted.

"Get it!" Ollie barked. Mark clambered back out of the rib and ran the short distance up the beach to where Caslin held Louise. Tentatively, he ducked low in order to keep out of his brother's line of fire. Grabbing the bag, he dragged it clear of Caslin. The exertion made him wince.

"What about my daughter?" Tarbet shouted from the boat. He and Mark had already turned the boat into the breakwater and Tarbet was firing up the outboard engine.

"Let her go," Ollie said.

"Not going to happen," Caslin whispered, his face pressed firmly against the back of Louise's head. Ollie looked towards his brother heaving the weighty rucksack out of the water and into the rib before clambering aboard himself. Then he spied the distance between them and the officers approaching as fast as they dared. Weapons were trained upon those below but they had to acknowledge from that range they would endanger everyone by firing. Likewise, to descend any faster could put themselves at risk. Should they receive fire, then they needed to be able to take cover. All this combined to make Caslin's wait feel like hours rather than minutes.

"Fair enough," Ollie said, squeezing the trigger twice in quick succession. The first round struck Louise in the chest and the second, her shoulder. The force of both shots struck her like hammer blows and she was punched from her feet and thrown backwards taking both her and Caslin to the ground. The air flew from his lungs as he hit the pebbles, Louise on top of him.

"No!" Tarbet screamed from the rib only a second before Mark Bridger put a round into him as well. Tarbet flipped backwards from the stern and into the shallow sea water. Caslin struggled to break free from the weight of Louise atop him in a desperate attempt to give him options. Ollie was coming to kill him, he was certain and he'd be damned if he would lie there and wait for it. His would-be assassin appeared in his peripheral vision and Caslin felt a surge of panic. Then there was a shot followed by another which caused Ollie to duck out of Caslin's view. Another round struck Louise. She didn't make a sound. Nor did she when there was a fourth.

Further shots came and Caslin angled his head to the bottom of the path where it met the beach. Chas Freeman and his team were on the beach and approaching. They were exchanging fire in the direction of the rib. Caslin felt a degree of safety and he managed to roll Louise off of him. He did so gently and once he was clear, he knelt alongside and looked at her. Her face was expressionless and her eyes wide. She was dead. A bullet fizzed past him far too close for comfort as he felt the change in the air pressure and what sounded like a crack as it went by. Throwing himself forward onto the beach, the overpowering smell of rotting seaweed filled his nostrils.

Staring towards the shoreline the rib was afloat, Mark Bridger hunkered in the stern attempting to steer them out to sea. Ollie was alongside, lying against the port side and sending volley after volley at the advancing police officers. The two were heavily out-gunned and now there were no hostages in play, Freeman's team openly returned fire. There was an audible bang as the outboard motor was struck and it gave out billowing smoke from within the housing. The rib floundered having not yet fully escaped the breakwater. With nowhere near enough momentum to carry them out to sea it was only a matter of time until the tide would return them to land.

Caslin wondered whether they would give up but he dismissed it rapidly. Mark Bridger turning his own weapon towards the beach answered that question. The Bridgers began firing in unison despite their vessel being holed in multiple places and the desperation of their situation acutely apparent. The battle was short lived. From Caslin's vantage point, he watched as Mark was struck first slumping backwards into the rib and disappearing from view. Ollie reached down, reappearing with his brother's gun and attempted to use both. He was hit in the chest a number of times and one final shot took him in the head and he fell forward dropping both weapons into the sea.

It was over.

With no one in charge of the rudder, the rib turned sideways and was carried to the beach by the swell. Caslin stood upon wobbly legs watching as the boat was first swamped by a large wave and then picked up and flipped by the next. Looking behind him, he saw the approaching forms of Hunter and Kyle Broadfoot, both bore concerned expressions. Hunter appeared relieved when she saw he was unhurt. Turning back towards the shore, Scott Tarbet's body was retrieved by two of the armed officers wading knee-deep into the water with the breakers crashing against them. Judging from their reaction, Caslin assumed he was also dead. They dragged his body further up the beach so that it wouldn't be carried back into the water and eyeing the tide as it retreated, Caslin saw it tinged red as blood flowed from the dead man.

"Are you okay?" Hunter asked, placing a hand on Caslin's forearm and noting how battered his face was.

"Yeah. It's fine," he said, with a weak smile. "I... I'm... fine."

"Is that all of them?" Broadfoot asked.

Caslin inclined his head in the direction of the lighthouse. "There are two more bodies back up there. MacEwan and one other. They're both dead. The Bridgers killed them."

"Right," Broadfoot said, glancing towards the water. Ollie's body was being carried to the beach, prostrate and face down among the breakers. Broadfoot flicked his eyes to Caslin and asked in a soft voice, "Jody?"

Caslin nodded, "Yes. I think Jody worked out what was going on and they used Scott Tarbet's daughter, Louise, to get close to him. A classic honey trap. Then they exploited Jody's connection with his business partner, Mason, and lured him into a situation where they killed him. I'm sorry."

Broadfoot's expression took on a far-away look, staring out to sea. "Thank you, Nathaniel. That's all of them then?"

Caslin felt a pang of guilt. Toby Ford was still at large. A serving police officer and a senior rank. A man supposedly held to a higher standard than most in society but how Caslin could square this circle, he didn't know. The Bridgers were right. In bringing down Ford, his own father's involvement would be revealed. Morally, there was only one course of action but loyalty to his father was pushing him in another direction.

"I believe so," Caslin said quietly. Hunter caught his eye. She knew him well. Very well. Broadfoot reached across and offered Caslin his hand. He took it. The handshake was brief and Broadfoot turned away setting off to speak with Freeman. There were tears in his eyes. Caslin felt for him. He had lost his godson, someone he loved and cared for. Caslin chose to keep Wyer's motivations for his investigation to himself. Destroying the lad's reputation in death wasn't necessary and would serve no purpose. Whether he was looking to lay his hands on the proceeds of the robbery was largely irrelevant now. Besides, the Bridgers were hardly the most credible of witnesses.

"There's more, isn't there?" Hunter asked once their senior officer was out of earshot.

"Later," Caslin said. "I've got one more conversation to have first," he added, making it very clear he held no desire to discuss it further and walked away.

CHAPTER THIRTY-ONE

DURING THE DRIVE back to York, Caslin found himself ruminating on the complexity and intrigue of this case. For all the horrendous actions carried out by the Bridger brothers enacting their Machiavellian revenge plot, Ollie made one point that Caslin found undeniable as much as it was inescapable. It was this thought that kept repeating on him. Many times, throughout his career, he chose to look the other way and on those occasions the decision was always related more to his inherent sense of justice rather than a desire to circumvent the law. People often referred to such moral dilemmas as grey areas. A case could be made for acting in whichever way necessitated their desired outcome. No matter which angle of approach he took in his reasoning, this wasn't one of those times.

Arriving at the hospital, Caslin was lucky to find an empty parking bay and left the car. Every step towards the entrance felt heavy, weighed down by the decision he knew was inevitable. To keep his father from suffering, Caslin had to allow another to walk free – a murderer, a thief, a disgrace to the uniform – none other than Chief Superintendent Toby Ford. He fed the Bridgers all of the information they needed and may well have influenced their course of action. All to ensure that he would walk away without ever needing to look over his shoulder. All to fulfil one of the negative base desires of humanity – that of greed. There was no way Caslin could bring a case against Ford without, as Ollie so colourfully described it, burning his own father. There was a distinct possibility that even if he was prepared to do so, it may not lead to a successful conviction. If they could attribute any of the money to Ford or find some communication between him and the Bridgers, then maybe. However, if Ford was adept at covering his tracks as so many others in this case appeared to be, then Caslin could see his father on trial and gain nothing in return.

Taking the stairs rather than the lift, Caslin made his way up to the second floor. A memory came to mind. When he and his brother, Stefan, were children they found themselves momentarily unsupervised in the local newsagent. Their mother was searching for something, he couldn't recall what it was and as a result the member of staff was with her at the rear of the shop. The two boys, no strangers to mischief, saw an opportunity to help themselves to the sweets their mother had already denied them. Egging each other on they took as much as they dared. Leaving the shop minutes later exhilarated by their achievements, both he and Stefan shared satisfied looks with one other. The scale of their theft was completely missed by the adults. Only much later when their father stumbled across them sharing out the stash was the truth revealed.

Caslin remembered anticipating his father's wrath, expecting a beating or at the very least to be verbally abused but no, his father sat calmly with them and talked. The image of that face, one of such profound disappointment remained fresh in his mind to this day. They discussed what they had done why it was wrong as well as what the consequences should be. Following that conversation both boys made the walk back to the shop to not only return what they had taken, pay for what they couldn't but also to apologise. That walk – a very long walk at the age of seven – carried with it the strongest sense of shame that he could remember. Of all the words his father said to him that day one sentence crystallised in his mind.

"*You can't hide from what you've done,*" his father had told them, "*and you have to accept the consequences of your actions. Only then, can you move forward.*"

The message was understood, even at such a young age. The current situation he found himself in was worth far more than a handful of sweets but the path forward was clear. No matter how painful it would be to walk it.

Coming to the ward's entrance, a young couple were leaving and kindly held the door open for him and Caslin slipped through, avoiding the wait to be buzzed in by the staff. The nurses' station was unmanned as he walked past heading for his father's room. Strangely, the armed guard was no longer present which irritated him. News travelled fast but until he was certain the threat had passed, he would have expected the protection to remain in place. He tapped lightly on the door and entered.

The curtains were open with sunshine streaming in but he found the room empty. The bed was made with fresh linen. Monitoring equipment was switched off and pushed to the side of the room. Caslin noted the absence of personal effects and considered whether his father had been discharged without his knowledge. Perhaps they had switched him to an open ward. Turning on his heel he left the room and walked back to the nurses' station. At which point he was met by Karen. Caslin's felt his face light up as he was able to confirm the case was over and their children were safe but something struck him as odd. A subtle shift in her demeanour as she set eyes on him. Her response was fleeting and yet telling.

He approached her. "Karen? What is it?"

She opened her mouth but words didn't follow. She met his eye and tears welled. The nurse accompanying her stepped forward. Her expression was solemn.

"Mr Caslin," she began. "We've been trying to reach you for the past few hours."

"My phone..." Caslin said, moving to retrieve the mobile from his pocket before remembering Ollie Bridger smashing it at the lighthouse. "Why? What's..." the words tailed off. Karen came closer and reached out, taking his hand in hers.

"I... I'm so sorry, Nate," she said, tears on her cheeks. Caslin looked into her eyes and then to the nurse alongside.

"I'm afraid there were complications overnight," the nurse explained. "I'm sorry but your father passed away this morning."

"No... no, that can't be right." Karen threw her arms around him and Caslin crumpled. His legs felt hollow, almost unable to take his weight and he felt the strangest sensation pass over him. They took a step backwards and Caslin almost stumbled but Karen guided him to a chair set against the wall in the corridor. He sat down. She knelt before him. "But... he was going to be okay..."

"I'm so sorry," Karen repeated, staring into his eyes and cupping his cheeks with the palms of her hands. She pressed gently and Caslin's head dropped into them, tears flowing. She pulled his head into her chest. "There was nothing anyone could do."

They stayed like that for the next five, maybe ten minutes. Caslin didn't know how long for sure. The moment passed and he regained his composure. Moving his head away, Karen stroked the side of his face, smiling.

"Your father loved you, Nate. I know he had a hard time showing it but he did... very much."

Caslin nodded. "I know," he replied. The statement felt inadequate under the circumstances. His father was a man who struggled to convey positive emotions. They were far more alike than either cared to admit.

"They said they can arrange for you to spend some time with him, if you would like," Karen said.

"I would like that very much," Caslin replied, standing. He

approached the nurse sitting behind her workstation. "Could I borrow your telephone? I need to make a call."

"Of course."

Caslin withdrew from Karen's grasp, she was reluctant to let him go. "I can come with you," she said. He smiled. Following the nurse, she led him into an adjoining office to give him privacy.

"I'll just be a moment," Caslin said, using the back of his hand to clear his eyes. Picking up the receiver, he dialled Kyle Broadfoot's personal mobile. The call was answered within three rings.

"Nathaniel," he said. "I'm terribly sorry to hear about…"

"Thank you, sir. That's very kind," Caslin cut him off. "There's one more name we have to pick up, sir."

"There is?" Broadfoot said, surprised.

"Chief Superintendent Ford, sir."

There was a moment of silence at the other end of the line. "On what charge?"

"Start with conspiracy to commit the murder of Jody Wyer… misconduct in public office… and then we can go from there…"

"Understood, Nathaniel," Broadfoot said, his tone conveying his shock at the revelation. "Do you want to make the arrest?"

"No, sir," Caslin replied. "This one is all yours," he said and hung up. Replacing the receiver, he took a deep breath and closed his eyes. "I love you too, Dad," he said quietly to himself.

FREE BOOK GIVEAWAY

Visit the author's website at **www.jmdalgliesh.com** and sign up to the VIP Club and be first to receive news and previews of forthcoming works.

Here you can download a FREE eBook novella exclusive to club members;

Life & Death - A Hidden Norfolk novella

Never miss a new release.

No spam, ever, guaranteed. You can unsubscribe at any time.

ARE YOU ABLE TO HELP?

Enjoy this book? You could make a real difference.

Because reviews are critical to the success of an author's career, if you have enjoyed this novel, please do me a massive favour by entering one onto Amazon.

———

Type the following link into your internet search bar to go to the Amazon page and leave a review;

http://mybook.to/Blood_Money

———

If you prefer not to follow the link please visit the Amazon sales page where you purchased the title in order to leave a review.

THE SIXTH PRECEPT - PREVIEW

DARK YORKSHIRE - BOOK 6

THE CELLS ON THE SPREADSHEET MERGED as eye-strain overcame her. She pressed thumb and forefinger to the lids and gently squeezed them towards one another, meeting at the bridge of her nose. Blinking furiously, she waited until her eyes refocussed. Glancing at the mobile on her desk, she noted the missed call. The second of the evening. Checking the time, it was pushing eight o'clock.

She saved the document and resolved to pick up where she left off first thing in the morning. Closing down the applications, she switched off the monitor and detached the laptop from the hub, sliding it into her carry bag. Lastly, she turned off the desk lamp and got to her feet. Crossing the office and taking her coat from the stand, she put it on and slipped the straps of her bag over her shoulder and left, closing the door behind her.

The carpeted corridors were deserted and were now illuminated only by secondary lighting, in place to allow the contract cleaners to set about their routines. They paid her no attention as she reached the lift, accompanied by the grating sound of a vacuum cleaner. Summoning the lift to the fourth floor, she waited, checking her watch once more. Thomas would be annoyed. Another figure came into view, rounding the corner at the far end. Despite the lack of light, the sizeable frame gave away the identity of the night shift security guard. He smiled at her as he approached.

"Working late again, Miss Ryan?"

"Heading home now, Marcus."

"You work too hard."

"Isn't that the truth." A ping sounded and the doors parted before her. Entering the lift, she turned and pressed the button for the basement parking level. "Goodnight, Marcus."

"Goodnight, Miss Ryan."

The doors closed and the lift began the descent. Moments later, she stepped out into the underground basement. There were perhaps a dozen cars scattered around the parking level. Apparently, there were employees outdoing even her with their commitment to the cause. She moved to the left, her heels echoing through the parking level the only sounds that carried. Descending a ramp to the lower level, she set eyes on her BMW, parked in her designated space. Alongside was a transit van and she was irritated by the proximity of it to her own. To be fair, the spaces were narrow and not marked out with wider vehicles in mind but even so, she cursed the driver under her breath for being so thoughtless.

Approaching the car, the keyless entry system registered her presence and the car unlocked itself. Opening the boot, she placed the shoulder bag containing her laptop flat inside. Removing her coat, she lay that alongside it too. Shutting the tailgate, she was forced to turn sideways and slip down between the two vehicles. Whilst assessing how much of a gap would be needed to enable her to get into the driving seat, something in the corner of her eye caught her attention. Looking across the parking level, she tried to see what it was. For a moment she thought she'd heard something and seen a flicker of movement.

The level was well lit with only the huge concrete supporting pillars and the occasional parked car interrupting her line of sight for fifty yards in every direction. She waited, straining to see or hear what had alerted her – but nothing. Only the muted drumming from within the ventilation duct overhead could now be heard. Realising she was holding her breath, she dismissed her overactive imagination. The mobile phone in her pocket began to vibrate and she took it out. It was Thomas again. She directed the call to voicemail, putting the handset back in her pocket and grasped the door handle. The sliding door of the van opened and before she could react, something struck her in the back. Intense pain tore through her as her body went into spasm moments before her legs gave out and she collapsed, falling against the car on her way down. The fluorescent strip lights hanging from the roof appeared to swing from left to right as strong hands took a firm hold of her.

Then, there was only darkness.

Something was wrong. Opening her eyes, her lids felt heavy. Gritty. The darkness of the night was all-encompassing. The smell of the outdoors; damp soil. Something was wrong... very wrong. Attempting to stand, she found herself held in place somehow, panic flared; she feared she'd been in an accident and was paralysed or worse still: dead. Her left ankle throbbed. Although unable to move her foot, any flexing of the muscles in her leg caused a sharp painful sensation. Relieved she could still feel all of her extremities, despite their apparent cold, she cast her mind back. Leaving the office, speaking to Marcus and arriving at her car... but then, nothing. Breathing was difficult. There was something restricting her mouth, taut and unforgiving. She couldn't move her lips. Trying to call out gave off a muffled sound, elevating to a scream. Only when trying to reach up with her hand to free her mouth did she realise that she couldn't move at all.

No amount of struggling or exertion, using all of the strength she could muster, could move her even the slightest. She cried out again, as loudly as she could, but her muffled screams passed into despairing tears as frustration turned to fear and then panic. A thud sounded nearby, not particularly loud but it drew her attention. Her eyes were slowly beginning to adjust to the darkness and she looked around but couldn't make out what had made the noise. Then there was another, only this time much closer. A third sounded behind her, a little way off. Then silence returned.

The wind whispered from nearby trees and then came the realisation. She was by woodland. The damp soil, the trees... the cold. Shadows moved. It was hard to judge but she thought it was a person, perhaps twenty feet away but she couldn't be sure. Craning her neck, she tried to make out any detail but moving caused her discomfort. All of a sudden, she was bathed in bright light. Screwing her eyes tightly shut, she screamed again. Slowly opening her eyes, she squinted against beams of car headlights. They illuminated everything around her.

Nearby, she saw a rock, perhaps the size of a closed fist. To the right was another. They looked somehow out of place, as if recently deposited. Another thud. Another rock, landing to the left of her head. She screamed. Something struck the top of her head sending a shooting pain across her skull. Her screaming ceased, replaced by confusion. Then another. This one struck her forehead before dropping to the ground in front of her. Liquid flowed across her eyebrow and trickled into her eye.

She was bleeding. Something else passed through her line of sight, striking her on the cheek. Horrified, she silently begged for help but none was forthcoming.

Another strike. Her vision swam... and the darkness returned.

ALSO BY J M DALGLIESH

The Dark Yorkshire Series

Divided House

Blacklight

The Dogs in the Street

Blood Money

Fear the Past

The Sixth Precept

Box Sets

Dark Yorkshire Books 1-3

Dark Yorkshire Books 4-6

The Hidden Norfolk Series

One Lost Soul

Bury Your Past

Kill Our Sins

Tell No Tales

Hear No Evil

Life and Death**

**FREE eBook - A Hidden Norfolk novella - visit jmdalgliesh.com

Audiobooks

The entire Dark Yorkshire series is available in audio format, read by the award-winning Greg Patmore.

Divided House

Blacklight

The Dogs in the street

Blood Money

Fear the Past

The Sixth Precept

Audiobook Box Sets

Dark Yorkshire Books 1-3

Dark Yorkshire Books 4-6

*Hidden Norfolk audiobooks arriving 2020

Made in the USA
Las Vegas, NV
22 August 2021